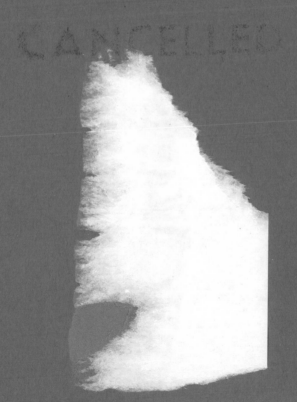

BEST SF: 75

Also by HARRY HARRISON

NOVELS

Deathworld
Deathworld 2
Deathworld 3
Planet of the Damned
Bill, the Galactic Hero
Plaque from Space
Make Room! Make Room!
The Technicolor Time Machine
Captive Universe
The Daleth Effect
The Stainless Steel Rat
The Stainless Steel Rat's Revenge
The Stainless Steel Rat Saves the
    World
A Transatlantic Tunnel, Hurrah!
Montezuma's Revenge
Queen Victoria's Revenge
Stonehenge
            (with Leon E. Stover)
Star Smashers of the Galaxy Rangers

SHORT STORY COLLECTIONS

War with the Robots
Two Tales and 8 Tomorrows
Prime Number
One Step from Earth

JUVENILES

Spaceship Medic
Worlds of Wonder (Editor)
The Man from P. I. G.

EDITED

The Year 2000
John W. Campbell: Collected Editori-
    als from Analog
SF: Authors' Choice 1
SF: Authors' Choice 2
SF: Authors' Choice 3
SF: Authors' Choice 4
Best SF: 67
Best SF: 68
Best SF: 69
Best SF: 70
Best SF: 71
Best SF: 72
Best SF: 73
Best SF: 74
Four for the Future
The Light Fantastic
Nova 1
Nova 2
Nova 3
Nova 4
Nebula Award Stories 2
            (with Brian W. Aldiss)
Apeman, Spaceman
            (with Leon E. Stover)
Ahead of Time
    (with Theodore J. Gordon)
The Astounding-Analog Reader
    (with Brian W. Aldiss)
Science Fiction Reader
        (with Carol Pugner; high
                    school text)
Astounding: John W. Campbell Me-
    morial Anthology

BEST SF :

75757575

THE NINTH ANNUAL

EDITED BY

HARRY HARRISON

AND

BRIAN W. ALDISS

THE BOBBS-MERRILL COMPANY, INC.
Indianapolis/New York

ISBN 0-672-52197-0
Library of Congress catalog card number 74-116158
Designed by Jacques Chazaud
Manufactured in the United States of America

First printing

Acknowledgments

"A Scraping at the Bones," by Algis Budrys, copyright © 1975 by the Conde Nast Publications, Inc.; reprinted by permission of the author and Candida Donadio and Associates, Inc. First published in *Analog Science Fact/Science Fiction.*

"Changelings," by Lisa Tuttle, copyright © 1975 by UPD Publishing Corporation; reprinted by permission of the author. First published in *Galaxy/If.*

"The Santa Claus Compromise," by Thomas M. Disch, copyright © 1974 by Crawdaddy Publishing Co., Inc.; reprinted by permission of the author. First published in *Crawdaddy.*

"A Galaxy Called Rome," by Barry N. Malzberg, copyright © 1974 by Mercury Press; reprinted by permission of the author. First published in the *Magazine of Fantasy and Science Fiction.*

"A Twelvemonth," by Peter Redgrove, copyright © 1975 by Peter Redgrove; reprinted by permission of the author. First published in *The Times Literary Supplement,* London.

"The Custodians," by Richard Cowper, copyright © 1975/1976 by Colin Murry; reprinted by permission of the author and his agent, Harold Matson Co., Inc. First published in the *Magazine of Fantasy and Science Fiction.*

"The Linguist," by Stephen Robinett, copyright © 1975 by UPD Publishing Corporation; reprinted by permission of the author. First published in *Galaxy/If.*

ACKNOWLEDGMENTS

"Settling the World," by M. John Harrison, copyright © 1975 by Thomas M. Disch; reprinted by permission of the author. First published in *The New Improved Sun*.

"The Chaste Planet," by John Updike, copyright © 1975 by The New Yorker Magazine, Inc.; reprinted by permission of the author. First published in *The New Yorker*.

"End Game," by Joe Haldeman, copyright © 1975 by the Conde Nast Publications, Inc.; reprinted by permission of the author and his agent, Robert P. Mills, Ltd. First published in *Analog Science Fact/Science Fiction*.

"The Lop-Eared Cat That Devoured Philadelphia," by Louis Phillips, copyright © 1975 by Louis Phillips; reprinted by permission of the author. First published in *Cornudo*.

"A Dead Singer," by Michael Moorcock, copyright © 1974 by Michael Moorcock; reprinted by permission of the author. First published in *Factions*.

Contents

INTRODUCTION   *Harry Harrison*   *xi*

A SCRAPING AT THE BONES   *Algis Budrys*   *1*

CHANGELINGS   *Lisa Tuttle*   *20*

THE SANTA CLAUS COMPROMISE   *Thomas M. Disch*   *35*

A GALAXY CALLED ROME   *Barry N. Malzberg*   *42*

A TWELVEMONTH   *Peter Redgrove*   *65*

THE CUSTODIANS   *Richard Cowper*   *67*

THE LINGUIST   *Stephen Robinett*   *109*

SETTLING THE WORLD   *M. John Harrison*   *126*

THE CHASTE PLANET   *John Updike*   *154*

END GAME   *Joe Haldeman*   *160*

THE LOP-EARED CAT THAT DEVOURED PHILADELPHIA
Louis Phillips   *208*

A DEAD SINGER   *Michael Moorcock*   *210*

AFTERWORD: SCIENCE FICTION ON THE *Titanic*
Brian W. Aldiss   *234*

Introduction

by **HARRY HARRISON**

So one day I suggested to Brian Aldiss that what this world really needed was a good annual anthology of the best SF of the year. Judy Merrill had done an admirable job with her best, but she was out of business and the libraries would be crying for their annual fix of a hardbound volume of this prose category. A fine idea, Brian said, and agreed that we were just the chaps to do it.

Nine years later . . .

Here is the Ninth Annual, and where *has* the time gone? It has been hard and interesting work putting together these volumes, and productive in unexpected ways. By reading everything written, every year, I have had a continuing perspective of the development of science fiction, something I would never have had by remaining inside my ivory rocket ship and writing in solitude. It has been a very interesting decade to watch.

I would not say that SF was in disarray nine years ago. It was just not as booming, nor did it smell as good as it does now. The SF films were all about glop monsters pouncing on screaming girls. *2001: A Space Odyssey* changed all that, and now *Newsweek* is proud to announce that "the recent wave of disaster films will be succeeded by a spate of science fiction movies." And they casually mention twenty-million-dollar budgets. Well, good—if they *are* good SF, but we have been fooled before.

Even before the films discovered our strengths, academia had already latched onto us with a firm grip. Hundreds of college SF courses are being taught, thousands of high school ones. Success in teaching rides so high that this year the University of Kansas had an "Intensive English Institute on the Teaching of Science Fiction." Science fiction conventions, once organized as a labor of love by dedicated fans, have grown so big that some of them have gone commercial and reaped handsome profits. Star Trek conventions have had gates of over 10,000, while the world conventions have been so snowed under by attenders that they are going to limit the number who can come in the future. A fringe benefit for authors is the fact that they will now be *paid* for attending conventions, which can only be a good thing.

What I find most interesting is the growing international popularity of our favorite drug. Perhaps the old fans were right and we may take over world literature yet. There were conventions all over the globe this year: Mexico had its first, while the European one was in Poland. But Italy outdid them all with a festival in Rome that ran for fifty-seven days with 110,000 paid admissions.

All this feverish activity among science fiction readers and viewers has of course been of benefit to the authors who produce the stuff. Translation sales not only put a little more money into the author's pocket but increase his readership and prestige as well. Alongside the growth in translations has been the development of national schools of science fiction writing. Finally—and it has been long overdue—a First International Science Fiction Authors Convention will be held in October 1976, in Dublin, with the cooperation of the Irish Government and the Tourist Board. This will be the first time ever that SF authors have had a chance to meet, and the outcome can only be of benefit to everyone. There will be authors there not only from America and Western Europe, but from the Soviet Union, Poland, and Hungary, as well as a delegation from Japan.

There has also been a rush of books ancillary to science fiction. Not only nostalgia books, like Brian Aldiss's handsome *Science Fiction Art,* but things like Franz Rottensteiner's *The Science Fiction Book,* which is subtitled "An Illustrated History." Illustrated it is; history it is not, except as seen in a warped and highly idiosyncratic mirror. The author apparently loves only Lem, whom he calls the greatest contemporary SF writer (certainly an opinion open to some disagreement), and hates almost everyone else: Heinlein is known for his "ultramilitaristic philosophy" and "diffuse mysticism" which "inspired the drug commune leader and murderer Charles Manson." The author also believes that Theodore Sturgeon "has merely adapted soap opera to science fiction, presenting schmaltz and tears rather than genuine feeling." A book not to be recommended to those watching their blood pressure. This year also featured the long-awaited return of L. Sprague de Camp's *Science Fiction Handbook, Revised.* This book was first published in 1953, and, I must sorrowfully advise, you should get the excellent original if you can. For some reason de Camp seems scarcely aware of SF developments since that first edition. What can we think of an SF handbook that does not have the names of Thomas Disch, Barry Malzberg, Robert Sheckley, Damon Knight and Harry Harrison in its index, to name but a few? Nor can we take seriously advice to young writers about selling to magazines, most of which are tottering toward extinction, but never mentioning the large and flourishing original-anthology market. Most troubling to me was the omission from a list of reference works of Amis's *New Maps of Hell* and the most important book in this field, Aldiss's *Billion Year Spree.*

All of this eager attention can only have a salutary effect on the fiction produced. This year our anthology contains tried and true names along with a sprinkling of inspired newcomers. It is interesting to note that most of the stories are of novelette length, some bordering on novellas. It was not planned that way; these were just the best pieces of fiction to be found. Happily we have no restrictions on length—no restrictions of any kind—in this anthology. We simply read it all and try to give you the best. As always, Brian Aldiss has winnowed the British and other-language sources, while our stalwart Managing Editor, Bruce McAllister, has been bent under the masses of the American printed word.

Please enjoy these stories and poems. We did.

HARRY HARRISON

BEST SF: 75

A Scraping at the Bones

by **ALGIS BUDRYS**

Algis Budrys has been writing too little of late, so it is a pleasure to welcome him back to *Best SF* with this quick glimpse into a crowded future. Here we see some of the problems—with their not-too-nice solutions—that may be lurking beyond tomorrow's threshold.

The Wastes Processing foreman was doughy and soft; looking at his greenish pallor and watching the convulsed workings at the corners of his mouth, Ned Brosmer wondered what would happen if the man lost hold of himself and began puking. Would it all come up—first the stomach, and then the very nearly similar material of the limbs, and then the pelvis and torso and ears, until finally the empty royal-blue slick-finish coverall would be lying at his feet under a heap of something like oatmeal? "It's in there, Officer," the foreman was saying with a relinquishing gesture toward the open inspection plate, the wave of his arm ending with his hand in front of his mouth.

"All right," Brosmer said. "I'll look."

Down here, many levels below the dwelling units that clambered skyward in the complex shape of Panorama Tower, it was all pumps and tubing and worklights. The particular duct from which the smell came was four feet in diameter and

1

was painted an ivory white. Coded red decal symbols identified it as the north tower branch feed to the central waste
macerater.

The hatch was a three-by-two plate, swung back and up;
an extension light dangled over it, swaying from the cord as
the constant air currents within the duct came gusting out.
"Are we going to get flooded?" Brosmer asked, and the foreman shook his head violently.

"Hell, no!" he said. "We got this branch shut off back
there, where the tube comes straight down from upstairs and
makes that bend, see? There's this surge tank there, like you
got to have, and you can use that big valve to block everything
between it and here."

"Got you," Brosmer said. "Would a body pass through
that valve?"

"No way. Jam it, maybe. But most likely it would just stay
in the tank until the next time we cleaned it out."

"So it probably went into the duct right through this
hatch."

"That would figure, yeah. Somebody came down here and
put it in."

"Or it's suicide."

"You're kidding! Who would want to drown himself
in—"

"I was kidding," Brosmer said. He had taken a respirator
from his kit bag and was putting it on. His voice sounded
remote in his ears, as if he were on dope. He sighed and
looked into the duct.

The air flow was backing up from the hydrolizing tanks
beyond the macerater, whistling against the torn edges of
the thin metal blade that terminated the duct. The blade
was designed to rotate at high rpm; it had shattered
against something in the body, which had been passing
feet-first through it without incident up to that point. Brosmer clenched his teeth, grasped one of the shoulders, and
turned it over. A white male, middle-aged, hair gray, eyes

2

brown, several post-mortem abrasions and superficial lac-
erations, and the apparently fatal puncture wound in the
upper right-hand quadrant of the thorax. Made with a thin,
long, sharp weapon, Brosmer decided, for he had seen the
exit wound below the left shoulder blade. It wouldn't have
bled very much; whatever rags had mopped up the spill
had probably preceded the corpse down the duct and were
on their way to the farmers by now. And—Brosmer looked
more closely. Right. A stainless steel replacement ball and
Teflon socket for the original left hip joint. That was what
had stopped the blade.

Brosmer drew his head and shoulders back out of the
inspection hatchway. "Recognize him, Mr. Johnson?" he said
to the foreman. "Take a good look. Sorry." He kept himself
out of the way and put a hand on Johnson's elbow to urge him
forward.

Johnson craned briefly, then stepped back. "No—I don't
know him."

"He's just about got to live in this unit," Brosmer said.

"I don't see none of them. They're up there and I'm down
here. There's thousands of them and three guys in my crew
and me. That's the way they want it, and that's the way I want
it. This is a different kind of place down here."

"Okay," Brosmer said. No matter what, the longest delay
in making an identification would be a routine four-hour
turnaround time for the Social Security print files in Omaha;
sooner if anybody wanted to rush it. He stripped off his exam-
ining gloves and dropped them in a waste can. "Somebody'll
be along to pick it up."

"Is this all?" the foreman asked.

Brosmer looked at him with the appearance of great wisdom. "You mean, where's the sergeant and the lieutenant and
the Chief Medical Examiner of New York City? Well, the
sergeant's tied up collating officers' reports, and the lieutenant's in a conference with some sergeants. There'll be a photographer with the meat-wagon crew. You see," he explained

patiently, "this isn't a stage set; this is real. We don't need a lot of mouths full of dialogue to establish the plot."

"You're all the cop we're going to get on this case?"

"I'm 3-D and in color, Mr. Johnson. You can even feel me, if you don't get personal. That's good enough for an unidentified male found in a sewer."

"Well, you sure as hell look young to me, to be handling something like this all by yourself."

"That's right, I do," Brosmer said, packing away his respirator. "You've got my card. Call me if anybody starts asking you questions about the plumbing. I'm getting out of here. I hate dismal places." He turned back once. "Don't tell anybody about this, or I'll bust your ass to someplace where they use buckets."

At the lobby level, Brosmer walked through one Kasuba environment after another, eschewing their invitations to energy or lassitude, until he had reached the lobby area. He rang Building Management.

"Please state your business," the hologram said, and then caught itself. "Oh, it's you, Officer." Her lips took on fullness, but her eyes widened with something other than love. "I'll put you through to Mr. Vermeil." She faded, to be replaced by a naïvely interesting sculpture that rotated gently under lights, and with the sound of Japanese wind chimes, which in turn yielded to a representation of a man all in body-fitting burgundy crushed velvet. It seemed to Brosmer it was a little early in the evening for that, but perhaps the manager was an early riser.

"Yes, Officer?" Vermeil said busily, not having bothered to put down his frappé.

"There'll be a mortuary truck to get the body, so you'll want to alert your perimeter security people," Brosmer said. "A police photographer will take ID shots; you'll be expected to look at them, in case you can identify the victim. It's almost a sure thing he's one of your residents."

4

"Good heavens, Officer, *I* don't know every Tom, Dick and Harry who lives here! Why on earth should I?"

"Nobody ever calls you up about anything? You know, there was a time when tenants hammered on pipes for more heat, or had their dripping faucets fixed by the super. And the manager came around every month to collect the rent. They've got to be in touch with you now and then."

"I *don't* remember them, Officer. The bank evicts them if their credit goes, and Central Services has the building maintenance contract. They can hammer all they want to on their . . . *pipes,* did you say? Why, yes, Officer, there *was* a time when pipes brought on the heat, wasn't there?" He smirked.

"Vermeil, when the photographer calls you up and shows you the pictures, look at them. And remember it's a sworn admissible communication, whatever you tell him. I'll be in touch when I need you." Brosmer rang off. He went to the lobby doors and flashed his buzzer at the sensing devices. The inner doors opened, and he stepped into the lock. "NYPD Shield number 062-26-8729," he said perfunctorily. "One man going out."

There was a pause, and the intervening sound of wind chimes. Then the outer doors opened. He stepped into the raw air, grimacing, and walked toward the transit station, keeping clear of low walls and shrubbery. Above him, the brownish precast concrete settings clambered heavenward to frame waterfalls of reflectorized glass. As he walked, he rang a police channel and talked to his sergeant, telling him the story.

"What do you think, Ned?" the sergeant asked when he had all the data.

"I think somebody knows in his heart he got away with it. Thinks our victim's a bag of nutrient for the rutabaga. I'm going to get that sucker."

"Why do you suppose he wanted to obliterate the body? How'd he know how plumbing works?"

"What are you, Sarge—an old fire horse? Those are *my* questions."

"All right. You gonna be home?"

"Ten minutes transit time first. Thereafter."

"Good. I'll call you on a landline as soon as we have a working collation."

"I'll be there when I'm needed."

"Say hello to Dorrie for me."

"Should I give any particular name?"

Once on the train, he punched his destination on the coder in his armrest. When the straps went around him, the back of his mind thought of Dorrie. The train took off as soon as his interlock was made, and the front of his mind busied itself reviewing the people in the other seats. There were two or three persons with lunch-bucket faces: technicians. The rest were pimps and whores. All of us personal servants make up the subway-riding public, he thought.

In the middle of his mind, he pondered an individual who could stuff a stripped corpse into the jakes but was too overwhelmed by his or her accomplishment to cut down through an old orthopedic scar and just check to see what might lie behind it. An amateur. But then, professionals just left 'em lying. There weren't any more feckless people. Everyone was numbered. When they died, there was a hole in the credit banks, the dwelling occupancy budget, the place where ongoing supermarket billings might be. There were no unmarked graves; IBM's tombstone punches represented more substance than the incidental flesh could ever show.

Please note, he told the place where he stored his experience: With the lower limbs absent, the free-floating position is face down.

He lived in Riverscene Heights. In the lobby lock, he said, "City civil servant," which put him in the system's admissible tenant class, and then gave his Social Security number. "One man coming in," he said for the voiceprint. In the motionless elevator, he gave his apartment number. In this building, the systems played music during intervals. When he had been properly scanned, the elevator unlocked and took him to his floor. He got out and walked down Hall 114, which also recognized him, and came to Door 11489, which let him in. Dorrie moved toward him out of the forefront of a crowd of dancers.

She was slight and dark, wearing black openwork hip-huggers and bronze jewelry; her long ashy hair fell over one eye; the apartment lights reflected from the amber lens over the other.

"Hello," he said.

She touched her upper lip with her tongue. "Welcome home," she said softly. They touched each other.

He couldn't get enough of her. Wincing, he pulled his shirt open so more of them would be touching. "Can't stay long," he said. "Working." She had put perfume on the top of her head. Her hands passed gently over his deltoid musculature.

"Home tonight?" she asked softly.

"Don't know. Probably not."

"I'll go down the hall, then. Iris Ruthven asked me to join her Bezant class with her."

He grimaced into her hair.

"You know," she said quickly, "that's not something you can do by phone." She leaned back in his arms, took off her glasses, and looked directly into his eyes. "I mean, when you all get around the table, you actually have to *touch* hands, or it doesn't work."

"Does it work if you do?"

"Oh, don't be so *rational!*" She tapped his biceps mock-pettishly with her glasses.

And don't be such a liar, he thought. Another thing worked better in the flesh, too. Why she thought she had to be so convincing and yet so transparent, he couldn't imagine.

Husbands weren't supposed to be selfish, were they? But he was; he was, and he was pretty sure she lied to reproach him subtly, come to think of it.

"Rational is as rational does," he said. "There's one fresh soul I'd sure like to contact. I'll bet he's got a story he'd love to tell."

She danced away from him a little, replacing her glasses. "Are you on a murder?" she asked, her lips parting.

"Over at Panorama." He moved toward a chair.

"Where the *artists* live? Did you go inside? What are the units like? I'll bet they're *fabulous!*"

"They don't get any more cubic feet per body than we do," he said, dropping into the chair. "Besides, I wasn't up on the dwelling levels." He put his feet up on the edge of the daybed and sighed. He reached out and touched Dorrie's thigh as she moved about him. "Listen, I hate to cut off the party, but I want to watch the news."

She nodded. " 'S okay." He switched off the hi-fi and the dancers winked out. Moving toward the bar, Dorrie rummaged, keeping one hip cocked so as not to break the contact between his hand and her leg. "Stick?" she asked.

Dialing the phone for Laurent Michaelmas, he shook his head. "Working," he reminded her.

"You're funny," she murmured fondly as the Michaelmas hologram formed a few paces to her left. "You wouldn't even be back downstairs before your head was all straight again."

"Working *now,*" he said, evading the central issue.

"Good evening," Michaelmas said. He was, as usual, in a plain black suit. Looking at him, Brosmer thought that the self-contained, square-bodied man, with his economical gestures and his lively, intelligent face, might understand him. He hoped that someday an assignment would let them meet. But it seemed hardly likely; Brosmer wasn't even sure whether Michaelmas lived in Manhattan, and he worked all over the world.

"I just want *local crime,*" Brosmer said to him, uttering the last two words distinctly.

Michaelmas nodded. There was a slight flicker. "Local crime," he said. He began a series of expositions, some of which involved Brosmer in the chase of a stolen boat, hunting over the riparian complexes like a midge among the stock shelves of a glass shoe store, sweeping down over the Hudson with a flurry of vanes and surging rpm changes in the turbines, whirling skyward again among the glittering windows as the thieves throttled down and circled disconsolately in the bay. In another sequence, ambulances ran mugging victims toward resuscitation centers, whistling among the pylons and freight ramps of the streets. Michaelmas' voice was crisp and measured, his data succinct. Dorrie, the broken end of a stick trailing between her enameled nails, smiled roguishly toward Brosmer and intertwined her limbs with Michaelmas, running her hands over the back shoulders of the suit, miming with such casual skill that Brosmer had to laugh as Michaelmas continued to speak and move obliviously. Only a few of his gestures surpassed her anticipation; at one point, his left arm protruded between her shoulder blades, but in the next she had recovered and was mock-biting gently with her white teeth along his forearm.

There was nothing about Panorama.

"All right," Brosmer said to himself, and to Michaelmas by way of good-bye as he dialed him off. The hologram disappeared from Dorrie's caresses. She turned and faced Brosmer slump-shouldered, dangling her glasses in one hand against her thigh and looking at him through her lashes. Her lower lip was tentatively between her teeth. She moved her feet. She reached behind her to fully opaque the window wall.

Grinning awkwardly, Brosmer shook his head. "You know we're on open police landline. George Holmeir could be calling any time now."

Well, what would he see that he didn't know first-hand?

Brosmer thought as Dorrie smiled at him sadly. But her expression did change slightly at the mention of the sergeant's name. What would he see? Brosmer finished the thought. He'd see me. He might feel it was inappropriate.

And in fact Holmeir formed without preliminaries, between Dorrie and Brosmer. "Okay, Ned," he said. "Here's what there is."

Brosmer shifted in his chair so the pickup would give Holmeir eye contact with him. "Go ahead."

"Your DOA is Charles Castelvecchio. Resident at 25609 Panorama North, accompanied by Nola Furness Castelvecchio and one infant son. Castelvecchio was a writer on the *Warbirds of Time* series. Here's the stats on them; want to take it?" Holmeir held up the sheet. Brosmer nodded and activated his camera.

"Got it."

Holmeir put the sheet down on his desk. "Okay. Now that's a positive ID. Positive. Fingerprints, dental charts, surgical records, every way we could do it."

Brosmer raised his eyebrows. "Thorough."

"Had to be. He's still doing business; we reviewed his phone calls. He was part of a story conference half an hour ago. Seemed a little jumpy, but did his fair share."

"While he was down in that duct all the time."

"Dead twelve hours, Forensics says, and soaking in that thing for an hour before he was found."

"Killed in the building."

"Had to be. He didn't just materialize." Holmeir looked at Brosmer expectantly.

"How do you mean?"

"He never went in or out through any door. But the elevator wasn't used once all day. That's what the building tapes say."

"It's a glitch. You're getting a false memory readout."

Holmeir nodded. "Sure. Something screwed up in the

building system. It happens. Of course, maybe nobody *did* use
the elevator. That happens, too. So maybe somebody's found
a way to make a hologram you can feel. Only which one is it
—the dead one or the one that suggested sending a squadron
of Spads to strafe Charlemagne?"

"Come off it, Sarge."

"Well, I'll be damned if I can explain it. But I don't have
to. Sergeants sit and officers walk."

"How about the widow? Did you talk to her?"

"Come off it, Ned. How would I know she didn't do it? It's
all yours. He's not even officially dead."

Brosmer nodded. "It's a sweetheart of a case."

Holmeir grinned. "Yeah. I never heard of an MO like this.
You're gonna be breaking new ground. They'll give it your
name at the Academy—every time it ever comes up again,
they'll call it a Brosmer. It'll be good for you when you're
tired enough to apply for sergeant."

"And I'll apply for green feathers and fly to the moon,"
Brosmer said, trying to picture himself as Holmeir, and wincing.

"Okay," he said. "I'll call in when I've got something."

"Right. I'm going off-shift in about an hour. But I'll leave
a cue in my phone for you."

"Okay."

Dorrie had moved around to where the pickup could find
her. "Hello, George," she said.

"Hello, Dorrie."

"See you, Sarge," Brosmer said.

As soon as he was gone, Dorrie turned to Brosmer with
her glasses off and her eyes full of stick. Hearing himself gasp,
he knew there was nothing he could do to prevent it, or
wanted to. Afterward, soft in his arms, blurred with lassitude,
full of confidentiality, she murmured: "You silly, don't you
know I don't see George anymore; I've even mostly forgotten
where he lives in this building. And besides, it's *you* I want to

live with. You're so gentle with me," and he wished she didn't try so hard to teach a coherent understanding of the world to him.

It was funny how it all fell together. He had decided to call on the widow and see if there was any sense to be made of it. Appropriately dressed, his pockets full of supporting data, he walked up to her door as if it hadn't been his buzzer that had gotten him in, but when he rang at the door, nothing happened for a while. Brosmer stood plumply in the hall, thinking now about calling in for a warrant unlock, but instead the next door opened, and a man was standing there. "May I help you?" he said from under unceasingly restless eyes.

Brosmer shifted his feet in awkwardness and scratched the back of his neck. "Well, I don't know . . ." he said.

The man was tall and fleshy, dressed in a floor-length robe of figured iridescent orange. The flesh under one eye was jumping regularly, and his upper lip was wet. "It's all right. It's all right. I often come out," he said reassuringly. "The Castelvecchios aren't home; were they expecting you?"

"Well, yeah, Charlie left a cue in the system for me, and . . ."

"Strange. Yet he's not here. I'm Timothy Fortnum."

"Lou Marchant," Brosmer said. "I'm his cousin."

"Of this city?"

"Chicago," Brosmer said, having been there on a fugitive pickup once. Originally, he had been a young writer from the Bronx, for the widow's benefit, and he was shifting things around inside, watching Fortnum, looking nonplused, wondering how a man could look so guilty and still keep talking.

Fortnum was calming down. "I knew he had no relatives in New York," he said. "Well, come in—let me offer you some hospitality while we straighten this thing out." He took Brosmer by the upper arm to urge him inside. Brosmer had to relax his muscles instantly to come off the pressure plates in the police undersuit beneath his garments, but his arm was only humanly resistant when Fortnum's hand closed on it.

Fortnum was much bolder now. His hip swung to bump Brosmer past him. Most of his attention was concentrated on closing and locking the door with swift, complex motions of his fingers.

"Sit down . . . sit down!" Fortnum said heartily, moving up behind him. "This is my wife, Martita. Darling, this is Mr. Marchant, Charles Castelvecchio's Chicago cousin, come to us unexpectedly."

Brosmer found himself having to look up. Martita Fortnum was leaning over the railing of an area to his left whose floor began at normal ceiling height. She was a slim, blond woman in a red veil caftan, her limbs long and straight, but aging as she descended a circular staircase. The elevated area, he saw, occupied the unit's worth of space above the Castelvecchio unit. Over his head, the ceiling, two ceilings high, supported a crystalline chandelier with soft lights playing upon it. Hanging gardens of opaque silky fabric draped the wall where three window frames ought to have been visible.

"I've never seen a place like this!" Brosmer said.

"Yes. I'm an architect. It's amazing what you can do. *Sit* down, Mr. Marchant. Tell us about yourself." His hand pressed Brosmer's shoulder. "Martita—bring our guest something, will you?"

The wall in the far corner was for shelves of books, a swing-down drawing board, and a prose encoder. Beside the encoder was a roughly similar machine—if he had not seen one in a documentary on popular music, he would not have known it was for editing tune material. All that space was occupied. These people had no visible food preparation area.

Fortnum's hand was still pressing. Brosmer let himself fall into the chair beside the wall between the Fortnum and Castelvecchio units.

Martita Fortnum had reached this floor. She turned with a fluidity strongly reminiscent of youth and passed through an

13

opening behind the staircase. Its edges were fresh; unfinished. There were wallboard fragments on a dropcloth laid in the opening, and it led into the next unit. Martita Fortnum threw Brosmer a fleeting smile as she moved out of sight.

"What are you *doing?*" Brosmer asked, turning his face up to Fortnum.

"Why, we're entertaining you," Fortnum said heartily. "There's so much I want to know about you. Any visitor of Charlie's is bound to be such a surprise to me. He was saying to me just yesterday that he never received any callers." Fortnum put one buttock on the arm of another chair, which stood where the daybed ought to have been, and eyed Brosmer's face intently. A pair of huge antique geometrician's dividers, massive in bronze, each slender two-foot arm ending in a glistening steel point, hung on the wall near his right shoulder.

"It's an old cue," Brosmer said. "I called him weeks ago and said I'd be in town on business, and he put it into the building system for me right then."

"What business are you in, Mr. Marchant?"

"I'm a writer," Brosmer answered, slapping his pocket so Fortnum could hear the impact on the cassette he'd put there when he still thought Castelvecchio had survivors.

"Like Charles. Talent runs in families. Ah, here's Martita with some refreshment. Do you have any gifted children, Mr. Marchant? But you're so young—are you even married?"

"I'm a bachelor," Brosmer said. "In fact, I'm an orphan. Charlie's my only relative." He watched Fortnum's eyes widen in satisfaction. It was always so easy to believe what you hoped for. Brosmer reached out and took the goblet Martita Fortnum handed him silently, her broad mouth pursed quizzically, her eyes peering pale blue amid dark cosmetics.

"Have a drink," she said in a husky whisper when he held the rim to his lips. "Both of us have just had some, or we'd join you."

Ah, Jesus, he thought as he inhaled. It was a thing they

called Swindle on the street; none of the successful pimps would use it, but the whores all did. It made things so easy. And she hadn't lied; you could see it in both their eyes—they were drifting and dreaming of tense cleverness, lazily riding the hurtling nightmare.

"A harmless relaxant," Fortnum was saying.

Oh, yes, yes, yes, Brosmer thought. In a little while, you can play music and I can dance, I can toss up my hair and be one with the wind, and when you speak to me, I shall answer in tongues that I learned as a child and forgot that I knew.

He pressed his arm against his side, firing Dexedrine into his body, and took a long draught. Amateur animals, he thought, gazing amiably, his nostrils tingling with fumes.

"Isn't that better?" Martita Fortnum whispered.

"Mm-hmm." He smiled at Fortnum. "Do you know where Charlie is? He must have taken his whole family with him."

"Oh, as a matter of fact, they went slightly ahead of him," Fortnum said, and Martita Fortnum giggled.

He could feel it working on him; not just the Swindle gradually winning over the clumsily saurian rages of the Dexedrine, but the rightness, the inevitability of these monsters and what had been swimming in their systems long before entertainment chemistry had come along with snappily salable products to validate it. What the hell am I doing here? he thought. I fly a Spad and these people are propelled by turbines.

He lolled his head back in his chair and looked up. There were brass placards in bronze frames hanging over where the door to 25709 could still be faintly made out in midair. Over the door to 25711, and over a bed, he imagined, was a nearly wall-width painting which, he deduced from what he could see of it, was of the ocean as one might glimpse it from a bower in a sea cave. The brass placards over the (permanently locked) door to 25709 were bas-reliefs of people in coveralls tearing patches off their clothing, baring buttocks and breasts.

"You killed them for their space," he whispered. "You

15

chewed away their walls, and you stuffed them in the duct for their dwelling allocations."

Fortnum sprang to his feet. Martita recoiled. Fortnum stared at him goggle-eyed: "You're a cop!"

Brosmer lolled in his chair. He gestured idly with his goblet. "Cousin Fuzz." He keyed his phone to the DA's channels. "NYPD shield number 062–26–8729 arresting Timothy and Martita Fortnum, 25609 North Panorama, charge Murder 1 three counts with additional pending. Attempted Murder of Police Officer, one count. Stand by and monitor. Sit down, Fortnum," he said.

Martita Fortnum sat down at the foot of the circular stairs, one hand over her eyes, the other wandering idly, clambering unconsciously up the banister to its fullest extension, then trailing swiftly back down to the newel post and clambering again.

Brosmer smiled from very far away. He held out his goblet to Fortnum. "Drink me," he said. "That's an order. You are being questioned."

Breathing sharply through white nostrils, Fortnum complied.

"How do you do it?" Brosmer said after the proper interval.

Fortnum sprawled. "Do what? Get through the walls? That's no trick—you just scrape away the material without nicking the sensors; you know, they're just all elementary. Thermocouples and manometers and things; standard hardware. After you get the wall structure cleared out, you swing all the wiring up so the sensors are reading each other; all the damn building systems care about is whether things are burning or flooding, or if the windows are broken. Then you hang drapes over it."

"Do architects know about plumbing?"

Fortnum raised his head and snorted. "What the hell do you think architecture is, these days? Everybody's got the same space allocation, and the building code's uniform, isn't it? What the hell makes a difference between units except the efficiency of the services? The hell, man, *you* could do it—dial up the library. It's all in there. Plumbing, phone systems . . . everything." A spasm crossed his face. "But *you* never thought of that. You're going home to your place, wherever it is, and dial up *Warbirds,* or do you watch cop shows?"

"I get along," Brosmer said. "Is that how you got to the elevator memory? Do you know about that from the library?"

*"You'*d have to. I *learned* it." It was amazing how much scorn and pride were getting through the Swindle. Brosmer took it in through the buzzing in his ears.

"The story conference," he said. "I can see how you might have learned to intercut tapes of Castelvecchio, but how did you fake being a writer?"

Fortnum giggled shockingly. He wiped his open lips. "Fake being a writer," he grinned. "Fake. Writers." He stood up suddenly and pulled the covering off the chair. Underneath was a metal cabinet. "There she is," he said fondly, running his hands over the home-joined crackled panels. He peered over his shoulder at Brosmer. "This is what it takes," he said, "you know. It's just an assembly of standard logic circuits. Nothing Buck Rogers about it. It's a synthesizing phone switchboard. You give it a lot of tapes of Charlie Castelvecchio sitting in a chair and babbling his life away, and when you speak into it, it puts his face on the phone and talks in his voice. Every time it can't match a lip movement, it shows him turning his face away from the point of view or putting his hand in front of his mouth. It makes him look like he's got the jerks, but who's gonna notice that?"

"And it does the writing for you?"

"Writing? You simple boob, all you need is a hero the audience can identify with, and you give him an immediate serious problem. Then you introduce complications that get him in deeper and deeper, but in the end he does something characteristic on his own hook, and gets out of it. The rest is just atmosphere. You think that stuff in your living room is *art?* Listen—" He waved his arm and dialed. Music swelled up in the room. It thrummed and shook in the air. "That's art," Fortnum said, bracing himself against the wall with one hand. "That's a little ditty called "Jesu, Joy of Man's Desiring," by Johann Sebastian Bach, the mightiest voice in the Public Domain." He dialed it off hastily. "You know what you can do with that? You can give it an up-tempo, write a set of words that make sounds like screwing but don't use the word, and you're rich. That's how that *momser* upstairs makes his living," Fortnum gasped, waving at the chandelier. "And over *there,*" he panted, pointing into the emptiness above his bed, "is the woman who sculpts by dipping paper strands in epoxy and throwing them into the air just before they harden. I can be any of them. I can be all three of them and me, too, all at the same time. And what do you think of that, cop?" He turned, and for a moment his hand rested on the antique scriber. He looked over his shoulder guiltily at Brosmer. Brosmer shook his forefinger at him.

It was the woman who moved—who sprang from her place and flew to the wall, and so it developed that it was for her —for the To Be Widow Fortnum—that Brosmer had worn his suit. She gaped at him unbelievingly as his servos operated the auxiliary mesh skin over his body and gave him the speed and strength of ten, so that though she flew as the gannet, he struck as the hawk. And then it was over; she and her husband sat comforting each other with justifications, a police lock on their open phone and police locks on their door(s) as Brosmer made his way home.

Dorrie greeted him. Her eyes did not meet his. "You— you're home very soon," she said. "I haven't left yet. Do you want me to stay?"

He went over to his chair, walking around her as best he could, thinking. He thought of what would happen. Perhaps already the libraries were being restricted in access. Only those with certain credentials, such as police buzzers, would be able to obtain certain classes of data.

"Ned?"

"What? Oh—no, no. You go ahead and do what you've promised. I've been thinking," he said. "Panorama owes me the standard rate on about seven Murder 1's, and even after I give George his twenty-five percent commission, and pay the bill from Forensic, that's pretty good. I think maybe we should get mirrors put in. On the walls . . . maybe on the ceiling."

Dorrie put her fingertip to her mouth. "It'll make it so much sexier in here," she murmured.

"Bigger," he said. "For a while."

Changelings

by **LISA TUTTLE**

Without trying to sound too sexist, we must go on record as saying we enjoy the works of female SF writers and enjoy including them in this annual. In the past we have anthologized Doris Piserchia, Sydney J. Van Scyoc, Angela Carter, Kit Reed, Cynthia Ozick, Naomi Mitchison and Ursula LeGuin. We now welcome Lisa Tuttle to these honored ranks.

Ryan turned away from the window, looking down and turning his glass so that the ice cubes spun. The house felt empty; the silence was not right. He knew that he should hear the soft sounds of his wife getting his daughter ready for bed.

Ryan felt lonely, and went to the portable bar for another drink. The bar looked like an antique wooden globe when it was closed. Ryan had bought it in Spain, where he and May had gone on their honeymoon, the year before civilian passports were revoked.

Annie walked in naked.

"Annie," Ryan said, gently reproving. He set his glass down on the stereo and went to kneel beside her. Her hair lay in moist curls around her head, and there were tiny droplets of water all over her body. The damp patch on the carpet where she stood began to spread. She turned her brilliant blue eyes, her mother's eyes, on Ryan and said accusingly, "Mommy didn't come dry me off."

Ryan smoothed her damp hair. Russet, he thought, auburn. The loveliest words for the loveliest color. It reminded him of autumn. He pressed his face against her head, but she smelled of Ivory soap and childhood, not of apples or leaves.

She pulled away, putting her hands on her hips, and made a mouth at him, the way she had seen her mother do. "Daddy. It's my bedtime."

"I'll put you to bed," he said. "You shouldn't run around naked, you know."

"Well, Mommy didn't *come*. I was looked for her."

"A child."

Ryan and Annie looked up together. May stood in the doorway, her hair mussed, her face soft and slightly puffy, as if she had been asleep.

"There's a child, a little girl. Ryan?"

No, he thought belatedly. He wished he had not been drinking, or that he had drunk himself into insensibility. But there was Annie.

"Annie, sweetheart—"

But she had run to her mother. "I waited and waited but you didn't come."

"Ryan?"

"Annie, sweetheart," Ryan said. "Run to your room and put on your jammies. Mommy and I will be in to kiss you goodnight in a minute."

"Mommy, why didn't you come dry me? Mommy? Why? Mommy?" Annie tugged at May's full skirt. Ryan caught the note in her voice that presaged tears. Poor Annie. She knew. She could sense it.

Dawning panic on May's face as she bent to enfold Annie's wet body to her. Her eyes did not leave Ryan's. "Oh, Ryan. This is—oh, Ryan—"

"Annie."

"Annie," May murmured. She stood up, holding Annie,

and bent her face into Annie's neck. "Annie, Annie. Oh, Annie."

Annie threw her arms around her mother's neck and buried her face against her. But she said nothing. She was not reassurred.

"I'll take her to bed?" May asked.

"At the end of the hall."

"Wait for me."

Ryan sank into the couch and stared at the Van Gogh print on the opposite wall. Crazy old Van Gogh. He had cut off his own ear. Ryan wondered what they had done to him after that.

"Five years, Ryan. At least five years." May came and sat beside him on the couch, taking his hand between hers. "How old is she? Of course we called her Annie, after my sister, right?"

Ryan nodded wearily.

"This has happened before, hasn't it, Ryan? It's happened before? Has it?"

"Yes."

"But I don't remember! I don't! We were married, the two of us, together, here—" she touched the couch and looked around. "Here, in this house. But no Annie, no children. Oh, Ryan, what does it mean? How could I lose—five years? Or more? How could it happen? Why? What is it?"

"You just forget things," he said very softly.

"But why? Always? Will my memory come back? Why?"

"The operation. It's something to do with that."

She stared at him in a panic and snatched her hand from his. "What op—I don't remember! What's wrong with me— is this me?" Turning her face away from him, she began to cry.

Ryan stood and went to the window, where he stared out at the placid streets. The pools of light beneath each street-lamp were empty. The neighborhood was silent. People didn't go out much after dark anymore, though the streets were safer than they had ever been. He turned back into the room. May had stopped crying. She had never been one for crying.

She said, "When I was little my sister Annie told me that every seven years each cell in a person's body has been replaced. I guess I was about five then. It really worried me. She told me that every seven years you become a completely new person. A *different* person. I used to be afraid. I thought that when I was seven I wouldn't remember the old me. I thought that if my brain cells were all replaced then," she turned her palms upward into the air, "poof go my memories."

"But by the time you were seven you had forgotten about it. Until Annie reminded you."

"I've told you this before?"

Ryan nodded.

"The last time I forgot? Is it like this every time?"

"Not exactly."

"How often? How long has this been going on? Have we been to the doctor?"

"More than one. There's nothing . . . nothing that can be done. It might be just an immediate reaction, and it should stop soon." But her periods of amnesia had been increasing in frequency.

"What operation was this?" May asked.

"Government sponsored for a better future."

She glanced at him sharply. "A volunteer thing?"

"Not in the least. People turned each other in—and then, of course, there were the criminals, and those on file as subversives."

"Of course. I was a subversive in college. A teenage radical. What did the operation do to me?"

"Made you a better, happier citizen. The object was to remove your destructive tendencies and install something, a tracer device, so that if you should backslide, they could find you."

"Are you . . . ?"

"No. There's a new bill up, though, about 'testing for

23

subversive and criminal potentiality,' and if it passes, which it will . . .''

May stared at the floor. "I don't remember. I could have been in fairyland for the past five years. Or what Annie told me about being made new, or—"

"Or you could be a changeling."

She looked up. "How did you know—"

"That was the story Annie wanted?"

She nodded. "I told her no story tonight."

"But she never goes to sleep without a story."

"She was very good about it. Very quiet. She—I suppose she could feel there was something wrong, that I was different. I didn't even know what drawer her pajamas were in. Oh, Ryan, can't we do something? When will I be all right again?"

Ryan shrugged, caught her look of need. "I'm sorry, but it varies. A few hours or a few days."

"Never any longer?"

He shook his head. Last time it had been six days before her memory came back. The duration grew longer, and the time between occurrences lessened. The first time she had been set back only to the time of the operation.

"Can we call a doctor?"

"I told you—"

"Oh, please, darling—just let's call Ben. It will make me feel better to talk to him. He knows about me?"

Ryan nodded. "I'll call him."

She leaned across the couch to hug him, and he pulled her to him, holding on tight.

May went back into the bedroom while Ryan called Ben. "I'll just lie down for a while," she said.

Ben would come, of course. He was the family doctor and a long-time family friend. He promised to be by within an hour.

Ryan went into the bedroom. It was dark, but the curtains were open, and there was some light from the street. He saw the gleam of May's eyes.

"I didn't mean to disturb you," he said.

"I'm not sleepy. He's coming?"

"In about an hour."

"Oh?"

"I told him it wasn't an emergency. Really, darling, we can't just break up his whole evening."

"I'm sorry."

"Don't be silly."

He went to the dresser, to the box that held the cuff links and tie clips he never wore, relics of a time past.

He took out a folded, brittle newspaper clipping and unfolded it by the window in a shaft of light from the streetlamp, although he knew the picture well enough to look at it in the dark.

It had been a front-page photo. May's head was sandwiched between two others, leaning out of the window of an occupied building. A banner proclaiming the building's liberation stretched below them. Three arms thrust forward in jubilant fists. And May's face, smiling, alive, victorious . . . holy.

"For this," he said softly.

"Ryan? What are you—oh. I wish you'd throw that away. I don't like it." He turned and saw that she had raised herself on her elbows. "That's not me. It was a stupid, violent time that we grew up in. You had the sense then . . . I didn't. I'm a different person now, though. I don't know how I could have ever been like that . . . I can't even remember what it felt like."

"Of course you can't." He folded the paper and put it in his back pocket.

"Ryan? Come here." Her voice was shy.

"Not now," he said, as gently as he could, and left the room without touching her.

He didn't like the way the living room felt, and he knew the rest of the house would be no better. He felt like a deserter, but he went outside. He would walk for a few minutes.

Outside was no better. It was quiet and the air felt thick and still. He could taste the smog. He began to walk, hoping he would see someone to speak to, but he saw no one. He headed up toward the highway, toward a diner he had occasionally stopped in for a cup of coffee.

The diner, when he reached it, was empty except for the counterman, its emptiness made the more vivid by the merciless fluorescent lights shining down endlessly on all the hard, clean, bright surfaces.

"Evening," said the counterman cheerily. "What can I do for you?"

Ryan straddled one of the high brown stools. "Just a Coke. Thanks."

"This is a slow time," the counterman said. "Past the regular dinner hour, but not so late that other places are closed. You live nearby, don't you? We don't get many walking in—when I saw you didn't have a car, I knew you must be from nearby. There y'are—anything else?"

"No, thanks."

"Walk for your health?"

"I just wanted some air."

"Nice night for walking, I guess. Real warm for this late in the season."

Ryan wished another customer would come in. The counterman's persistent friendliness made him uncomfortable, and his physical appearance inspired dislike in Ryan: the shining head beneath thinning hair, the watery blue eyes, the horsey teeth beneath the stiff ginger mustache. . . . Ryan turned his attention to the voice from the radio that was playing at the end of the counter. It was a news broadcast, full of hopeful messages about the state of the union. There was less and less coverage given to the rest of the world these days —no one wanted to hear about wars or crime.

The counterman seemed to follow Ryan's attention. "Gives you hope, doesn't it?"

"What?"

"The news. It's all good now, or nearly. Just remember how it was ten years ago—or even five. People didn't go out on the streets—you wouldn't have gone out for fresh air unless you were crazy. You would have been beaten up and robbed. Mugged." He said the word as if it were foreign and he wasn't sure of the pronunciation.

"Thanks to the operation," Ryan said.

"That, and other things. The government finally cracking down on criminals. Democracy is great, but people have to *deserve* it. There were a lot of changes that had to be made."

"Did you have the operation?" Ryan asked.

"Me? No. I've always been a good citizen. I've always done my duty." The way the counterman looked at him made Ryan uneasy, and he had to caution himself against paranoia. The day May was in the hospital he had gone around all day suspecting people of spying on him, of being out to get him, of making accusations disguised as innocuous conversation.

Ryan realized that he was standing, fumbling in his pocket for change.

"I've got to be going," he said. "I didn't tell my wife I was going out—she'll worry—"

"But you didn't drink your Coke."

"I guess I'm not thirsty." He put a quarter on the counter.

The counterman pushed it back. "I won't charge you for it, then. Drink it myself." He smiled. "Have a good walk." His "Come back again" was cut off by the closing of the heavy glass door.

Headlights cut across Ryan's face as he turned up his driveway, and he felt the familiar paranoid beating of his heart as he realized the car was turning into his driveway just behind him.

"Ryan? Is anything wrong?"

It was Ben.

"No, no. I just stepped out for some air."

"Well, you stepped into the wrong place for it," Ben said, getting out of his car. "Phew. It stinks tonight. Supposed to clear by tomorrow, though."

Ben was one year away from compulsory retirement. He'd chosen to continue working through the past two optional years. They went into the house together.

"May's in the bedroom, resting."

"Fine." He scrutinized Ryan's face. "You shouldn't let this get to you, you know. I'm sure it's only some preliminary adjustment."

"Why don't you go in and see her?" Ryan knew that Ben would catch the hard edge of dismissal in his voice, knew also that Ben would not be offended by it.

"Sure, sure," Ben said. He put his hand on Ryan's shoulder. "Take it easy."

Ryan sank into the couch, ignoring the voices that came quietly from the other room.

"She'll sleep now," Ben said when he came out of the bedroom. "Could I trouble you for a cup of coffee?" He followed Ryan into the kitchen.

"What did you tell her?"

"She just wanted to talk."

"She's sleeping, you said?"

"No, but it shouldn't be long."

"Why didn't you just turn her off?"

"I wouldn't do that, Ryan."

"Why not? You're a doctor; you should know all about implants. I turned her off myself, once. Accidentally. I was frantic until I found the place again to turn her back on."

"The little death," said the doctor.

"No. More like turning off and turning on a doll. Ben, they've taken my wife away from me and given me a docile robot-housekeeper. They destroyed her! Now she's losing her past—"

"It's nothing to worry about, Ryan. This whole business of the memory—it will pass, I promise you."

"How do you know? Maybe for some people—but when they're tampering with minds—it could get worse. She'll be nothing but a shell, without memories, and they'll reprogram her into a model citizen—that's what they—"

"Your voice, Ryan—lower your voice."

Ryan took a coffee cup and saucer out of the cupboard, his hands shaking.

"How did we let this happen, Ben? How could we? It won't stop. It was only the criminals at first—but they took my wife, my sweet, beautiful May just because she was on their bloody list."

"She wasn't harmed, Ryan. You're being overly dramatic. You must face up to the fact that May had certain . . . tendencies and beliefs that could be harmful."

"She never did anything! They forced her to have this op—"

"Calm down, Ryan. If May had had an illness you would have wanted it operated on, removed—"

"The analogy doesn't hold, *Doctor*. May used to be interested and aggressive and very alive. She wanted to change things—she was a constructive person, not a destructive one. You've seen the change—you can't say it's for the better. I can't believe this is you, Ben, spouting—" Ryan stopped, comprehension dawning. "You. You've had the operation, too. You have an implant like May, haven't you, Ben?"

"Yes. Yes, I have. But don't you see—"

"Why you?" Ryan asked softly. "God knows you've never been a radical. What was your crime? Membership in the JDL?"

"I was against the operations at first. I thought that they removed the will. Now I understand—"

"Of course. And now you're a puppet as well."

"You're being paranoid. There is no great 'they' corrupting us—we run our own lives."

"Oh, we let it happen, all right. We wanted to burn out the badness in our criminals. Then in our potential criminals.

Then in anyone who disagrees. Change their minds. Indoctrinate our children."

"Ryan, it's all for the good."

"It always is. The good of the State. Well, goddamn the State!"

"As your doctor and your friend I must advise you to stop this foolish talk. Get some sleep. Take a vacation. Don't worry so much."

"That's a great prescription. This country has gone to hell precisely because we've closed our eyes."

Ben turned away. "I'd better leave now."

Ryan saw his own hand go out toward the back of Ben's neck. His fingers found it, pressed, and he caught Ben before he could hit the floor. The implant was in the same place as May's.

"How convenient," he murmured. He looked up from the sleeping Ben to see Annie standing in the doorway in a long blue nightgown, her little bare feet curling on the linoleum as she watched in silence. In a year she would have to go to kindergarten, and they would begin on her, feeding her drugs for docility and propaganda in the name of education.

"Is Doctor Ben sick?"

"Just sleeping, hon. Run back to bed now."

"Can't sleep."

"Sure you can."

"No story," she said, widening her eyes at him. A finger went to her mouth, and she chewed it thoughtfully, staring at him.

"Run back to bed, and Daddy will come tell you a story."

When she had gone, he laid Ben down in some semblance of comfort. He thought about going to Canada. He had thought about it before. Things weren't much better up there, but in Canada and in the northwestern states like Washington and Oregon the underground was supposed to be strong. May had told him that, before the operation. They should have gotten out then, but when you've spent your whole life, as Ryan had, accepting and obeying, it was hard to give up everything and go.

If he went now he would have to leave May. He couldn't take her—the implant was part tracer, and the police would have them back as soon as they were missed.

He went back into the bedroom.

"Darling? Has Ben gone?"

"Yeah."

"I didn't hear his car. I was listening for it."

"You should be asleep."

"I know. Is Annie still up?"

"Yes, she came out and saw Ben."

"Oh. I heard her—I didn't hear any other voices—I don't know, I thought she was playing with the phone. I must have been dozing."

"Of course you were. Go back to sleep. The sooner you do, the sooner it will be morning."

She laughed. "Like Christmas. If I wait for Santa, he'll never come. Ryan . . ."

He went to her, bent over, and kissed her. His hand went behind her neck and pressed, and her lips fell slack and asleep beneath his.

He went into Annie's room and helped her to dress, telling her that they were going for a ride.

"But it's late."

"Not for grown-up people. And you're not asleep, anyway. You like to go for rides."

"Yes," she said doubtfully. "Will Mommy come?"

"No. Mommy's sleeping."

"Like Doctor Ben?"

He looked down at her sharply.

"You turned him off, didn't you?"

"What do you mean?"

"You turned off Doctor Ben."

"What do you know about things like that? Where did you hear it?"

"I just know." Her eyes grew vague. She looked away. "Can I bring Raggedy Ann?" Ryan picked up the doll from the bedside table, where it slumped against the pink Princess telephone.

The streets were eerily empty. Didn't people go out anymore? Ryan turned on the radio in the car and settled into driving.

"The President spoke to the nation this afternoon, expressing his gratitude to the people of the United States for making such a drastic drop in the crime rate possible. Reminding his listeners that 'Eternal Vigilance is the price of freedom,' Mr.—"

Ryan punched the key for another station and got some bouncy, innocuous music.

"We learned that in school," Annie said suddenly.

"What?"

"Eternal vigilance."

"Annie, you don't go to school."

"Ballet school. I do so."

"You learned that in ballet school?"

"Miss Fontaine tells us lots of things."

"Not always about ballet, I take it." He had convinced May that ballet lessons would be more useful to Annie than nursery school. There were no more safe places.

"You shouldn't have," she said.

"What?" She was as uncanny as her mother about reaching into his thoughts.

"Done what you did to Doctor Ben. That's against the law. And the things you said to him. They were wrong, too."

"How long were you spying on us?" Fat, ugly spiders were crawling up his spine. His sweat made him cold. He looked at her. She was leaning away from him, her face close to the window, fogging it with her breath and tracing lines with one finger. "Answer me!" Her left hand crept to her mouth at the sharpness in his voice.

"It was against the law," she whispered.

32

"Annie—" With an effort he gentled his voice, returned most of his attention to the road. They were on the freeway now, heading out of town, and there was some traffic. "Annie, you know your Daddy wouldn't do anything wrong. Sometimes the laws are wrong, and people must change them."

"People change laws by voting. People who break laws are sick and they must be helped." The words were not hers; her voice was virtuous and intent.

"Does Miss Fontaine tell you that, too?"

"Nuh-uh. That's Sargent Dare."

"Who's Sargent Dare?"

"*You* know. On TV."

"The TV doesn't always tell you the truth, punkin. Life isn't that simple. The TV is wrong sometimes, but what your parents tell you—"

"Tell me a story. You said you would. Tell me the one about the changeling."

"I don't know that one."

"Yes you *do*. About how the fairies come and steal away the human baby and put a fairy child in its place—yes you *do* know it. Tell me."

"Not while I'm driving, sweetheart." Glancing down at her, he saw that she was near tears. She should have been asleep long ago, poor kid. "Look, why don't you climb over into the back seat and lie down and go to sleep?"

"Story first."

"You'll have to give me time to think of one, then."

"Okay."

But all he could think of was May, how she had been before, and the way they had changed her. Annie began to speak then, and he pulled himself out of bitterness to listen.

"On Sargent Dare there was this show where this boy's parents were very bad people." She was speaking to her Raggedy Ann doll, Ryan saw. She used that ploy often, dragging the doll into a room where her parents were occupied, and talking to it, meaning for them to hear as well. "They weren't really bad people, but they were sick. They had bad thoughts, and so they broke the law. They broke the law a whole lot, but nobody knew about it except their little boy. Then he learned in school about the law and so he called the police and told them. He remembered the number.

"But don't worry, Raggedy, they didn't put his parents in jail. The police are our friends. They help us. They took his parents and did a little operation and made them happy. They came home and they smiled and they never broke the law again and they gave the little boy presents. And they all lived happily ever after."

There was a road block up ahead. A routine police check. One of the measures that was ridding the country of crime. Ryan had been through a dozen of them, at least. He slowed the car, his throat tight.

He felt Annie sliding closer to him on the seat. She put her hand on his arm.

"We'll live happily?" she asked. "Happily ever after?"

The Santa Claus Compromise

by **THOMAS M. DISCH**

Well, yes, it must be a good thing to lower the voting and drinking age. If someone can be drafted and shot in his country's service at the age of eighteen, he should also be allowed to drink to numb the pain. But why stop at eighteen? Sixteen—or lower perhaps, or . . . or let Disch outline what the eventual end might be.

The first revelations hit the headlines the day after Thanksgiving, less than a year from the Supreme Court's epochal decision to extend full civil liberties to five-year-olds. After centuries of servitude and repression the last minority was finally free. Free to get married. Free to vote and hold office. Free to go to bed at any hour they wanted. Free to spend their allowances on whatever they liked.

For those services geared to the newly liberated young it was a period of heady expansion. A typical example was Lord & Taylor's department stores, which had gone deeply into the red in the two previous years, due to the popularity of thermal body-paints. Lord & Taylor changed its name to Dumb Dresses and Silly Shoes, and its profits soared to record heights in the second quarter of '79. In the field of entertainment, the Broadway musical *I See London, I See France* scored a similar success with audiences and critics alike. "I think it

35

shows," wrote *Our Own Times* Drama Critic Sandy Myers, "how kids are really on the ball today. I think everyone who likes singing and dancing and things like that should go and see it. But prudes should be warned that some of the humor is pretty spicy."

It was the same newspaper's team of investigative reporters, Bobby Boyd and Michelle Ginsberg, who broke the Santa Claus story one memorable November morning. Under a banner headline that proclaimed: "THERE IS NO SANTA CLAUS!" Bobby told how, months before, rummaging through various trunks and boxes in his parents' home in Westchester, he had discovered a costume identical in every respect with that worn by the "Santa Claus" who had visited the Boyd household on the previous Christmas Eve. "My soul was torn," wrote the young Pulitzer Prize winner, "between feelings of outrage and fear. The thought of all the years of imposture and deceit that had been practiced on me and my brothers and sisters around the world made me furious. Then, when I foresaw all that I'd be up against, a shiver of dread went through me. If I'd known that the trail of guilt would lead me to the door of my father's bedroom, I can't be sure that I'd have followed it. I had my suspicions, of course."

But suspicions, however strong, weren't enough for Bobby and Michelle. They wanted evidence. Months of back-breaking and heart-breaking labor produced nothing but hearsay, innuendo, and conflicting allegations. Then, in mid-November, as the stores were already beginning to fill with Christmas displays, Michelle met the mysterious Clayton E. Forster. Forster claimed that he had repeatedly assumed the character and name of Santa Claus, and that this imposture had been financed from funds set aside for this purpose by a number of prominent New York businesses. When asked if he had ever met or spoken to the real Santa Claus, Forster declared outright that *there wasn't any!* Though prevented from confirming Forster's allegations from his own lips by the municipal authorities (Forster had been sent to prison on a vagrancy charge), reporters were able to listen to Michelle's tape recording of the interview, on which the self-styled soldier-of-fortune could be heard to say: "Santa Claus? Santa's just a pile of (expletive deleted), kid! Get wise—there ain't no (expletive deleted), and there never was one. It's nothing but your (expletive deleted) mother and father!"

The clincher, however, was Bobby's publication of a number of BankAmericard receipts, charging Mr. Oscar T. Boyd for, among much else, "2 rooty-toot-toots and 3 rummy-tumtums." These purchases had been made in early December of the previous year and coincided *in all respects* with the Christmas presents that the Boyd children subsequently received, presumably from Santa Claus. "You could call it circumstantial evidence, sure," admitted *Our Own Times'* Senior Editor Barry "Beaver" Collins, "but we felt we'd reached the point when we had to let the public know."

The public reacted at first with sheer, blank incomprehension. Only slowly did the significance and extent of the alleged fraud sink in. A Gallup poll, taken on December 1, asked voters aged five through eight: "Do you believe in Santa Claus?" The results: Yes, 26%; No, 38%; Not sure, 36%. Older children were even more skeptical. A Harris poll taken at the same time seemed to show a more widespread faith in Santa: 84% of all younger voters replied "Yes" when asked if they expected Santa to leave presents for them on Christmas morning. Only the grownup-oriented media saw fit to point out that a Santa who didn't exist could not very well leave presents.

On December 12, an estimated 300,000 children converged on the Boyd residence in Westchester from every part of the city and the state. Chanting "Poop on the big fat hypocrites," they solemnly burned no less than 128 effigies of Santa Claus in the Boyds' front yard. Equivalent protests took place in every major city.

The height of the scandal—and of the protests—came the following day, when the two young reporters revealed that

Dorothy Biddle, personnel director of the vast Macy's Toy Store, had ordered the contents of three personnel department files shredded and burned on the very day the *Times'* story had broken. The employee who had carried out this task, Miss Charlotte Olson, contacted Bobby and Michelle after hearing Baby Jesus sing "Jingle Bells" in a vision. Though Miss Olson claimed not to have examined the documents she shredded, the implication was irresistible that these were the employment records of the "False Santas" spoken of by Clayton Forster. Director Biddle would neither confirm nor deny the *Times'* sensational charges, insisting that whether or not they were true, the *real* Santa Claus might nevertheless exist. For many young people, however, this argument was no longer persuasive. As Bobby later wrote, looking back on those momentous days, "It had become something bigger than just Santa Claus. We began to question everything our daddies and mommies told us. It was scary. You know?"

The real long-range consequences of the scandal did not become apparent for much longer, since they lay rather in what wasn't done than in what was. People were acting as though not only Santa but Christmas itself had been called in question. Log-jams of unsold merchandise piled up in stockrooms and warehouses, and the streets filled up with forests of brittle evergreens.

Any number of public figures tried, unavailingly, to reverse this portentous state of affairs. The Congress appropriated $3 million to decorate the Capitol and the White House with giant figures of Santa and his reindeer, and the Lincoln Memorial temporarily became the Santa Claus Memorial. Reverend Billy Graham announced that he was a personal friend of both Santa Claus and his wife, and had often led prayer meetings at Santa's workshop at the North Pole. But nothing served to restore the public's confidence. By December 18, one week before Christmas, the Dow-Jones industrial average had fallen to an all-time low.

In response to appeals from businessmen all over the country, a national emergency was declared and Christmas was pushed back one month, to the 25th of January, on which date it continues to be celebrated. An effort was made by the National Association of Manufacturers to substitute their own Grandma America for the disgraced Santa Claus. Grandma America had a distinct advantage over her predecessor, in that she was invisible and could walk through walls, thereby eliminating the age-old problem of how children living in chimneyless houses get their presents. There appeared to be hope that this campaign would succeed, until a rival group of businesses which had been excluded from the Grandma America franchise introduced Aloysius the Magic Snowman, and the Disney Corporation premiered their new nightly TV series, *Uncle Scrooge and the Spirit of Christmas Presents.*

The predictable result of the mutual recriminations of the various franchise-holders was an even greater dubiety on the part of both children and grownups. "I used to be a really convinced believer in Santa," declared Bobby's mother in an exclusive interview with her son, "but now with all this fufa-raw over Grandma America and the rest of them, I just don't know. It seems sordid, somehow. As for Christmas itself, I think we may just sit this one out."

"Bobby and I, we just felt *terrible,*" pretty little (3′ 11″) Michelle Ginsberg said, recalling these dark mid-January days at the Pulitzer Prize ceremony. "We'd reported what we honestly believed were the facts. We never considered that it could lead to a recession or anything so awful. I remember one Christmas morning—what *used* to be Christmas, that is— sitting there with my empty pantyhose hanging from the fireplace and just crying my heart out. It was probably the single most painful moment of my life."

Then, on January 21, *Our Own Times* received a telephone call from the President of the United States, who invited its two reporters, Billy and Michelle, to come with him on the Presidential jet, *Spirit of '76,* on a special surprise visit to the North Pole!

What they saw there, and whom they met, the whole nation learned on the night of January 24, the new Christmas Eve, during the President's momentous press conference. After Billy showed his Polaroid snapshots of the elves at work in their workshop, of himself shaking Santa's hand and sitting beside him in his sleigh, and of everyone—Billy, Michelle, Santa Claus and Mrs. Santa, the President and the First Lady —sitting down to a big turkey dinner, Michelle read a list of all the presents that she and Billy had received. Their estimated retail value: $18,599.95. As Michelle bluntly put it: "My father just doesn't make that kind of money."

"So would you say, Michelle," the President asked with a twinkle in his eye, "that you do believe in Santa Claus?"

"Oh, absolutely, there's no question."

"And you, Billy?"

Billy looked at the tips of his new cowboy boots and smiled. "Oh, sure. And not just 'cause he gave us such swell presents. His beard, for instance. I gave it quite a yank. I'd take my oath that the beard was real."

The President put his arms around the two children and gave them a big warm squeeze. Then, becoming suddenly more serious, he looked right at the TV camera and said: "Billy, Michelle—your friends who told you that there is no Santa Claus were wrong. They have been affected by the skepticism of a skeptical age. They do not believe except they see. They think that nothing can be which is not comprehensible by their little minds. But all minds, Virginia—uh, that is to say, Billy and Michelle—whether they be men's or children's, are little. In this great universe of ours, man is a mere *insect,* an ant, in his intellect, as compared with the boundless world about him, as measured by the intelligence capable of grasping the *whole* of truth and knowledge.

"Not believe in Santa Claus? You might as well not believe in fairies. No Santa Claus! Thank God he lives, and he lives forever. A thousand years from now—nay, ten times ten thousand years from now, he will continue to make glad the hearts of childhood."

Then, with a friendly wink, and laying his finger aside of his nose, he added, "In conclusion, I would like to say—to Billy and Michelle and to my fellow Americans of every age —Merry Christmas to all, and to all a good night!"

A Galaxy Called Rome

by **BARRY MALZBERG**

Who said that Malzberg could not write "hard" science fiction? It is beginning to look as if Malzberg can do anything he sets his mind to. His novel, *Beyond Apollo,* won the John W. Campbell Memorial Award for the best novel of 1972. Perhaps that joining of names engendered this story, which is a memorial as well to that same master.

I

This is not a novelette but a series of notes. The novelette cannot be truly written, because it partakes of its time, which is distant and could be perceived only through the idiom and devices of that era.

Thus the piece, by virtue of these reasons and others too personal even for this variety of True Confession, is little more than a set of constructions toward something less substantial . . . and, like the author, it cannot be completed.

II

The novelette would lean heavily upon two articles by the late John Campbell, for thirty-three years the editor of *Astounding/Analog,* which were written shortly before his death untimely on July 11, 1971, and appeared as editorials in his magazine later that year, the second being perhaps the last piece which will ever bear his byline. They imagine a black galaxy which would result from the implosion of a neutron star, an implosion so mighty that gravitational forces unleashed would contain not only light itself but space and time; and *A Galaxy Called Rome* is his title, not mine, since he envisions a spacecraft that might be trapped within such a black galaxy and be unable to get out . . . because escape velocity would have to exceed the speed of light. All paths of travel would lead to this galaxy, then; none away. A galaxy called Rome.

III

Conceive then of a faster-than-light spaceship which would tumble into the black galaxy and would be unable to leave. Tumbling would be easy, or at least inevitable, since one of the characteristics of the black galaxy would be its *invisibility,* and there the ship would be. The story would then pivot on the efforts of the crew to get out. The ship is named *Skipstone.* It was completed in 3892. Five hundred people died so that it might fly, but in this age life is held even more cheaply than it is today.

Left to my own devices, I might be less interested in the escape problem than that of adjustment. Light housekeeping in an anterior sector of the universe; submission to the elements, a fine, ironic literary despair. This is not science

43

fiction, however. Science fiction was created by Hugo Gernsback to show us the ways out of technological impasse. So be it.

IV

As interesting as the material was, I quailed even at this series of notes, let alone a polished, completed work. My personal life is my black hole, I felt like pointing out (who would listen?); my daughters provide a more correct and sticky implosion than any neutron star, and the sound of the pulsars is as nothing to the music of the paddock area at Aqueduct racetrack in Ozone Park, Queens, on a clear summer Tuesday. "Enough of these breathtaking concepts, infinite distances, quasar leaps, binding messages amidst the arms of the spiral nebula," I could have pointed out. "I know that there are those who find an ultimate truth there, but I am not one of them. I would rather dedicate the years of life remaining (my melodramatic streak) to an understanding of the agonies of this middle-class town in northern New Jersey; until I can deal with those, how can I comprehend Ridgefield Park, to say nothing of the extension of fission to include progressively heavier gases?" Indeed, I almost abided to this until it occurred to me that Ridgefield Park would forever be as mysterious as the stars and that one could not deny infinity merely to pursue a particular that would be impenetrable until the day of one's death.

So I decided to try the novelette, at least as this series of notes, although with some trepidation, but trepidation did not unsettle me, nor did I grieve, for my life is merely a set of notes for a life, and Ridgefield Park merely a rough working model of Trenton, in which, nevertheless, several thousand people live who cannot discern their right hands from their left, and also much cattle.

V

It is 3895. The spacecraft *Skipstone,* on an exploratory flight through the major and minor galaxies surrounding the Milky Way, falls into the black galaxy of a neutron star and is lost forever.

The captain of this ship, the only living consciousness of it, is its commander, Lena Thomas. True, the hold of the ship carries five hundred and fifteen of the dead sealed in gelatinous fix who will absorb unshielded gamma rays. True, these rays will at some time in the future hasten their reconstitution. True, again, that another part of the hold contains the prostheses of seven skilled engineers, male and female, who could be switched on at only slight inconvenience and would provide Lena not only with answers to any technical problems which would arise but with companionship to while away the long and grave hours of the *Skipstone*'s flight.

Lena, however, does not use the prosthesis, nor does she feel the necessity to. She is highly skilled and competent, at least in relation to the routine tasks of this testing flight, and she feels that to call for outside help would only be an admission of weakness, would be reported back to the Bureau and lessen her potential for promotion. (She is right; the Bureau has monitored every cubicle of this ship, both visually and biologically; she can see or do nothing which does not trace to a printout; they would not think well of her if she were dependent upon outside assistance.) Toward the embalmed she feels somewhat more; her condition rattling in the hold of the ship as it moves on tachyonic drive seems to approximate theirs: although they are deprived of consciousness, that quality seems to be almost irrelevant to the condition of hyperspace; and if there were any way that she could bridge their mystery, she might well address them. As it is, she must settle for imaginary dialogues and for long, quiescent periods when she will watch the monitors, watch the rainbow of hy-

45

perspace, the collision of the spectrum, and say nothing what-soever.

Saying nothing will not do, however, and the fact is that Lena talks incessantly at times, if only to herself. This is good, because the story should have much dialogue; dramatic incident is best impelled through straightforward characterization, and Lena's compulsive need, now and then, to state her condition and its relation to the spaces she occupies will satisfy this need.

In her conversation, of course, she often addresses the embalmed. "Consider," she says to them, some of them dead eight hundred years, others dead weeks, all of them stacked in the hold in relation to their status in life and their ability to hoard assets to pay for the process that will return them their lives, "consider what's going on here," pointing through the hold, the colors gleaming through the portholes onto her wrist, colors dancing in the air, her eyes quite full and maddened in this light, which does not indicate that she is mad but only that the condition of hyperspace itself is insane, the Michelson-Morley effect having a psychological as well as physical reality here. "Why, it could be *me* dead and in the hold and all of you here in the dock watching the colors spin; it's all the same, all the same faster than light," and indeed the twisting and sliding effects of the tachyonic drive are such that at the moment of speech what Lena says is true.

The dead live; the living are dead; all slides and becomes jumbled together as she has noted; and were it not that their objective poles of consciousness were fixed by years of training and discipline, just as hers are transfixed by a different kind of training and discipline, she would press the levers to eject the dead one by one into the larger coffin of space, something which is indicated only as an emergency procedure under the gravest of terms and which would result in her removal from the Bureau immediately upon her return. The dead are precious cargo; they are, in essence, paying for the experiments and must be handled with the greatest delicacy.

"I will handle you with the greatest delicacy," Lena says in hyperspace, "and I will never let you go, little packages in my little prison," and so on, singing and chanting as the ship moves on somewhat in excess of one million miles per second, always accelerating; and yet, except for the colors, the nausea, the disorienting swing, her own mounting insanity, the terms of this story, she might be in the IRT Lenox Avenue local at rush hour, moving slowly uptown as circles of illness move through the fainting car in the bowels of summer.

VI

She is twenty-eight years old. Almost two thousand years in the future, when man has established colonies on forty planets in the Milky Way, has fully populated the solar system, is working in the faster-than-light experiments as quickly as he can to move through other galaxies, the medical science of that day is not notably superior to that of our own, and the human lifespan has not been significantly extended, nor have the diseases of mankind which are now known as congenital been eradicated. Most of the embalmed were in their eighties or nineties; a few of them, the more recent deaths, were nearly a hundred, but the average lifespan still hangs somewhat short of eighty, and most of these have died from cancer, heart attacks, renal failure, cerebral blowout, and the like. There is some irony in the fact that man can have at least established a toehold in his galaxy, can have solved the mysteries of the FTL drive, and yet finds the fact of his own biology as stupefying as he has throughout history. But every sociologist understands that those who live in a culture are least qualified to criticize it (because they have fully assimilated the codes of the culture, even as to criticism), and Lena does not see this irony any more than the reader will have to in order to appreciate the deeper and more metaphysical irony of the story, which is this: that greater speed, greater space, greater progress, greater sensation has not resulted in any definable expansion of the limits of consciousness and personality, and all that the FTL drive is to Lena is an increasing entrapment.

It is important to understand that she is merely a technician; that although she is highly skilled and has been trained through the Bureau for many years for her job as pilot, she really does not need to possess the technical knowledge of any graduate scientists of our own time . . . that her job, which is essentially a probe-and-ferrying, could be done by an adolescent; and that all of her training has afforded her no protection against the boredom and depression of her assignment.

When she is done with this latest probe, she will return to Uranus and be granted a six-month leave. She is looking forward to that. She appreciates the opportunity. She is only twenty-eight, and she is tired of being sent with the dead to tumble through the spectrum for weeks at a time, and what she would very much like to be, at least for a while, is a young woman. She would like to be at peace. She would like to be loved. She would like to have sex.

VII

Something must be made of the element of sex in this story, if only because it deals with a female protagonist (where asepsis will not work); and in the tradition of modern literary science fiction, where some credence is given to the whole range of human needs and behaviors, it would be clumsy and amateurish to ignore the issue. Certainly the easy scenes can be written and to great effect: Lena masturbating as she stares through the port at the colored levels of hyperspace; Lena dreaming thickly of intercourse as she unconsciously massages her nipples, the ship plunging deeper and deeper (as she does not yet know) toward the Black Galaxy; the Black Galaxy itself as some ultimate vaginal symbol of absorption whose Freudian overcast will not be ignored in the imagery of this story . . . indeed, one can envision Lena stumbling toward the Evictors at the depths of her panic in the Black Galaxy to bring out one of the embalmed, her grim and necrophiliac fantasies as the body is slowly moved upwards on its glistening slab, the way that her eyes will look as she comes to consciousness and realizes what she has become . . . oh, this would be a very powerful scene indeed—almost anything to do with sex in space is powerful (one must also conjure with the effects of hyperspace upon the orgasm; would it be the orgasm which all of us know and love so well, or something entirely different, perhaps detumescence, perhaps exaltation?)—and I would face the issue squarely, if only I could, and in line with the very real need of the story to have powerful and effective dialogue.

"For God's sake," Lena would say at the end, the music of her entrapment squeezing her, coming over her, blotting her toward extinction, "for God's sake, all we ever needed was a fuck, that's all that sent us out into space, that's all that it ever meant to us, I've got to have it, got to have it, do you understand?" jamming her fingers in and out of her aqueous surfaces. . . .

—But of course this would not work, at least in the story which I am trying to conceptualize. Space *is* aseptic; that is the secret of science fiction for forty-five years; it is not deceit or its adolescent audience or the publication codes which have deprived most of the literature of the range of human sexuality, but the fact that in the clean and abysmal spaces between the stars sex, that demonstration of our perverse and irreplaceable humanity, would have no role at all. Not for nothing did the astronauts return to tell us their vision of otherworldliness; not for nothing did they stagger in their thick landing gear as they walked toward the colonels' salute; not for nothing did all of those marriages, all of those wonderful kids undergo such terrible strains. There is simply no room for it. It does not fit. Lena would understand this. "I never thought of sex," she would say, "never thought of it once, not even at the end, when everything was around me and I was danc-ing."

VIII

Therefore it will be necessary to characterize Lena in some other way, and that opportunity will only come through the moment of crisis, the moment at which the *Skipstone* is drawn into the Black Galaxy of the neutron star. This moment will occur fairly early into the story, perhaps five or six hundred words deep (her previous life on the ship and impressions of hyperspace will come in expository chunks interwoven be-tween sections of ongoing action), and her only indication of what has happened will be when there is a deep, lurching shiver in the gut of the ship where the embalmed lay and then she feels herself falling.

To explain this sensation it is important to explain normal hyperspace, the skip-drive which is merely to draw the cur-tains and to be in a cubicle. There is no sensation of motion in hyperspace, there could not be, the drive taking the *Skip-stone* past any concepts of sound or light and into an area where there is no language to encompass or glands to regis-ter. Were she to draw the curtains (curiously similar in their frills and pastels to what we might see hanging today in lower-middle-class homes of the kind I inhabit), she would be de-prived of any sensation, but of course she cannot; she must open them to the portholes, and through them she can see the song of the colors to which I have previously alluded. Inside, there is a deep and grievous wretchedness, a feeling of terri-ble loss (which may explain why Lena thinks of exhuming the dead) that may be ascribed to the effects of hyperspace upon the corpus; but these sensations can be shielded, are not visible from the outside, and can be completely controlled by the phlegmatic types who comprise most of the pilots of these experimental flights. (Lena is rather phlegmatic herself. She reacts more to stress than some of her counterparts but well within the normal range prescribed by the Bureau, which admittedly does a superficial check.)

The effects of falling into the Black Galaxy are entirely different, however, and it is here where Lena's emotional equipment becomes completely unstuck.

IX

At this point in the story great gobs of physics, astronomical and mathematic data would have to be incorporated, hopefully in a way which would furnish the hard-science basis of the story without repelling the reader.

Of course one should not worry so much about the repulsion of the reader; most who read science fiction do so in pursuit of exactly this kind of hard speculation (most often they are disappointed, but then most often they are after a time unable to tell the difference), and they would sit still much longer for a lecture than would, say, readers of the fictions of John Cheever, who could hardly bear sociological diatribes wedged into the everlasting vision of Gehenna which is Cheever's gift to his admirers. Thus it would be possible without awkwardness to make the following facts known, and these facts could indeed be set off from the body of the story and simply told like this:

It is posited that in other galaxies there are such as neutron stars, stars of four or five hundred times the size of our own or "normal" suns, which in their continuing nuclear process, burning and burning to maintain their light, will collapse in a mere ten to fifteen thousand years of difficult existence, their hydrogen fusing to helium, then nitrogen, and then to even heavier elements, until with an implosion of terrific force, hungering for power which is no longer there, they collapse upon one another and bring disaster.

51

Disaster not only to themselves but possibly to the entire galaxy which they inhabit, for the gravitational force created by the implosion would be so vast as to literally seal in light. Not only light but sound, and properties of all the stars in that great tube of force . . . so that the galaxy itself would be sucked into the funnel of gravitation created by the collapse and be absorbed into the flickering and desperate heart of the extinguished star.

It is possible to make several extrapolations from the fact of the neutron stars—and of the neutron stars themselves we have no doubt; many nova and supernova are now known to have been created by exactly this effect, not *ex-* but *im*-plosion —and some of them are these:

(a) The gravitational forces created, like great spokes wheeling out from the star, would drag in all parts of the galaxy within their compass; and because of the force of that gravitation, the galaxy would be invisible . . . these forces would, as has been said, literally contain light.

(b) The neutron star, functioning like a cosmic vacuum cleaner, might literally destroy the universe. Indeed, the universe may be in the slow process at this moment of being destroyed as hundreds of millions of its suns and planets are being inexorably drawn toward these great vortexes. The process would be *slow,* of course, but it is seemingly inexorable. One neutron star, theoretically, could absorb the universe. There are many more than one.

(c) The universe may have, obversely, been *created* by such an implosion, throwing out enormous cosmic filaments that, in a flickering instant of time which is as eons to us but an instant to the cosmologists, are now being drawn back in. The universe may be an accident.

(d) Cosmology aside, a ship trapped in such a vortex, such a "black," or invisible, galaxy, drawn toward the deadly source of the neutron star would be unable to leave it through normal faster-than-light drive . . . because the gravitation would absorb light; it would be impossible to build up any level of acceleration (which would at some point not exceed the speed of light) to permit escape. If it were possible to emerge from the field, it could only be done by an immediate switch to tachyonic drive without accelerative build-up . . . a process which could drive the occupant insane and which would, in any case, have no clear destination. The black hole of the dead star is a literal vacuum in space . . . one could fall through the hole, but where, then, would one go?

(e) The actual process of being in the field of the dead star might well drive one insane.

For all of these reasons Lena would not know that she had fallen into the Galaxy Called Rome until the ship simply did so.

And she would instantly and irreparably become insane.

X

The technological data having been stated, the crisis of the story—the collapse into the Galaxy—having occurred early on, it would now be the obligation of the writer to describe the actual sensations involved in falling into the Black Galaxy. Since little or nothing is known of what these sensations would be—other than that it is clear that the gravitation would suspend almost all physical laws and might well suspend time itself, time being only a function of physics—it would be easy to lurch into a surrealistic mode here; Lena could see monsters slithering on the walls—two-dimensional monsters, that is, little cut-outs of her past; she could re-enact her life *in full consciousness* from birth until death; she could literally be turned inside out anatomically and perform in her imagination or in the flesh gross physical acts upon herself; she could live and die a thousand times in the lightless, timeless expanse of the pit . . . all of this could be done within the confines of the story, and it would doubtless lead to some very powerful material. One could do it picaresque fashion, one perversity or lunacy to a chapter—that is to say, the chapters spliced together with more data on the gravitational excesses and the

53

fact that neutron stars (this is interesting) are probably the pulsars which we have identified, stars which can be detected through sound but not by sight from unimaginable distances. The author could do this kind of thing, and do it very well indeed; he has done it literally hundreds of times before, but this, perhaps, would be in disregard of Lena. She has needs more imperative than those of the author, or even those of the editors. She is in terrible pain. She is suffering.

Falling, she sees the dead; falling, she hears the dead; the dead address her from the hold, and they are screaming, "Release us, release us, we are alive, we are in pain, we are in torment"; in their gelatinous flux, their distended limbs sutured finger and toe to the membranes which hold them, their decay has been reversed as the warp into which they have fallen has reversed time; and they are begging Lena from a torment which they cannot phrase, so profound is it; their voices are in her head, pealing and banging like oddly shaped bells. "Release us!" they scream; "we are no longer dead; the trumpet has sounded!" and so on and so forth, but Lena literally does not know what to do. She is merely the ferryman on this dread passage; she is not a medical specialist; she knows nothing of prophylaxis or restoration, and any movement she made to release them from the gelatin which holds them would surely destroy their biology, no matter what the state of their minds.

But even if this were not so, even if she could by releasing them give them peace, she cannot, because she is succumbing to her own responses. In the black hole, if the dead are risen, then the risen are certainly the dead; she dies in this space, Lena does; she dies a thousand times over a period of seventy thousand years (because there is no objective time here, chronology is controlled only by the psyche, and Lena has a thousand full lives and a thousand full deaths), and it is terrible, of course, but it is also interesting, because for every cycle of death there is a life, seventy years in which she can meditate upon her condition in solitude; and by the two-hundredth death, the fourteen-thousandth year or more (or less: each of the lives is individual; some of them long, others short), Lena has come to an understanding of exactly where she is and what has happened to her. That it has taken her fourteen thousand years to reach this understanding is in one way incredible, and yet it is a kind of miracle as well, because in an infinite universe with infinite possibilities, all of them reconstituted for her, it is highly unlikely that even in fourteen thousand years she would stumble upon the answer, had it not been for the fact that she is unusually strong-willed and that some of the personalities through which she has lived are highly creative and controlled and have been able to do some serious thinking. Also there is a carry-over from life to life, even with the differing personalities, so that she is able to make use of preceding knowledge.

Most of the personalities are weak, of course, and not a few are insane, and almost all are cowardly, but there is a little residue; even in the worst of them there is enough residue to carry forth the knowledge, and so it is in the fourteen-thousandth year, when the truth of it has finally come upon her and she realizes what has happened to her and what is going on and what she must do to get out of there, and so it is [then] that she summons all of the strength and will which are left to her, and stumbling to the console (she is in her sixty-eighth year of this life and in the personality of an old, sniveling, whining man, an ex-ferryman himself), she summons one of the prostheses, the master engineer, the controller. All of this time the dead have been shrieking and clanging in her ears, fourteen thousand years of agony billowing from the hold and surrounding her in sheets like iron; and as the master engineer, exactly as he was when she last saw him fourteen thousand years and two weeks ago, emerges from the console, the machinery whirring slickly, she gasps in relief, too weak to even respond with pleasure to the fact that in this condition of antitime, antilight, anticausality the machinery still works. But then it would. The machinery always works, even in this final and most terrible of all the hard-science stories. It is not the machinery which fails but its operators, or, in extreme cases, the cosmos.

"What's the matter?" the master engineer says.

The stupidity of this question, its naïveté and irrelevance in the midst of the hell she has occupied, stuns Lena, but she realizes even through the haze that the master engineer would, of course, come without memory of circumstances and would have to be apprised of background. This is inevitable. Whining and sniveling, she tells him in her old man's voice what has happened.

"Why, that's terrible!" the master engineer says. "That's really terrible," and, lumbering to a porthole, he looks out at the Black Galaxy, the Galaxy Called Rome, and one look at it causes him to lock into position and then disintegrate, not because the machinery has failed (the machinery never fails, not ultimately) but because it has merely re-created a human substance which could not possibly come to grips with what has been seen outside that porthole.

Lena is left alone again, then, with the shouts of the dead carrying forward.

Realizing instantly what has happened to her—fourteen thousand years of perception can lead to a quicker reaction time, if nothing else—she addresses the console again, uses the switches and produces three more prostheses, all of them engineers barely subsidiary to the one she has already addressed. (Their resemblance to the three comforters of Job will not be ignored here, and there will be an opportunity to squeeze in some quick religious allegory, which is always useful to give an ambitious story yet another level of meaning.) Although they are not quite as qualified or definitive in their opinions as the original engineer, they are bright enough by far to absorb her explanation, and, this time, her warnings not to go to the portholes, not to look upon the galaxy, are heeded. Instead, they stand there in rigid and curiously mortified postures, as if waiting for Lena to speak.

"So you see," she says finally, as if concluding a long and difficult conversation, which in fact she has done, "as far as I can see, the only way to get out of this Black Galaxy is to go directly into tachyonic drive. Without any accelerative build-up at all."

The three comforters nod slowly, bleakly. They do not quite know what she is talking about, but then again, they have not had fourteen thousand years to ponder this point. "Unless you can see anything else," Lena says, "unless you can think of anything different. Otherwise, it's going to be infinity in here, and I can't take much more of this, really. Fourteen thousand years is enough."

"Perhaps," the first comforter suggests softly, "perhaps it is your fate and your destiny to spend infinity in this black hole. Perhaps in some way you are determining the fate of the universe. After all, it was you who said that it all might be a gigantic accident, eh? Perhaps your suffering gives it purpose."

"And then too," the second lisps, "you've got to consider the deads down there. This isn't very easy for them, you know, what with being jolted alive and all that, and an immediate vault into tachyonic would probably destroy them for good. The Bureau wouldn't like that, and you'd be liable for some pretty stiff damages. No, if I were you I'd stay with the dead," the second concludes, and a clamorous murmur seems to arise from the hold at this, although whether it is one of approval or of terrible pain is difficult to tell. The dead are not very expressive.

"Anyway," the third says, brushing a forelock out of his eyes, averting his glance from the omnipresent and dreadful portholes, "there's little enough to be done about this situation. You've fallen into a neutron star, a black funnel. It is utterly beyond the puny capacities and possibilities of man. I'd accept my fate if I were you." His model was a senior scientist working on quasar theory, but in reality he appears to be a metaphysician. "There are corners of experience in-

57

to which man cannot stray without being severely penalized."

"That's very easy for you to say," Lena says bitterly, her whine breaking into clear glissando, "but you haven't suffered as I have. Also, there's at least a theoretical possibility that I'll get out of here if I do the build-up without acceleration."

"But where will you land?" the third says, waving a trembling forefinger. "And when? All rules of space and time have been destroyed here; only gravity persists. You can fall through the center of this sun, but you do not know where you will come out or at what period of time. It is inconceivable that you would emerge into normal space in the time you think of as contemporary."

"No," the second says, "I wouldn't do that. You and the dead are joined together now; it is truly your fate to remain with them. What is death? What is life? In the Galaxy Called Rome all roads lead to the same, you see; you have ample time to consider these questions, and I'm sure that you will come up with something truly viable, of much interest."

"Ah, well," the first says, looking at Lena, "if you must know, I think that it would be much nobler of you to remain here; for all we know, your condition gives substance and viability to the universe. Perhaps you *are* the universe. But you're not going to listen anyway, and so I won't argue the point. I really won't," he says rather petulantly, and then makes a gesture to the other two; the three of them quite deliberately march to a porthole, push a curtain aside and look out upon it. Before Lena can stop them—not that she is sure she would, not that she is sure that this is not exactly what she has willed—they have been reduced to ash.

And she is left alone with the screams of the dead.

XI

It can be seen that the satiric aspects of the scene above can be milked for great implication, and unless a very skillful controlling hand is kept upon the material, the piece could easily degenerate into farce at this moment. It is possible, as almost any comedian knows, to reduce (or elevate) the starkest and most terrible issues to scatology or farce simply by particularizing them; and it will be hard not to use this scene for a kind of needed comic relief in what is, after all, an extremely depressing tale, the more depressing because it has used the largest possible canvas on which to imprint its message that man is irretrievably dwarfed by the cosmos. (At least, that is the message which it would be easiest to wring out of the material; actually I have other things in mind, but how many will be able to detect them?)

What will save the scene and the story itself, around this point, will be the lush physical descriptions of the Black Galaxy, the neutron star, the altering effects they have had upon perceived reality. Every rhetorical trick, every typographical device, every nuance of language and memory which the writer has to call upon will be utilized in this section describing the appearance of the black hole and its effects upon Lena's (admittedly distorted) consciousness. It will be a bleak vision, of course, but not necessarily a hopeless one; it will demonstrate that our concepts of "beauty" or "ugliness" or "evil" or "good" or "love" or "death" are little more than metaphors, semantically limited, framed-in by the poor receiving equipment in our heads; and it will be suggested that, rather than showing us a different or alternative reality, the black hole may only be showing us the only reality we know, but *extended,* infinitely extended, so that the story may give us, as good science fiction often does, at this point some glimpse of possibilities beyond ourselves, possibilities not to be contained in word rates or the problems of editorial qualification. And also at this point of the story it might be worthwhile to characterize Lena in a "warmer" and more "sympathetic" fashion so that the reader can see her as a distinct and admirable human being, quite plucky in the face of all her disasters and fourteen thousand years, two hundred lives. This can be

59

done through conventional fictional technique: individuation through defining idiosyncrasy, tricks of speech, habits, mannerisms, and so on. In common everyday fiction we could give her an affecting stutter, a dimple on her left breast, a love of policemen, fear of red convertibles, and leave it at that; in this story, because of its considerably extended theme, it will be necessary to do better than that, to find originalities of idiosyncrasy which will, in their wonder and suggestion of panoramic possibility, approximate the black hole . . . but no matter. No matter. This can be done; the section interweaving Lena and her vision of the black hole will be the flashiest and most admired but in truth the easiest section of the story to write, and I am sure that I would have no trouble with it whatsoever if, as I said much earlier, this were a story instead of a series of notes for a story, the story itself being unutterably beyond our time and space and devices and to be glimpsed only in empty little flickers of light much as Lena can glimpse the black hole, much as she knows the gravity of the neutron star. These notes are as close to the vision of the story as Lena herself would ever get.

As this section ends, it is clear that Lena has made her decision to attempt to leave the Black Galaxy by automatic boost to tachyonic drive. She does not know where she will emerge or how, but she does know that she can bear this no longer.

She prepares to set the controls, but before this it is necessary to write the dialogue with the dead.

XII

One of them presumably will appoint himself as the spokesman of the many and will appear before Lena in this newspace as if in a dream. "Listen here," this dead would say, one born in 3361, dead in 3401, waiting eight centuries for exhumation to a society that can rid his body of leukemia (he is bound to be disappointed), "you've got to face the facts of the situation here. We can't just leave in this way. Better the death we know than the death you will give us."

"The decision is made," Lena says, her fingers straight on the controls. "There will be no turning back."

"We are dead now," the leukemic says. "At least let this death continue. At least in the bowels of this galaxy where there is no time we have a kind of life, or at least that nonexistence of which we have always dreamed. I could tell you many of the things we have learned during these fourteen thousand years, but they would make little sense to you, of course. We have learned resignation. We have had great insights. Of course all of this would go beyond you."

"Nothing goes beyond me. Nothing at all. But it does not matter."

"Everything matters. Even here there is consequence, causality, a sense of humanness, one of responsibility. You can suspend physical laws, you can suspend life itself, but you cannot separate the moral imperatives of humanity. There are absolutes. It would be apostasy to try to leave."

"Man must leave," Lena says, "man must struggle, man must attempt to control his conditions. Even if he goes from worse to obliteration, that is still his destiny." Perhaps the dialogue is a little florid here. Nevertheless, this will be the thrust of it. It is to be noted that putting this conventional viewpoint in the character of a woman will give another of those necessary levels of irony with which the story must abound if it is to be anything other than a freak show, a cascade of sleazy wonders shown shamefully behind a tent . . . but irony will give it legitimacy. "I don't care about the dead," Lena says. "I only care about the living."

"Then care about the universe," the dead man says; "care about that, if nothing else. By trying to come out through the center of the black hole, you may rupture the seamless fabric of time and space itself. You may destroy everything. Past and present and future. The explosion may extend the funnel of

61

gravitational force to infinite size, and all of the universe will be driven into the hole."

Lena shakes her head. She knows that the dead is merely another one of her tempters in a more cunning and cadaverous guise. "You are lying to me," she says. "This is merely another effect of the Galaxy Called Rome. I am responsible to myself, only to myself. The universe is not at issue."

"That's a rationalization," the leukemic says, seeing her hesitation, sensing his victory, "and you know it as well as I do. You can't be an utter solipsist. You aren't God; there is no God, not here, but if there was, it wouldn't be you. You must measure the universe about yourself."

Lena looks at the dead, and the dead looks at her; and in that confrontation, in the shade of his eyes as they pass through the dull lusters of the neutron star effect, she sees that they are close to a communion so terrible that it will become a weld, become a connection . . . that if she listens to the dead for more than another instant, she will collapse within those eyes as the *Skipstone* has collapsed into the black hole; and she cannot bear this, it cannot be . . . she must hold to the belief that there is some separation between the living and the dead and that there is dignity in that separation, that life is not death but something else, because, if she cannot accept that, she denies herself . . . and quickly, then, quickly, before she can consider further, she hits the controls that will convert the ship instantly past the power of light; and then in the explosion of many suns that might only be her heart she hides her head in her arms and screams.

And the dead screams with her, and it is not a scream of joy but not of terror either . . . it is the true natal cry suspended between the moments of limbo, life and expiration, and their shrieks entwine in the womb of the *Skipstone* as it pours through into the redeemed light.

XIII

The story is open-ended, of course.

Perhaps Lena emerges into her own time and space once more, all of this having been a sheath over the greater reality. Perhaps she emerges into an otherness. Then again, maybe she never gets out of the black hole at all but remains and lives there, the *Skipstone* a planet in the tubular universe of the neutron star, the first or last of a series of planets collapsing toward their deadened sun. If the story is done correctly, if the ambiguities are prepared right, if the technological data is stated well, if the material is properly visualized . . . well, it does not matter then what happens to Lena, her *Skipstone* and her dead. Any ending will do. Any would suffice and be emotionally satisfying to the reader.

Still, there is an inevitable ending.

It seems clear to the writer, who will not, cannot write this story, but if he did he would drive it through to this one conclusion, the conclusion clear, implied really from the first, and bound, bound utterly, into the text.

So let the author have it.

XIV

In the infinity of time and space, all is possible, and as they are vomited from that great black hole, spilled from this anus of a neutron star (I will not miss a single Freudian implication if I can), Lena and her dead take on this infinity, partake of the vast canvas of possibility. Now they are in the Antares Cluster flickering like a bulb; here they are at the heart of Sirius the Dog Star five hundred screams from the hold; here again in ancient Rome watching Jesus trudge up carrying the Cross of Calvary . . . and then again in another unimaginable galaxy dead across from the Milky Way a billion light-years in span with a hundred thousand habitable planets, each of them with their Calvary . . . and they are not, they are not yet satisfied.

They cannot, being human, partake of infinity; they can partake of only what they know. They cannot, being created from the consciousness of the writer, partake of what he does not know but what is only close to him. Trapped within the consciousness of the writer, the penitentiary of his being, as the writer is himself trapped in the *Skipstone* of his mortality, Lena and her dead emerge in the year 1975 to the town of Ridgefield Park, New Jersey, and there they inhabit the bodies of its fifteen thousand souls, and there they are, there they are yet, dwelling amidst the refineries, strolling on Main Street, sitting in the Rialto Theatre, shopping in the supermarkets, pairing off and clutching one another in the imploded stars of their beds on this very night at this very moment, as that accident, the author, himself one of them, has conceived them.

It is unimaginable that they would come, Lena and the dead, from the heart of the Galaxy Called Rome to tenant Ridgefield Park, New Jersey . . . but more unimaginable still that from all the Ridgefield Parks of our time we will come and assemble and build the great engines which will take us to the stars, and some of the stars will bring us death and some bring life and some will bring nothing at all, but the engines will go on and on, and so—after a fashion, in our fashion—will we.

A Twelvemonth

by **PETER REDGROVE**

In the month called Bride
there is pale spectral honey
and in-laws made of chain-mail and whiskers.

In the month called Hue-and-Cry
green blood falls with a patter
and the pilchard-shoal flinches.

The month called Houseboat
is for conversing by perfume
and raising beer-steins:
great stone-and-foam masks.

In the month called Treasurechest
snails open french-windows onto their vitals,
become pollen-packed pinecones.

In the month called Brickbat
the sea is gorgeous with carpets
of orange squads of jellyfish:
and the people ride.

The month called Meatforest
is for flowers in the abattoirs,
catafalques for the steers.

In the month known as William
we watch the deer grazing on seaweed;
police open the strongroom of Christ.

In the month called Clocks
the poets decide
whether they shall draw salary,

And in the month called Horsewhip
they pluck their secret insurance
from the rotting rafters.

In the Mollycoddle month
barbers put up bearded mirrors
and no one is allowed to die.

In the month called Yellow Maze
all the teddy-bears
celebrate their thousandth birthday.

In the month called Sleep-with-your-wife
the sea makes a living
along this quiet shore, somehow.

The Custodians

by RICHARD COWPER

There has always been a strong sense of history present in science fiction, not only in the many parallel-world stories but in the firm realization that the past shapes the future. A proper study of history should extend in both directions in time. In this absorbing story Cowper takes us into the past, to an era when we will be in the future. It is strong and deeply moving.

Although the monastery of Hautaire has dominated the Ix valley for more than twelve hundred years, compared with the Jurassic limestone to which it clings, it might have been erected yesterday. Even the megaliths which dot the surrounding hillside predate the abbey by several millennia. But if, geologically speaking, Hautaire is still a newcomer, as a human monument it is already impressively ancient. For the first two centuries following its foundation, it served the faithful as a pilgrims' sanctuary, then, less happily, as a staging post for the Crusaders. By the thirteenth century, it had already known both fat years and lean ones, and it was during one of the latter that, on a cool September afternoon in the year 1272, a grey-bearded, sunburnt man came striding up the white road which wound beside the brawling Ix and hammered on the abbey doors with the butt of his staff.

67

There were rumors abroad that plague had broken out again in the southern ports, and the eye which scrutinized the lone traveler through the grille was alert with apprehension. In response to a shouted request the man snorted, flung off his cloak, discarded his tattered leather jerkin, and raised his bare arms. Twisting his torso from side to side, he displayed his armpits. There followed a whispered consultation within; then, with a rattle of chains and a protest of iron bolts, the oak wicket gate edged inward grudgingly and the man stepped through.

The monk who had admitted him made haste to secure the door. "We hear there is plague abroad, brother," he muttered by way of explanation.

The man shrugged on his jerkin, looping up the leather toggles with deft fingers. "The only plague in these parts is ignorance," he observed sardonically.

"You have come far, brother?"

"Far enough," grunted the traveler.

"From the south?"

The man slipped his arm through the strap of his satchel, eased it up onto his shoulder and then picked up his staff. He watched as the heavy iron chain was hooked back on to its staple. "From the east," he said.

The doorkeeper preceded his guest across the flagged courtyard and into a small room which was bare except for a heavy wooden trestle table. Lying upon it was a huge, leather-bound *registrum,* a stone ink pot and a quill pen. The monk frowned, licked his lips, picked up the quill and prodded it gingerly at the ink.

The man smiled faintly. "By your leave, brother," he murmured, and, taking the dipped quill, he wrote in rapid, flowing script: *Meister Sternwärts—Seher—ex-Cathay.*

The monk peered down at the ledger, his lips moving silently as he spelt his way laboriously through the entry. By the time he was halfway through the second word, a dark flush had crept up his neck and suffused his whole face. "Mea culpa, Magister," he muttered.

"So you've heard of Meister Sternwärts, have you, brother? And what have you heard, I wonder?"

In a rapid reflex action the simple monk sketched a flickering finger-cross in the air.

The man laughed. "Come, holy fool!" he cried, whacking the doorkeeper across the buttocks with his stick. "Conduct me to Abbé Paulus, lest I conjure you into a salamander!"

In the seven hundred years which had passed since Meister Sternwärts strode up the long white road and requested audience with the Abbé Paulus, the scene from the southern windows of the monastery had changed surprisingly little. Over the seaward slopes of the distant hills, purple-ripe clouds were still lowering their showers of rain like filmy nets, and high above the Ix valley the brown and white eagles spiraled lazily upwards in an invisible funnel of warm air that had risen there like a fountain every sunny day since the hills were first folded millions of years before. Even the road which Sternwärts had trodden, though better surfaced, still followed much the same path, and if a few of the riverside fields had expanded and swallowed up their immediate neighbors, the pattern of the stone walls was still recognizably what it had been for centuries. Only the file of high-tension cable carriers striding diagonally down across the valley on a stage of their march from the hydroelectric barrage in the high mountains thirty miles to the north proclaimed that this was the twentieth century.

Gazing down the valley from the library window of Hautaire, Spindrift saw the tiny distant figure trudging up the long slope, saw the sunlight glittering from blond hair as though from a fleck of gold dust, and found himself recalling the teams of men with their white helmets and their clattering machine who had come to erect those giant pylons. He remembered how the brothers had discussed the brash invasion of their privacy and had all agreed that things would never be the same again. Yet the fact remained that within a few short months they had grown accustomed to the novelty, and now Spindrift was no longer sure that he could remember exactly what the valley had looked like before the coming of the pylons. Which was odd, he reflected, because he recalled very clearly the first time he had set eyes upon Hautaire, and there had certainly been no pylons then.

May, 1923, it had been. He had bicycled up from the coast with his scanty possessions stuffed into a pair of basketwork panniers slung from his carrier. For the previous six months he had been gathering scraps of material for a projected doctoral thesis on the life and works of the shadowy "Meister Sternwärts" and had written to the abbot of Hautaire on the remote off-chance that some record of a possible visit by the Meister might still survive in the monastery archives. He explained that he had some reason to believe that Sternwärts might have visited Hautaire but that his evidence for this was, admittedly, of the slenderest kind, being based as it was on a single cryptic reference in a letter dated 1274, sent by the Meister to a friend in Basel.

Spindrift's enquiry had eventually been answered by a certain Fr. Roderigo, who explained that, since he was custodian of the monastery library, the Abbé Ferrand had accordingly passed M. Spindrift's letter on to him. He was, he continued, profoundly intrigued by M. Spindrift's enquiry, because in all the years he had been in charge of the abbey library, no one had ever expressed the remotest interest in Meister Sternwärts; in fact, to the best of his knowledge, he, Fr. Roderigo, and the Abbé Ferrand were the only two men now alive who knew that the Meister had spent his last years as an honored guest of the thirteenth-century abbey and had, in all probability, worked in that very library in which his letter was now being written. He concluded with the warm assurance that any such information concerning the Meister as he himself had acquired over the years was at M. Spindrift's disposal.

Spindrift had hardly been able to believe his good fortune. Only the most fantastic chance had led to his turning up that letter in Basel in the first place—the lone survivor of a correspondence which had ended in the incinerators of the Inquisition. Now there seemed to be a real chance that the slender corpus of the Meister's surviving works might be expanded beyond the gnomic apothegms of the *Illuminatum!* He had written back by return of post suggesting diffidently that he might perhaps be permitted to visit the monastery in person and give himself the inestimable pleasure of conversing with Fr. Roderigo. An invitation had come winging back, urging him to spend as long as he wished as a lay guest of the order.

If, in those far-off days, you had asked Marcus Spindrift what he believed in, the one concept he would certainly never have offered you would have been predestination. He had survived the war to emerge as a junior lieutenant in the Supply Corps and, on demobilization, had lost no time in returning to his first love, medieval philosophy. The mindless carnage which he had witnessed from the sidelines had done much to reinforce his interest in the works of the early Christian mystics, with particular reference to the *bons hommes* of the Albigensian heresy. His stumbling across an ancient handwritten transcript of Sternwärt's *Illuminatum* in the shell-shattered ruins of a presbytery in Armentières in April, 1918, had, for Spindrift, all the impact of a genuine spiritual revelation. Some tantalizing quality in the Meister's thought had called out to him across the gulf of the centuries, and there and then he had determined that if he was fortunate enough to emerge intact from the holocaust, he would make it his life's work to give form and substance to the shadowy presence which he sensed lurking behind the *Illuminatum* like the smile on the lips of the Gioconda.

Nevertheless, prior to his receiving Fr. Roderigo's letter, Spindrift would have been the first to admit that his quest for some irrefutable evidence that the Meister had ever really existed had reaped but one tiny grain of putative "fact" amid untold bushels of frustration. Apparently, not only had no one ever *heard* of Sternwärts; no one had expressed the slightest interest in whether he had ever existed at all. Indeed, as door after door closed in his face, Spindrift found himself coming to the depressing conclusion that the Weimar Republic had more than a little in common with the Dark Ages.

Yet, paradoxically, as one faint lead after another petered out or dissolved in the misty backwaters of medieval hearsay, Spindrift had found himself becoming more and more convinced not only that Sternwärts *had* existed, but that he himself had, in some mysterious fashion, been selected to prove it. The night before he set out on the last lap of his journey to Hautaire, he had lain awake in his ex-army sleeping bag and had found himself reviewing in his mind the odd chain of coincidences that had brought him to that particular place at that particular time: the initial stumbling upon the *Illuminatum;* the discovery of the cryptic reference coupling Sternwärts with Johannes of Basel; and, most fantastic of all, his happening to alight in Basel upon that one vital letter to Johannes which had been included as a cover-stiffener to a bound-up collection of addresses by the arch-heretic Michael Servetus. At every critical point it was as though he had received the precise nudge which alone could put him back on the trail again. "Old Meister," he murmured aloud, "am I seeking *you,* or are you seeking *me?"* High overhead, a plummeting meteorite scratched a diamond line down the star-frosted window of the sky. Spindrift smiled wryly and settled down to sleep.

At noon precisely the next day, he pedaled wearily round the bend in the lower road and was rewarded with his first glimpse of the distant abbey. With a thankful sigh he dismounted, leaned, panting, over his handlebars and peered up the valley. What he saw was destined to remain just as sharp and clear in his mind's eye until the day he died.

Starkly shadowed by the midday sun, its once red-tiled roofs long since bleached to a pale biscuit and rippling in the heat haze, Hautaire, despite its formidable mass, seemed oddly insubstantial. Behind it, tier upon tier, the mountains rose up faint and blue into the cloudless northern sky. As he gazed up at the abbey, Spindrift conceived the peculiar notion that the structure was simply tethered to the rocks like some strange airship built of stone. It was twisted oddly askew, and some of the buttresses supporting the Romanesque cupola seemed to have been stuck on almost as afterthoughts. He blinked his eyes, and the quirk of vision passed. The massive pile re-emerged as solid and unified as any edifice which has successfully stood foursquare-on to the elements for over a thousand years. Fumbling a handkerchief from his pocket, Spindrift mopped the sweat from his forehead; then, re-mounting his bicycle, he pushed off on the last lap of his journey.

Fifteen minutes later, as he wheeled his machine up the final steep incline, a little birdlike monk clad in a faded brown habit fluttered out from the shadows of the portico and scurried with arms outstretched in welcome to the perspiring cyclist. "Welcome, Señor Spindrift!" he cried. "I have been expecting you this half hour past."

Spindrift was still somewhat dizzy from his hot and dusty ride, but he was perfectly well aware that he had not specified any particular day for his arrival, if only because he had no means of knowing how long the journey from Switzerland would take him. He smiled and shook the proffered hand. "Brother Roderigo?"

"Of course, of course," chuckled the little monk, and glancing down at Spindrift's bicycle, he observed, "So they managed to repair your wheel."

Spindrift blinked. "Why, yes," he said. "But how on earth . . . ?"

"Ah, but you must be so hot and tired, Señor! Come into Hautaire where it is cool." Seizing hold of Spindrift's ma-

73

chine, he trundled it briskly across the courtyard, through an
archway, down a stone-flagged passage and propped it finally
against a cloister wall.

Spindrift, following a pace or two behind, gazed about him
curiously. In the past six months he had visited many ec-
clesiastical establishments, but none which had given him the
overwhelming sense of timeless serenity that he recognized
here. In the center of the cloister yard clear water was bub-
bling up into a shallow limestone saucer. As it brimmed over,
thin wavering streams tinkled musically into the deep basin
beneath. Spindrift walked slowly forward into the fierce sunlight and stared down into the rippled reflection of his dusty,
sweat-streaked face. A moment later his image was joined by
that of the smiling Fr. Roderigo. "That water comes down
from a spring in the hillside," the little monk informed him.
"It flows through the very same stone pipes which the Ro-
mans first laid. It has never been known to run dry."

A metal cup was standing on the shadowed inner rim of
the basin. The monk picked it up, dipped it, and handed it to
Spindrift. Spindrift smiled his thanks, raised the vessel to his
lips and drank. It seemed to him that he had never tasted
anything so delicious in his life. He drained the cup and
handed it back, aware as he did so that his companion was
nodding his head as though in affirmation. Spindrift smiled
quizzically. "Yes," sighed Fr. Roderigo, "you have come. Just
as he said you would."

The sense of acute disorientation which Spindrift had experienced since setting foot in Hautaire persisted throughout
the whole of the first week of his stay. For this, Fr. Roderigo
was chiefly responsible. In some manner not easy to define,
the little monk had succeeded in inducing in his guest the
growing conviction that his quest for the elusive Meister
Sternwärts had reached its ordained end; that what Spindrift
was seeking was hidden here at Hautaire, buried somewhere

among the musty manuscripts and incunabula that filled the oak shelves and stone recesses of the abbey library.

True to his promise, the librarian had laid before Spindrift such documentary evidence as he himself had amassed over the years, commencing with that faded entry in the thirteenth-century *registrum*. Together they had peered down at the ghostly script. "Out of Cathay," mused Spindrift. "Could it have been a joke?"

Fr. Roderigo pulled a face. "Perhaps," he said. "But the hand is indisputably the Meister's. Of course, he may simply have wished to mystify the brothers."

"Do you believe that?"

"No," said the monk. "I am sure that what is written there is the truth. Meister Sternwärts had just returned from a pilgrimage in the steps of Apollonius of Tyana. He had lived and studied in the East for ten years." He scuttled across to a distant shelf, lifted down a bound folio volume, blew the dust from it, coughed himself breathless, and then laid the book before Spindrift. "The evidence is all there," he panted with a shy smile. "I bound the sheets together myself some thirty years ago. I remember thinking at the time that it would make a fascinating commentary to Philostratus' *Life of Apollonius.*"

Spindrift opened the book and read the brief and firmly penned Prolegomenon. *"Being then in my forty-ninth year, Sound in Mind and Hale in Body, I, Peter Sternwärts, Seeker after Ancient Truths; Alerted by my Friends; Pursued by mine Enemies; did set forth from Würzburg for Old Buda. What here follows is the Truthful History of all that Befell me and of my Strange Sojourn in Far Cathay, written by my own hand in the Abbey of Hautaire in this year of Our Lord 1273."*

Spindrift looked up from the page, and as he did so, he gave a deep sigh of happiness.

Fr. Roderigo nodded. "I know, my friend," he said. "You do not have to tell me. I shall leave you alone with him."

But Spindrift was already turning the first page.

That evening, at Fr. Roderigo's suggestion, Spindrift strolled with him up onto the hillside above Hautaire. The ascent was a slow one, because every fifty paces or so Fr. Roderigo was constrained to pause awhile to regain his breath. It was then that Spindrift became aware that the friendly little monk was ill. Beneath that quick and ready smile were etched the deep lines of old familiar pain. He suggested gently that perhaps they might just sit where they were, but Fr. Roderigo would not hear of it. "No, no, my dear Spindrift," he insisted breathlessly. "There is something I must show you. Something that has a profound bearing upon our joint quest."

After some twenty minutes they had reached one of the fallen menhirs that formed a sort of gigantic necklace around the abbey. There Fr. Roderigo paused and patted his heaving chest apologetically. "Tell me, Señor," he panted. "What is your candid opinion of Apollonius of Tyana?"

Spindrift spread his hands in a gesture that contrived to be both noncommittal and expiatory. "To tell the truth, I can hardly be said to have an opinion at all," he confessed. "Of course I know that Philostratus made some extraordinary claims on his behalf."

"Apollonius made only one claim for *himself*," said Fr. Roderigo. "But that one was not inconsiderable. He claimed to have foreknowledge of the future."

"Yes?" said Spindrift guardedly.

"The extraordinary accuracy of his predictions led to his falling foul of the Emperor Nero. Apollonius, having already foreseen this, prudently retired to Ephesus before the monster was able to move against him."

Spindrift smiled. "Precognition obviously proved a most useful accomplishment."

"Yes and no," said Fr. Roderigo, ignoring the irony. "Have you reached the passage in the Meister's *Biographia* where he speaks of the Praemonitiones?"

"Do they really exist?"

The little monk seemed on the point of saying something and then appeared to change his mind. "Look," he said, gesturing around him with a sweep of his arm. "You see how Hautaire occupies the exact center of the circle?"

"Why, so it does," observed Spindrift.

"Not fortuitous, I think."

"No?"

"Nor did he," said Fr. Roderigo with a smile. "The Meister spent a whole year plotting the radiants. Somewhere there is a map which he drew."

"Why should he do that?"

"He was seeking to locate an Apollonian nexus."

"Meaning—"

"The concept is meaningless unless one is prepared to accept the possibility of precognition."

"Ah," said Spindrift guardedly. "And did he find what he was looking for?"

"Yes," said Fr. Roderigo simply. "There." He pointed down at the abbey.

"And then what?" enquired Spindrift curiously.

Fr. Roderigo chewed his lower lip and frowned. "He persuaded Abbé Paulus to build him an observatory—an *oculus,* he called it."

"And what did he hope to observe from it?"

"*In* it," corrected Fr. Roderigo with a faint smile. "It had no windows."

"You amaze me," said Spindrift, shaking his head. "Does it still exist?"

"It does."

"I should very much like to see it. Would that be possible?"

"It might," the monk admitted. "We would have to obtain the abbot's permission. However, I—" He broke off, racked by a savage fit of coughing that turned his face grey. Spindrift, much alarmed, patted his companion gently on the back and felt utterly helpless. Eventually the little monk recovered his breath and with a trembling hand wiped a trace of spittle from his blue lips. Spindrift was horrified to see a trace of blood on the white handkerchief. "Hadn't we better be making our way back?" he suggested solicitously.

Fr. Roderigo nodded submissively and allowed Spindrift to take him by the arm and help him down the track. When they were about halfway down, he was overcome by another fit of coughing which left him pale and gasping. Spindrift, now thoroughly alarmed, was all for going to fetch help from the abbey, but the monk would not hear of it. When he had recovered sufficiently to continue, he whispered hoarsely, "I promise I will speak to the abbot about the *oculus.*"

Spindrift protested that there was no hurry, but Fr. Roderigo shook his head stubbornly. "Fortunately there *is* still just time, my friend. Just time enough."

Three days later Fr. Roderigo was dead. After attending the evening Requiem Mass for his friend, Spindrift made his way up to the library and sat there alone for a long time. The day was fast fading and the mistral was beginning to blow along the Ix valley. Spindrift could hear it sighing round the buttresses and mourning among the crannies in the crumbling stonework. He thought of Roderigo now lying out on the hillside in his shallow anonymous grave. *The goal ye seek lies within yourself.* He wondered what had inspired the abbot to choose that particular line from the *Illuminatum* for his Requiem text and suspected that he was the only person present who had recognized its origin.

There was a deferential knock at the library door, and a young novice came in carrying a small, metal-bound casket. He set it down on the table before Spindrift, took a key from his pocket and laid it beside the box. "The father superior instructed me to bring these to you, sir," he said. "They were in Brother Roderigo's cell." He bowed his head slightly, turned, and went out, closing the door softly behind him.

Spindrift picked up the key and examined it curiously. It

was quite unlike any other he had ever seen, wrought somewhat in the shape of a florid, double-ended question mark. He had no idea how old it was or even what it was made of. It looked like some alloy—pewter, maybe?—but there was no discernible patina of age. He laid it down again and drew the casket towards him. This was about a foot long, nine inches or so wide, and perhaps six inches deep. The oak lid, which was ornately decorated with silver inlay and brass studding, was slightly domed. Spindrift raised the box and shook it gently. He could hear something shifting around inside, bumping softly against the sides. He did not doubt that the strange key unlocked the casket, but when he came to try, he could find no keyhole in which to fit it. He peered underneath. By the trickle of waning light through the western windows he could just discern an incised pentagram and the Roman numerals for 1274.

His pulse quickening perceptibly, he hurried across to the far end of the room and fetched an iron candlestick. Having lit the candle, he set it down beside the box and adjusted it so that its light was shining directly upon the lid. It was then that he noticed that part of the inlaid decoration appeared to correspond to what he had previously assumed to be the handle of the key. He pressed down on the silver inlay with his fingertips and thought he felt it yield ever so slightly.

He retrieved the key, adjusted it so that its pattern completely covered that of the inlay, and then pressed downwards experimentally. There was a faint *click!* and he felt the lid pushing itself upwards against the pressure of his fingers. He let out his pent breath in a faint sigh, detached the key, and eased the lid back on its hinge. Lying within the box was a vellum-covered book and a quill pen.

Spindrift wiped his fingers along his sleeve and, with his heart racing, dipped his hand into the casket and lifted out the book. As the light from the candle slanted across the cover, he was able to make out the faded sepia lettering spelling out the word: *PRAEMONITIONES,* and below it, in a darker ink, the cynical query—*Quis Custodiet Ipsos Custodes?*

Spindrift blinked up into the candlelight. "Who will watch the watchers?" he murmured. "Who, indeed?"

The wind snuffled and whimpered against the now dark window panes, and the vesper bell began to toll in the abbey tower. Spindrift gave a violent, involuntary shiver and turned back the cover of the book.

Someone, perhaps even Peter Sternwärts himself, had stitched onto the flyleaf a sheet of folded parchment. Spindrift carefully unfolded it and peered down upon what, at first glance, seemed to be an incomprehensible spiderweb of finely drawn lines. He had been staring at it for fully a minute before it dawned on him that the dominant pattern was remarkably similar to that on the lid of the casket and its weirdly shaped key. But there was something else too, something that teased at his recollection, something he knew he had once seen somewhere else. And suddenly he had it: an interlinked, megalithic spiral pattern carved into a rockface near Tintagael in Cornwall; here were exactly those same whorled and coupled S shapes that had once seemed to his youthful imagination like a giant's thumbprints in the granite.

No sooner was the memory isolated than he had associated this graphic labyrinth with the pagan menhirs dotting the hillside round Hautaire. Could *this* be the map Roderigo had mentioned? He held the parchment closer to the quaking candle flame and at once perceived the ring of tiny circles which formed a periphery around the central vortex. From each of these circles faint lines had been scratched across the swirling whirlpool to meet at its center.

Spindrift was now convinced that what he was holding in his hands was some arcane chart of Hautaire itself and its immediate environs, but at the precise point where the abbey itself should have been indicated, something had been written in minute letters. Unfortunately the point happened to coincide with the central cruciform fold in the parchment. Spindrift screwed up his eyes and thought he could just make out

80

the words *tempus* and *pons*—or possibly *fons*—together with a word which might equally well have been *cave* or *carpe*. "Time," "bridge," or perhaps "source." And what else? "Beware"? "Seize"? He shook his head in frustration and gave it up as a bad job. Having carefully refolded the chart, he turned over the flyleaf and began to read.

By the time he had reached the last page, the candle had sunk to a guttering stub, and Spindrift was acutely conscious of an agonizing headache. He lowered his face into his cupped hands and waited for the throbbing behind his eyeballs to subside. To the best of his knowledge, he had been intoxicated only once in his life, and that was on the occasion of his twenty-first birthday. He had not enjoyed the experience. The recollection of how the world had seemed to rock on its foundations had remained one of his most distressing memories. Now he was reminded of it all over again as his mind lurched drunkenly from one frail clutching point to the next. Of course it was a hoax, an extraordinarily elaborate, purposeless hoax. It *had* to be! And yet he feared it was nothing of the sort, that what he had just read was, in truth, nothing less than a medieval prophetic text of such incredible accuracy that it made absolute nonsense of every rationalist philosophy ever conceived by man. Having once read the *Praemonitiones,* one stepped like Alice through the looking glass into a world where only the impossible was possible. But *how?* In God's name *how?*

Spindrift removed his hands from before his eyes, opened the book at random and, by the vestige of light left in the flapping candle flame, read once more how, in the year 1492, Christobal Colon, a Genoese navigator, would bow to the dictates of the sage Chang Heng and would set sail into the west on the day of the Expulsion of the Jews from Spain. He would return the following year, laden with treasure and "companioned by those whom he would call Indians but who would in truth be no such people." At which point the candle flared up briefly and went out.

Next morning, Spindrift requested, and was granted, an audience with the abbot. He took with him the wooden casket and the mysterious key. His eyes were red-rimmed and bloodshot, and the dark rings beneath them testified to a sleepless night.

Abbé Ferrand was in his early fifties—a stalwart man with shrewd eyes, ash-grey hair and bushy eyebrows. His upright stance struck Spindrift as having more than a touch of the military about it. He wore the simple brown habit of his order, and only the plain brass crucifix, slung on a beaded leather thong about his neck, distinguished him from the other monks. He smiled as Spindrift entered the study, then rose from behind his desk and held out his hand. Spindrift, momentarily confused, tucked the casket under his left arm and then shook the proffered hand.

"And how can I be of service to you, M'sieur Spindrift?"

Spindrift took a breath, gripped the casket in both hands and held it out in front of him. "Abbé Ferrand, I . . . ," he began, and then dried up.

The corners of the abbot's lips were haunted by the ghost of a smile. "Yes?" he prompted gently.

"Sir," blurted Spindrift, "do you know what's in here?"

"Yes," said the abbot. "I think I do."

"Then why did you send it to me?"

"Brother Roderigo wished me to. It was one of his last requests."

"The book's a forgery, of course. But you must know that."

"You think so, M'sieur?"

"Well, of course I do."

"And what makes you so certain?"

"Why," cried Spindrift, "because it *has* to be!"

"But there have always been prophets, M'sieur Spindrift," returned the abbot mildly. "And they have all prophesied."

Spindrift waved a dismissive hand. "Nostradamus, you mean? Vague ambiguities. Predictions of disaster which could be interpreted to fit any untoward circumstance. But this . . ."

The abbot nodded. "Forgive my asking, M'sieur," he said, "but what was it exactly that brought you to Hautaire?"

Spindrift set the casket down on the desk in front of him and laid the key beside it. As he did so he realized, not for the first time, that the question Abbé Ferrand was posing could have no simple answer. "Principally, I believe, Peter Stern-wärts' *Illuminatum,*" he said. "I felt a compulsion to learn all I could about its author."

The abbot appeared to ponder on this reply; then he turned on his sandaled heel, walked over to a wall cupboard, opened it, and drew from within another vellum-covered notebook similar in appearance to that which Spindrift had replaced in the casket. Having closed the cupboard door, the abbot stood for a moment tapping the notebook against his finger ends. Finally he turned back to Spindrift. "I take it you have studied the *Praemonitiones,* M'sieur Spindrift?"

Spindrift nodded.

"Then you will perhaps recall that its forecasts end with the Franco-Prussian war. Unless my memory deceives me, the final entry concerns Bazaine's surrender at Metz in October, 1870; the capitulation of Paris in 1871; and the signing of the treaty at Frankfurt-sur-Main on May 10th of that same year?"

"Yes," said Spindrift, "that is perfectly correct."

The abbot opened the book he was holding, flipped over a few pages, glanced at what was written there, and then said, "Would you say, M'sieur Spindrift, that Europe has at last seen the end of war?"

"Why, certainly," said Spindrift. "The League of Nations has outlawed—"

"On September 1st, 1939," cut in the abbot, "Russia and Germany will, in concert, invade Poland. As a direct consequence of this, Britain and France will declare war on Germany."

"But that's preposterous!" exclaimed Spindrift. "Why, the

Versailles Treaty specifically states that under no circumstances is Germany ever again to be allowed to rearm!"

The abbot turned back a page. "In 1924—next year, is it
not?—Lenin will die and will be succeeded by"—here he
tilted the page to catch the light—"Joseph Vissarionovitch—
I think that's right—Stalin. An age of unparalleled tyranny
will commence in the so-called Soviet Republic which will
continue for fifty-one years." He flicked on. "In 1941 German
armies will invade Russia and inflict massive defeats on the
Soviet forces." He turned another page. "In July, 1945, the
fabric of civilization will be rent asunder by an explosion in
an American desert." He shrugged and closed up the book,
almost with relief.

"You are surely not asking me to believe that those fantastic predictions are the work of Peter Sternwärts?" Spindrift
protested.

"Only indirectly," said the abbot. "Without Meister Sternwärts they would certainly never have come into existence.
Nevertheless, he did not write them himself."

"Then who did?"

"These last? Brother Roderigo."

Spindrift just gaped.

The abbot laid the book down on the desk beside the
casket and picked up the key. "Before he died," he said,
"Brother Roderigo informed me that you had expressed a
desire to examine the *oculus.* Is this so?"

"Then it really does exist?"

"Oh, yes. Most certainly it exists. This is the key to it."

"In that case, I would very much like to see it."

"Very well, M'sieur," said the abbot, "I will conduct you
there myself. But first I should be intrigued to know what
makes you so certain that the *Praemonitiones* is a forgery?"

Spindrift looked down at the casket. The whorled inlay on
its lid seemed to spin like a silver Catherine wheel. He
dragged his gaze away with difficulty. "Because I have always

84

believed in free will," he said flatly. "To believe in the *Praemonitiones* would be to deny it."

"Oh," said the abbot, "is that all? I thought perhaps you had detected the alteration in the script which takes place at roughly fifty-year intervals. It is admittedly slight, but it cannot be denied."

"The light was not good in the library last night," said Spindrift. "I noticed no marked change in the cursive style of the entries."

The abbot smiled. "Look again, M'sieur Spindrift," he said. "By daylight." He pressed the key into the lock, removed the *Praemonitiones* from the casket and handed it over.

Spindrift leafed through the pages, then paused, turned back a few, nodded, and went on. "Why, yes," he said. "Here in this entry for 1527: 'The Holy City sacked by the armies of the Emperor Charles.' There *is* a difference. How do you account for it?"

"They were written by different hands," said the abbot. "Though all, I hazard, with that same pen."

Spindrift reached into the casket, took out the cut-down quill and examined it. As his fingers closed round the yellowed shaft, it seemed to twist ever so slightly between them as though endowed with some strange will of its own. He dropped it back hastily into the box and flushed with annoyance at his own childishness. "If I understand you, Abbé, you are saying that these predictions were made by many different hands over the past seven centuries."

"That is correct. It would appear that the horizon of foresight is generally limited to about fifty years, though in certain cases—notably Sternwärts himself—it reaches a good deal further." The abbot said this in a quiet matter-of-fact tone that Spindrift found distinctly disconcerting. He reached out tentatively for the second book which the abbot had placed on the desk, but, seemingly unaware of Spindrift's intention, the abbot had casually laid his own hand upon it. "Now, if you are ready, M'sieur," he said, "I suggest we might climb up and pay our respects to the *oculus*."

Spindrift nodded.

The abbot smiled and seemed pleased. He placed the two books within the casket and clapped the lid shut. Then he picked up the key, took down another bunch of keys which was hanging from a hook on the wall, and, nodding to Spindrift to follow him, led the way along a cool white corridor, up a flight of stone stairs and along a passage buttressed by slanting sunbeams. They took several turns and climbed yet another flight of stairs. Spindrift glanced out of a window as they passed and observed that they were now almost on a level with the ruin of the prehistoric stone circle. The abbot's leather sandals slapped briskly against the soles of his bare feet and made a noise like a razor being stropped.

At last they reached a small oak door. The abbot paused, selected one of the keys from the bunch, thrust it into the lock and twisted it. The hinges groaned and the door squealed inwards. "This leads to the dome of the rotunda," he explained. "The *oculus* is actually situated within the fabric of the northern wall. It is certainly an architectural curiosity."

Spindrift ducked his head, passed through the doorway, and found himself in a narrow crack of a curved passageway dimly lit by narrow barred slits in the outer stonework. Thick dust lay on the stone floor, which was caked with a crust formed from generations of bird and bat droppings. The floor spiraled upwards at an angle of some ten degrees, and Spindrift calculated that they had made at least one complete circuit of the rotunda before the abbot said, *"Ecce oculus!"*

Peering past the broad shoulder of his guide, Spindrift saw a second door, so narrow that a man could have passed through it only with extreme difficulty. The abbot squeezed himself backwards into a niche and allowed Spindrift to edge around him. Then he handed over the key to the casket, saying as he did so: "You will find that it operates in the normal way, M'sieur."

"Thank you," said Spindrift, taking the key from him and approaching the door. "Is there room for only one person inside?"

"Barely that," said the abbot. "The door opens outwards."

Spindrift inserted the key into the lock and twisted it. The wards grated reluctantly but still allowed the key to turn. Then, using it as a handle, for there was, indeed, no other, he pulled the door gently towards him. A moment later he had started back with a barely suppressed gasp of astonishment. The door had opened to disclose a sort of lidless limestone coffin, bare and empty, standing on its end, apparently cemented fast into the surrounding masonry. "What on earth is it?" he demanded.

The abbot chuckled. "That is your *oculus*, M'sieur."

Spindrift eyed the coffin uncertainly. "And you say Sternwärts built that?" he enquired dubiously.

"Well, certainly he must have caused it to be built," said the abbot. "Of that there can be little doubt. See there—" He pointed to some lettering carved on the limestone corbel which framed the "head" of the casque—*Sternwärts hoc fecit*. "Not proof positive, I grant you, but good enough for me." He smiled again. "Well, now you are here, M'sieur Spindrift, are you not tempted to try it?"

Spindrift gazed at the Latin lettering. "Sternwärts made this," he muttered, and, even as he spoke the words aloud, he knew he would have to step inside that stone shell, if only because to refuse to do so would be to deny the noble and courageous spirit of the man who had penned the *Illuminatum*. Yet he could not disguise his reluctance. How dearly at that moment he would have liked to say: "Tomorrow, perhaps, or next week, if it's all the same to you, Abbé." But he knew he would be allowed no second chance. It was now or never. He nodded, drew a deep breath, swallowed once, stepped resolutely forward and edged himself backwards into the cold sarcophagus.

Gently the abbot closed the door upon him and sketched over it a slow and thoughtful sign of the Cross.

For no particular reason that he was aware of, Spindrift had recently found himself thinking about Fr. Roderigo. Once or twice he had even wandered out into the abbey graveyard and tried to locate the spot where the bones of the little monk were buried. He had pottered about, peering vaguely among the hummocks, but he found that he could no longer recall precisely where the body of his friend had been interred. Only the abbots of Hautaire were accorded head-stones, and even Abbé Ferrand's was by now thickly en-crusted with lichen.

Spindrift found a piece of dry twig and began scratching at the lettered limestone, but by the time he had scraped clean the figures 1910–1937, he found the impulse had already waned. After all, what was the point? That was the surprising thing about growing old: nothing seemed quite so urgent or important any more. Sharp edges became blunt; black and white fudged off into grey; and your attention kept wandering off after stupid little tidbits of memory and getting lost among the flowery hedgerows of the Past. *Quis Custodiet . . . ?*

The old librarian straightened up, released the piece of twig he was holding and began massaging his aching back. As he did so, he suddenly recalled the letter. He had been carry-ing it around with him all day and had, in fact, come out into the graveyard on purpose to try to make up his mind about it. Obscurely he felt he needed the ghostly presence of Roderigo and the Abbé Ferrand to help him. Above all he needed to be *sure.*

He peered around for a convenient seat, then lowered himself creakily so that his back rested against the abbé's sun-warmed headstone. He dipped around inside his woolen habit for his spectacles and the envelope, and having at last settled everything to his comfort and satisfaction, he extracted the letter, unfolded it, cleared his throat and read out aloud:

Post Restante
Arles
Bouches du Rhône.

June 21, 1981.

Dear Sir,

I have recently returned to Europe after four years' travel and study in India, Burma and Nepal, during which one of my teachers introduced me to your marvelous edition of the *Biographia Mystica* of Meister Sternwärts. It was a complete revelation to me and, together with the *Illuminatum,* has radically changed my whole outlook on life. *"The truly aimed shaft strikes him who looses it"* (Ill.XXIV)!!

I could not permit myself to quit Europe and return home to Chicago without having made an effort to thank you in person and, perhaps, to give myself the treat of conversing with you about the life and works of the Meister.

If you could possibly see your way towards gratifying my wish sometime—say within the next month or so?— would you be so good as to drop me a line at the above address, and I will come with all speed to Hautaire.

Yours most sincerely,
J. S. Harland

Spindrift concluded his reading, raised his head and blinked out over the valley. *"Quis Custodiet?"* he murmured, remembering suddenly, with quite astonishing clarity, how once, long ago, Brother Roderigo had handed him a cup of ice-cool water and had then nodded his head in affirmation. How had *he* known?

Hurtling out of the northern sky, three black planes, shaped like assegais, rushed down the length of the valley, drowning it with their reverberating thunder. Spindrift sighed, refolded the letter and fumbled it back into its envelope. He reached out, plucked a leaf of wild sage, rubbed it between finger and thumb and held it under his nose. By then the planes were already fifty miles away, skimming low over the distant, glittering sea, but the ripples of their bullying passage still lapped faintly back and forth between the ancient hills.

"Very well," murmured Spindrift, "I will write to this young man. *Ex nihilo, nihil fit.* But perhaps Mr. Harland is not 'nothing.' Perhaps he is something—even, maybe, my own successor, as I was Roderigo's and Roderigo was Brother Martin's. There always has *been* a successor—a watcher—an eye for the eye." He grunted, heaved himself up from the grave on which he was sitting and shuffled off towards the abbey, a slightly dotty old lay brother, muttering to himself as he went.

The counter clerk at the Bureau des Postes sniffed down her nose, glared at the passport which was held out to her and then, reluctantly, handed over the letter, expressing her profound disapproval of the younger generation.

The slim, deeply tanned, blond girl in the faded blue shirt and jeans examined the postmark on the letter and chuckled delightedly. She hurried out into the sunny square, sat herself down on a low wall, carefully tore off a narrow strip from the end of the envelope and extracted Spindrift's letter. Her sea-blue eyes flickered rapidly along the lines of typescript. "Oh, *great!*" she exclaimed. "Gee, isn't that *mar*-velous?"

Judy Harland, who, in her twenty-second year, still contrived to look a youthful and boyish eighteen, had once written on some application form in the space reserved for "occupation" the single word "enthusiast." They had not offered her the job, but it can hardly have been on the grounds of self-misrepresentation. Her letter to Spindrift had been dashed off on the spur of the moment when she had discovered that the Abbey of Hautaire was an easy day's hitchhike down the coast from Arles. Not that the information which she had given Spindrift was untrue—it *was* true—up to a point, that point being that her interest in Meister Sternwärts was but one of several such enthusiasms among which, over the past eight years, she had zoomed back and forth like a tipsy hummingbird in a frangipani forest. She had already sampled Hatha Yoga, the teachings of Don Carlos, Tarot, Zen Buddhism, and the *I Ching*. Each had possessed her like an ardent lover to the exclusion of all the others—until the next. The *Illuminatum* and the *Biographia Mystica* represented but the most recent of her spiritual love affairs.

Her signing of her letter with her initials rather than her Christian name had been an act of prudence induced by certain awkward experiences in Persia and Afghanistan. She had survived these unscathed, just as she had survived everything else, because her essential self was hedged about by an inviolable conviction that she had been chosen to fulfil some stupendous but as-yet-unspecified purpose. The fact that she had no very clear idea of what the purpose might be was immaterial. What counted was the strength of the conviction. Indeed, in certain respects, Judy had more than a little in common with Joan of Arc.

A little deft work on her hair with a pair of scissors and a concealed chiffon scarf wound round her chest soon transformed her outwardly into a very passable boy. It was as James Harland that she climbed down from the cab of the friendly *camion* driver, shouldered her well-worn rucksack and strode off, whistling like a bird, up the winding, dusty road towards Hautaire. Just as Spindrift himself had done some sixty years before, and at precisely the same spot, she paused as she came within sight of the abbey and stood still for a moment, staring up at it. She saw a brown and white eagle corkscrewing majestically upwards in an invisible funnel of warm air, and as she watched it, she experienced an almost overwhelming impulse to turn round and go back. Perhaps if she had been under the aegis of the *I Ching,* she would have obeyed it, but Hautaire was now to her what fabled Cathay had once been to Peter Sternwärts—a challenge to be met and overcome. Shrugging aside her forebodings, she hooked her thumbs more firmly under the straps of her pack and marched on up the road.

Old age had lengthened Spindrift's vision. From the library window he had picked out the determined little figure when it was still three-quarters of a mile away. Something about it touched his heart like a cold finger. *"Golden-haired like an angel."* Had he not himself written that long, long ago, after his last visit to the rotunda? How many years was it now? Fifty at least. As far as the eye could see. Why then had he not gone back? Was it fear? Or lack of any real religious faith to sustain him? Yet everything he had "seen" had come to pass just as he had described it. Such crazy things they had seemed too. Sunburst bombs shattering whole cities in the blink of an eye; men in silver suits walking on the face of the moon; an assassin's bullets striking down the President who would put them there; the endless wars; the horror and anguish of the extermination camps; human bestiality. Pain, pain, always pain. Until he had been able to endure no more. His last entry in the *Praemonitiones* must surely be almost due now. Did that mean he had failed in his bounden duty? Well, then, so he had failed, but at least he had given the world the *Biographia,* and none of his predecessors had done that. And there was still the marvel of the *Exploratio Spiritualis* to come—that masterpiece which he alone had unearthed, translated, and pieced together. Perhaps one day it would be published. But not by him. Let someone else shoulder that burden. He knew what it would entail. And surely he had done enough. But the chill lay there in his heart like a splinter of ice that would not melt. *"Golden-haired like an angel."* Muttering to himself, he turned away from the window, shuffled across the library and began making his way down to the abbey gate to greet his visitor.

As a child Judy had sometimes toyed with a fanciful notion that people grew to resemble the names they had been born with. She was reminded of it when she first set eyes on Spindrift. His hair was as white and soft as the wisps of foam on a weir pool, and he blinked at her waterily through his steel-rimmed glasses as he shook her by the hand. "You are very young, Mr. Harland," he observed. "But, then, to you I dare-say I must seem very old."

"Are you?" she asked in that blunt way of hers which some people found charming and others simply ill-mannered.

"I am exactly as old as this century," he replied with a smile. "Which makes me four score and one. A goodly stretch by any reckoning, wouldn't you say?"

"And you've lived here all your life?"

"Most of it, to be sure. I first came to Hautaire in 1923."

"Hey! My *father* was born in 1923!"

"An *annus mirabilis,* indeed," the old man chuckled. "Come along, Mr. Harland. Let me be the first to introduce you to Hautaire."

So saying, he led her through the outer courtyard and down into the cloisters where, like dim autumnal leaves, a few of the brothers were wandering in silent meditation. Judy's bright magpie glance darted this way and that. "Say," she whispered, "this sure is some place."

"Would you care for a drink?" asked Spindrift, suddenly recalling his own introduction to the abbey and hoping, vaguely, that by repeating the pattern he would be vouchsafed a sign of some kind.

"I surely would," said Judy. "Thanks a lot." She shrugged off her rucksack and dumped it down beside the basin of the fountain while Spindrift groped around short-sightedly for the cup.

"Here, let me," she said, and, scooping up the cup, she dipped it into the basin and took a hearty swig.

Spindrift adjusted his spectacles and peered at her. A solitary drop of water hung for a moment like a tear from her square firm chin, and then she had brushed it away with the back of her hand. "That was great," she informed him. "Real cool."

Spindrift nodded and smiled. "That fountain was here

even before the abbey was built," he said.

"Is that so? Then Meister Sternwärts may have done just what I've done."

"Yes," agreed Spindrift. "It is more than likely."

"That's really something," sighed Judy. "Hey, I've brought my copy of the *Biographia* for you to autograph. It's right here in my pack. I carry it around every place I go."

"Oh, really?" said Spindrift, flushing with pleasure. "I must say I regard that as a great compliment."

"The *Biographia*'s one of the world's great books," averred Judy stoutly. "Possibly the greatest."

Spindrift felt appropriately flattered. "Perhaps you would be interested to see the original manuscript?" he suggested diffidently.

"*Would* I! You mean you have it right here in the abbey?"

"It's in the library."

"Well, what are we waiting for?" demanded Judy. "I mean —that is—if it's convenient."

"Oh, yes, yes," Spindrift assured her. "We'll just call in at the guest wing first, and I'll show you your quarters. We can go straight on up from there."

Judy's unfeigned enthusiasm for the Meister was all the old man could have wished for. He laid out the original manuscript of the *Biographia Mystica* before her and guided her through it while she gave little gasps and exclamations of wonder and pleasure. "It's just as if you'd known him personally, Mr. Spindrift," she said at last. "You make him come alive."

"Oh, he *is*, Mr. Harland. It is a gross error on our part to assume that life is mere physical existence. The *élan vital* lives on in the sublime creations of human genius. One only needs to study the *Exploratio Spiritualis* to realize that."

"And what's the *Exploratio Spiritualis*, Mr. Spindrift?"

"One day, I hope, it will be recognized as the *Biographia Mystica* of the human mind."

"You don't say!"

"But I *do,* Mr. Harland. And, what is more, I have the best of reasons for saying so."

Judy looked up at him curiously. "You don't mean that you've dug up *another* work by Meister Sternwärts?"

Spindrift nodded emphatically.

"Why that's marvelous!" she cried. "Sensational! Can I see it?"

"It would mean very little to you, I'm afraid, Mr. Harland. The *Spiritualis* was written in cipher."

"And you've cracked it? Translated it?"

"I have."

"Wow!" breathed Judy.

"I have spent the last twenty-five years working at it," said Spindrift with more than a trace of pride in his voice. "It is, I might pardonably claim, my swan song."

"And when's it going to be published?"

"By me—never."

"But why on earth not?"

"The responsibility is too great."

"How do you mean?"

Spindrift lifted his head and gazed out of the open library window towards the distant invisible sea. "The world is not yet ready for the *Spiritualis,"* he murmured. "Peter realized that, which is why he chose to write it in the form he did."

Judy frowned. "I'm afraid I'm still not with you, Mr. Spindrift. Why isn't it ready?"

"To accept a determinist universe as a proven fact?"

"Who says we're not?"

Almost reluctantly Spindrift withdrew his gaze from the far horizon and blinked down at her. "You mean you *can* accept it, Mr. Harland?" he asked curiously.

"Well, I certainly accept the *I Ching."*

"But you must, surely, believe in free will?"

"Well, up to a point, sure I do. I mean to say *I* have to consult the *I Ching.* It doesn't decide *for* me that I'm going to consult it, does it?"

It seemed to Spindrift at that moment that he had reached the final crossroads. But he was still not sure which path was the right one. He stirred the air vaguely with his fingers. "Then tell me, Mr. Harland," he said, "for the sake of the supposition, if you wish—what do you suppose would follow if one succeeded in convincing the human race that everything in life *was* preordained?"

Judy smiled. "But most of them believe it anyway. Astrology, Tarot, *I Ching*—you name it, we'll believe it. The fault, Mr. Spindrift, lies not in ourselves but in our stars."

"Really?" said Spindrift. "I must say that you astonish me."

"Well, a lot's happened in the last thirty years. We're the post-H-bomb generation, remember. We got to see where reason had led us. Right bang up to the edge of the precipice."

Spindrift nodded. "Yes, yes," he murmured. "I know. I saw it."

"Come again?"

"The *Pikadon.* That's what they called it." He closed his eyes and shuddered. A moment later he had gripped her by the arm. "But imagine *knowing* what was going to happen and that you were powerless to prevent it. What then, Mr. Harland?"

"How do you mean 'knowing'?"

"Just that," Spindrift insisted. "Seeing it all happening *before* it *had* happened. What then?"

"Are you serious?"

"It's all there in the *Spiritualis,*" said Spindrift, releasing his hold on her arm and gripping the back of her chair with both hands. "Peter Sternwärts rediscovered what Apollonius of Tyana had brought back with him from the East. But he did more than that. He devised the means whereby this knowledge could be handed down to future generations. He was a seer who bequeathed his eyes to posterity."

Judy's eyes narrowed. "Just let me get this straight," she said slowly. "Are you telling me that Meister Sternwärts could actually *see* the future?"

"Yes," said Spindrift simply.

"What? *All* of it?"

"No. Only the biggest storms on the horizon—the crises for civilization. He called them 'Knots in Time.' "

"But how do you know that?"

"He wrote them down," said Spindrift. "In a book he called *Praemonitiones.* "

"Holy Moses!" Judy whispered. "You just *have* to be kidding!"

"Sternwärts' own forecasts extend only as far as the fifteenth century, but, as I said before, he bequeathed his eyes to posterity."

"And just what does that *mean,* Mr. Spindrift?"

Spindrift drew in his breath. "Wait here a moment, Mr. Harland," he said, "and I will do my best to show you what it means."

A minute later he was back carrying the first volume of the *Praemonitiones.* He opened it at the frontispiece map and spread it out before her. Then he settled his spectacles firmly on his nose and began to explain what was what.

"This was drawn by Peter Sternwärts himself," he said. "There can be no question of that. It represents a bird's-eye view of the area within which Hautaire is situated. These dots represent the Neolithic stone circle, and the straight lines radiating from the menhirs all cross at this point here. I thought at first that these spirals were some primitive attempt to represent lines of magnetic force, but I know now that this is not so. Nevertheless, they do represent a force field of some kind—one, moreover, which was undoubtedly first detected by the ancient race who raised the original stone circle. Sternwärts realized that the menhirs acted as some sort of focusing device and that the area of maximum intensity would probably occur at the point where the intersection of the chords was held in equilibrium by the force field—what he called the *mare temporis*—sea of time."

Judy nodded. "So?" she said.

"He deduced that at this particular point he would find what he was seeking. I have since unearthed among the archives a number of sketches he made of similar stone circles in Brittany. And just off the center of each he has written the same word *oculus*—that is the Latin word for 'eye.' "

"Hey," said Judy, "you don't mean . . ."

"Indeed I do," insisted Spindrift. "After an immense amount of trial and error he succeeded in locating the precise point—and it is a very small area indeed—right here in Hautaire itself. Having found it, he built himself a time observatory and then proceeded to set down on record everything he saw. The results are there before you. The *Praemonitiones!*"

Judy stared down at the map. "But if that's so, why hasn't anyone else discovered one? I mean there's Stonehenge and Carnac and so forth, isn't there?"

Spindrift nodded. "That mystified Peter too, until he realized that the focal point of each circle was almost invariably situated a good twenty or so meters above ground level. He postulates that in the days when the circles were first raised, wooden towers were erected in their centers. The seer, who would probably have been a high priest, would have had sole access to that tower. In the case of Hautaire, it just so happened that the site of the long-vanished tower was occupied by the rotunda of the Abbey."

"And that was why Sternwärts came here?"

"No, Peter came to Hautaire because he had reason to believe that Apollonius of Tyana had made a special point of visiting this particular circle. There was apparently still a pagan shrine and a resident oracle here in the first century A.D."

Judy turned over some pages in the book before her, but she barely glanced at what was written there. "But how does it *work?*" she asked. "What do you do in this *oculus?* Peek into a crystal ball or something?"

"One sees," said Spindrift vaguely. "Within the mind's eye."

"But *how?*"

"That I have never discovered. Nor, I hazard, did Peter. Nevertheless that is what happens."

"And can you choose what you want to see?"

"I used to think not," said Spindrift, "but since I stumbled upon the key to the *Exploratio Spiritualis*, I have been forced to revise my opinion. I now believe that Peter Sternwärts was deliberately working towards the goal of a spiritual and mental discipline which would allow him to exert a direct influence upon what he saw. His aim was to become a shaper of the future as well as a seer."

Judy's blue eyes widened perceptibly. "A *shaper?*" she echoed. "And did he?"

"It is impossible to tell," said Spindrift. "But it is surely not without significance that he left Hautaire before he died."

"Come again?"

"Well, by the time he left he knew for certain that chance does nothing that has not been prepared well in advance. He must have realized that the only way in which he could exert an influence upon the future would be by acting in the present. If he could succeed in tracing the thread backwards from its knot, he might be able to step in and adjust things at the very point where only the merest modicum of intervention could affect the future. Of course, you must understand that this is all the purest supposition on my part."

Judy nodded. "And these disciplines—mental what's-its— what were they?"

"They are expressly designed to enable the seer to select his own particular vision. Having seen the catastrophe ahead, he could, if he were successful, feel his way backwards in time from that point and, hopefully, reach a *junctura criticalis*—the precise germinal instant of which some far-off tragedy was the progeny."

"Yes, I understand that. But what *sort* of disciplines were they?"

"Ironically, Mr. Harland, they appear to have had a good deal in common with those which are still practiced today among certain Eastern faiths."

"What's ironical about that?"

"Well, surely, the avowed aim of the Oriental sages is to achieve the ultimate annihilation of the self—of the ego. What Peter Sternwärts was hoping to achieve seems to me to have been the exact opposite—the veritable apotheosis of the human ego! Nothing less than the elevation of Man to God! He had a persistent vision of himself as the potter and the whole of humanity as his clay. That explains why, throughout the *Exploratio,* he constantly refers to himself as a 'shaper.' It also explains why I have shunned the responsibility of publishing it."

"Then why are you telling me?" demanded Judy shrewdly.

Spindrift removed his spectacles, closed his eyes, and massaged his eyelids with his fingertips. "I am very old, Mr. Harland," he said at last. "It is now over fifty years since I last visited the *oculus,* and the world is very close to the horizon of my own visions. Ever since Abbé Ferrand's untimely death forty years ago, the secret of the *oculus* has been mine alone. If I were to die this minute, it would perish with me, and I, by default, would have betrayed the trust which I believe has been reposed in me. In other words, I would die betraying the very man who has meant far more to me than any I have ever known in the flesh—Peter Sternwärts himself."

"But why choose *me?*" Judy insisted. "Why not one of the other brothers?"

Spindrift sighed. "I think, Mr. Harland, that it is perhaps because I recognize in you some of my own lifelong reverence for Peter Sternwärts. Furthermore, in some manner which I find quite impossible to explain, I am convinced that you are associated with the last visit I paid to the *oculus*—with my final vision."

"Really? And what was that?"

Spindrift looked down at the parchment which had absorbed so much of his life, and then he shook his head. "There was a girl," he murmured. "A girl with golden hair . . ."

"A *girl?*"

Like a waterlogged corpse rising slowly to the surface, the old man seemed to float up from the troubled depths of some dark and private nightmare. His eyes cleared. "Why, yes," he said. "A *girl.* Do you know, Mr. Harland, in all these years that point had never struck me before! A girl, *here in Hautaire!"* He began to chuckle wheezily. "Oh dear, oh dear, oh dear! Why, that would be the end of the world indeed!"

In spite of herself Judy was deeply moved by the old man's transparent relief. Instinctively she put out her hand and laid it on his. "I don't know what your vision was, Mr. Spindrift," she said. "But if you feel I can be of help to you in any way . . ."

Spindrift brought his other hand across and patted hers abstractedly. "That is most kind of you, Mr. Harland," he murmured. "Really, most kind . . ."

At supper that evening the abbot stepped up to the lectern in the refectory and raised a hand for silence. The murmur of voices stilled as the brothers turned their wondering eyes towards their father superior. He surveyed them all in silence for a long moment and then said, "Brethren and honored guests . . . my friends. Here at Hautaire, we live a life whose fundamental pattern was laid down for us more than a thousand years ago. I believe it is a good life, one which has accordingly found favor in the eyes of God. My cherished hope is that a thousand years from now its pattern will have remained, in all essential respects, as it is today—that the spiritual verities enshrined in our foundation will be what they have always been—a source of comfort and reassurance to all God-loving men, a harbor of hope and tranquillity in a storm-tossed world."

He paused as though uncertain how to continue, and they all saw him close his eyes and turn his face upwards in mute prayer for a long, long minute. When at last he looked down upon them again, the silence in the hall was almost palpable.

"My friends, I have just learnt that certain European powers, acting in concert with Israel and the United States of America, have this afternoon launched an armed invasion of Saudi Arabia and the Trucial States."

There was a concerted gasp of horror and a sudden burst of whispering. The abbot raised his voice to carry over the hubbub.

"Their avowed aim is to secure for themselves access to the oil supplies which they deem essential to their national, political and economic survival. Under the terms of the Baghdad Treaty of 1979, the Arabs have called upon the Soviet Union for immediate armed assistance, and Russia and its allies have demanded the instant and total withdrawal of the invading forces. Failure to comply with this demand will, they say, bring about inevitable consequences."

He paused again and regarded them somberly. "I shall personally conduct a service for Divine Intercession immediately after complin. It will be held in the main chapel. It goes without saying that all our guests are invited to attend. *Dominus vobiscum.*" He sketched the sign of the Cross over them, stepped down from the lectern, and strode swiftly out of the hall.

In the outburst of chattering which erupted immediately the abbot had left the hall, Spindrift turned to Judy and seized her by the arm. "You must come with me, Mr. Harland," he whispered urgently. "At once."

Judy, who was still groping to come to terms with all the implications of what she had heard, nodded submissively and allowed the old man to shepherd her out of the refectory and up into the library. He unearthed the keys to the *oculus* and the rotunda, then hurried her up the stairs and along the deserted passages to the door which had remained locked for more than half a century. He was possessed by an almost feverish impatience and kept up an incessant muttering to himself the whole way. Judy could hardly make out a word of what he was saying, but more than once she thought she caught the strange word *Pikadon.* It meant nothing to her at all.

So much rubbish had accumulated in the narrow passage that they had to lean their combined weight against the rotunda door before they managed to force it open. They squeezed through into the crevice beyond, and Spindrift lit a candle he had brought with him. By its wavering light the two of them scuffled their way forward to the *oculus.*

When they reached it, Spindrift handed the key to Judy and held the candle so that she could see what she was doing. A minute later the door had creaked open to expose the sarcophagus, standing just as it had stood for the last seven hundred years.

Judy gaped at it in astonishment. "You mean you go in *there?*"

"*You* must, Mr. Harland," said Spindrift. "Please, hurry."

"But *why?*" demanded Judy. "What good could it do?"

Spindrift gripped her by the shoulder and almost succeeded in thrusting her bodily into the casque. "Don't you understand, Mr. Harland?" he cried. "It is *you* who must prove my final vision false! *You have to prove me wrong!*"

Into her twenty-two years of life Judy had already packed more unusual experiences than had most women three times her age, but none of them had prepared her for this. Alone with a looney octogenarian who seemed bent on stuffing her into a stone coffin buried somewhere inside the walls of a medieval monastery! For all she knew, once he had got her inside, he would turn the key on her and leave her there to rot. And yet, at the very moment when she most needed her physical strength, it had apparently deserted her. Her arms, braced against the stone slabs, seemed all but nerveless; her legs so weak she wondered if they were not going to fold under her. "The key," she muttered. "Give me the key. And you go away. Right away. Back to that other door. You can wait for me there."

The pressure of Spindrift's hand relaxed. Judy stepped back and fumbled the key out of the lock. Then, feeling a little more confident, she turned to face the old man. By the trembling light of the candle she glimpsed the streaks of tears on his ancient cheeks.

"Please go, Mr. Spindrift," she pleaded. *"Please."*

"But you will do it?" he begged. "I must *know*, Mr. Harland."

"Yes, yes," she said. "Sure I will. I give you my word."

He shuffled backwards a few doubtful paces and stood watching her. "Would you like me to leave you the candle?" he asked.

"All right," she said. "Put it down there on the floor."

She waited until he had done it, and then, aloud, she started to count slowly up to sixty. She had reached barely halfway before the rotunda was buffeted by the massive reverberating thunder of warplanes hurtling past high overhead. Judy shivered violently and, without bothering to finish her count, stepped the two short paces back into the casque until her shoulders were pressed against the cold stone. "Please, dear God," she whispered, "let it be all—"

She was falling, dropping vertically downwards into the bowels of the earth as if down the shaft of an elevator. Yet the candle, still standing there before her just where the old man had left it and burning with its quiet golden flame, told her that her stomach lied. But her sense of vertigo was so acute that she braced her arms against the sides of the coffin in an effort to steady herself. Watery saliva poured into her mouth. Certain she was about to faint, she swallowed and closed her eyes.

Like magenta fire balloons, the afterimages of the candle flame drifted across her retina. They changed imperceptibly to green, to dark blue, to purple, and finally vanished into the velvety darkness. Her eyelids felt as though lead weights had been laid upon them.

Suddenly—without warning of any kind—she found herself gazing down, as if from a great height, upon a city. With the instant familiarity bred of a dozen high-school civics assignments, she knew it at once for her own hometown. The whole panoramic scene had a strange, almost dreamlike clarity. The air was unbelievably clear; no trace of smoke or haze obscured the uncompromising grid of the streets. Northwards, Lake Michigan glittered silver-blue in the bright sunshine, while the plum-blue shadows of drifting clouds ghosted silently across its placid waters. But this was no longer the Chicago she remembered. The whole center of the metropolis was gone. Where it had been was nothing but a vast circular smudge of grey rubble, along the fringes of which green shrubs were already growing. No factory stacks smoked; no glittering lines of automobiles choked these expressways; no freight trains wriggled and jinked through these latticed sidings; all was as dead and still as a city on the moon. This was indeed Necropolis, City of the Dead.

At last the vision faded and its place was taken by another. She now found herself gazing out across a vast plain through which wound a great river. But the endless golden Danubian wheatfields which she remembered so well had all vanished. The winds which sent the towering cloud schooners scudding across this sky blew only through the feathered heads of weeds and wild grasses which stretched out like a green and rippling sea to the world's end. Of man, or cattle, or even flying bird there was no sign at all.

When Spindrift returned some twenty minutes later, it was to discover Judy crouched in the bottom of the sarcophagus, curled up like a dormouse with her head resting on her bent knees. Fearfully he stooped over her and placed his hand on her shoulder. "Mr. Harland," he whispered urgently. "Mr. Harland, are you all right?"

There was no response. He knelt down, thrust his hands beneath her arms and, by a mighty effort, succeeded in dragging her clear of the casque. She flopped sideways against the door, then sprawled forwards beside him. He fumbled his hand inside the neck of her shirt, felt for the beating of her heart, and so discovered who she was. The last dim flicker of hope died within him.

He patted her deathly cheeks and chafed her hands until at last her eyelids fluttered open. "What happened?" he asked. "What did you see?"

She raised a cold hand and wonderingly touched his wrinkled face with her fingertips. "Then it *hasn't* happened," she whispered. "And it was *so* real."

"It *will* happen," he said sadly. "Whatever it was you saw must come to pass. It always has."

"But there was no one," she mourned. "No one at all. What happened, Mr. Spindrift? Where had they all gone?"

"Come, my dear," he urged, gently coaxing her to her feet. "Come with me."

The air on the hillside was still warm, drowsy with the summer scents of wild sage, lavender and rosemary, as the old man and the girl made their way up the dim path towards the ridge where the ancient neoliths still bared themselves like broken teeth against the night sky. Below them, the abbey lights glowed out cheerfully, and small figures could be seen moving back and forth behind the chapel windows.

They reached a point where an outcrop of limestone had been roughly shaped into a seat. Spindrift eased himself onto it, drew Judy down beside him and spread out the wide skirt of his habit to cover her. As he did so, he could feel her trembling like a crystal bell that, once struck, goes on quivering far below the threshold of audible sound. An enormous, impotent grief seized him by the throat. Too late he saw what he should have done, how he had betrayed the trust that Brother Roderigo and the Abbé Ferrand had laid upon him. But he saw too, with a sort of numb clarity, how he, Spindrift, could not have done it, because, within himself, some vital spark of faith in humanity had been extinguished far back in the blood-stained ruins of 1917. He could no longer believe that men were essentially good, or that the miracle which the genius of Peter Sternwärts had created would not be used in some hideous way to further the purposes of evil.

Yet what if he *had* gone that one step further, *had* published the *Exploratio Spiritualis* and given to all men the means of foreseeing the inevitable consequences of their insane greed, their overweening arrogance, their atavistic lust for power? Who was to say that Armageddon might not have been averted, that Peter's miracle might not have succeeded in shaping anew the human spirit? *Quis custodiet ipsos custodes?* Ah, who indeed, if not God? And Spindrift's God had died in the mud of Ypres.

The full knowledge of what he had done rose as bitter as bile at the back of the old man's throat. Desperately he sought for some words of comfort for the girl who crouched beside him and could not stop quivering. Some lie, some little harmless lie. "I did not tell you before," he said, "but I believe you are destined to publish the *Spiritualis* for me. Yes, I remember now. That was how you were to be associated with my final vision. So, you see, there *is* still hope."

But even as he spoke, the distant eastern horizon suddenly flickered as though with summer lightning. His arm tightened involuntarily around the girl's shoulders. She stirred. "Oh God," she moaned softly. "Oh God, oh God, oh God." A harsh, grating sob shook her, and then another and another.

A second flash threw the low clouds into sharp relief, and then the whole arching roof of the world was lit up like the day. An urgent bell began tolling in the abbey.

Something scratched a line like a blood-red stalk high up into the southern sky, and a ball of blue-white fire blossomed in strange and sinister silence.

And later a wind got up and blew from the north.

The Linguist

by STEPHEN ROBINETT

I hope that it won't sadden the readers too much, but most SF writers tend to look more like round-shouldered bookkeepers rather than like the strong-thewed heroes of their stories. Steve Robinett is, I believe, the only exception to this firm rule, looking more like Flash Gordon than Buster Crabbe ever did. I doubt if this fact would relate at all to his excellent story here (other than echoing a hint of pot-bellied jealousy) if it weren't that the story's hero is a two-fisted intellectual. You will see what I mean.

I

I *won't have my brain picked,"* shouted Eberly, squinting over the rear sight of the 30–30 and aligning the bead on the rocks below. *"Not this time! Not again!"*

A faint shadow dodged from rock to rock. Eberly squeezed the trigger. The rifle bucked against his shoulder. Dirt puffed in front of the rocks. The shot had fallen short.

"Eberly, give up," came Plagio's voice, amplified by a bull-horn. *"You haven't got a chance. You can't fight us. There are too many of us."*

"Where there's life," responded Eberly, wishing he had something pithier and more original to say, *"there's hope."* He

109

squeezed off another round. Rock shattered. A man screamed.

"You made a contract, Eberly."

"An illegal contract."

"But an enforceable contract."

Bullets splattered on the rocks around Eberly, punctuating Plagio's comment about the contract's enforceability. Specific Performance? Was that what they called making someone fulfill his contract? Eberly shrugged. Maybe they called it Specific Performance. Maybe they called it Fred. Eberly had studied law once, but that, too, was gone, plucked from his head for a fee.

He dusted the rock chips from his sleeve and decided to change position. Plagio and his men were too close. Soon they would know his exact position. Knowing it, they could surround him and wait. Even if the Mohave sun failed to cook him, hunger and thirst would eventually defeat him; if he lost consciousness even for a minute, Plagio would sweep down on him, sedate him, carry him off and pick his brain.

Eberly shoved two replacement shells into the 30–30. He stuck a bookmark into the tattered copy of *Don Quixote* and stuffed it into his coat pocket with the box of shells. This time, he would finish the book. If he had to shoot Plagio himself, he would follow *Don Quixote* to the end.

Quietly, keeping low behind the rocks, Eberly scurried toward the ledge he had spotted earlier. He slung the rifle across his back, but hesitated before continuing the climb, glancing down. Over the ledge, the cliff fell away for two hundred meters to the desert. One slip would leave him flattened on the sand or draped over a cactus, a sack of broken bones. Yet, death with honor—even without honor—had advantages. It would cheat Plagio of his pound of engrams. Momentarily, Eberly considered jumping, then rejected the idea. Any satisfaction he might feel at cheating Plagio would be only transitory. Better to climb higher and hope for total victory.

He began a sideways shuffle along the ledge, fingertips straining in fissures to hold his body against the rock wall. Once, he glanced down. His head swirled. He looked away, stopping and leaning his sweating forehead against the cool rock. He tried to breathe deeply to calm his nerves.

"Eberly!"

"Not now," muttered Eberly. "Don't distract me."

"We see you moving, Eberly. We have heat scanners on you."

Eberly inched toward the next outcropping, trying to ignore the distracting voice.

"Submit, Eberly. You've done it before. It takes only a few seconds. It is painless. Think of your wife and children. If you submit, they will continue to live in luxury. If you are killed, they will have to go on welfare. Your wife is too slow-witted to be of use to us."

Now Plagio was insulting Gloria. True, Gloria was a slow learner. It had taken her four years just to master the fundamentals of Rumanian grammar, a skill Eberly sold Plagio for fifty dollars, flat fee. Considering Gloria's faulty preterit and weak future subjunctive, along with her complete inability to understand the Rumanian relative pronoun, it was probably a good price. Still, Plagio had no reason to insult her.

"Your own wife pronounced French like a Bulgarian," shouted Eberly.

An angry burst of rifle fire answered.

Eberly reached the outcropping and relative safety. To the west, the sun, an elongated orange ball on the desert horizon, was setting. No one would try to cross the ledge at night. If he could hold them off until after dark, he could finish the last two hundred pages of *Don Quixote*.

Eberly unslung the rifle and positioned himself behind a tall rock with a V-shaped notch in the top, resting the gun barrel in the notch. At this distance, he would need all the stability he could find to keep Plagio pinned down. Below, he heard gravel slip. He fired twice.

"No," he muttered. "Save the ammunition. Only shoot when I see something worth shooting."

He got out the box of shells and opened it, replacing the two spent rounds and counting the rest in the fading light. Thirty rounds, including those in the rifle. Hardly enough for a war but adequate to hold off Plagio.

"Eberly!"

"Brain picker!" shouted Eberly. *"Filthy brain picker!"*

"I harvest a crop. Nothing more. We have had a profitable arrangement in the past, Eberly. Why can't it continue?"

"Why can't I finish Don Quixote?"

"I am a reasonable man. How—"

"You are a pig and a brain picker!"

"As I was saying, I am a reasonable man, a businessman. How much do you have to go to finish it?"

"About two hundred pages."

A pause ensued. *"How long will it take you?"*

"In this light? All night. Maybe longer."

"How long with a good reading lamp?"

"Four or five hours."

"It's too long. The customer is waiting. He has a final exam in Spanish tomorrow at eleven A.M. *He's paid in advance. We have to set up the equipment, make the extraction and the implant, then get him back to Los Angeles for the exam. Submit, Eberly. You can finish the book next time."*

Next time. Eberly had already learned Spanish seven times. Each time, when he mastered the ability sufficiently to read Don Quixote, Plagio, who used Don Quixote as the objective test of Spanish mastery, extracted the skill from him, leaving Don Quixote or Sancho Panza or the beautiful Dulcinea or the not so beautiful Rosinante in some dire situation and Eberly unable to find out what happened. He was thankful, at least, that he could remember the plot. Plagio took only the language skill, not the information it conveyed.

"Plagio!" yelled Eberly.

"What?"

"You said the same thing last time and the time before that. It's no go. You'll never let me finish. Next time will be exactly like this time. As soon as I can read it, you'll pick my brain. I won't even know how to say buenos días.*"*

"Read it in translation."

Infuriated by Plagio's aesthetic insensitivity, Eberly muttered, *"Caramba,"* and squeezed off three rounds. His ears rang from the explosions.

"Eberly, what was that for?"

"Because it's never the same in translation, you philistine!"

Eberly sat down behind the rocks, planning to take advantage of the last rays of sunlight. He opened *Don Quixote* and began looking for his place.

"Let's see, they came to the inn and Don Quixote fell asleep and—ah, here it is. The curate has just said the original cause of Don Quixote's madness was from reading books."

Eberly became immersed in his book. Eventually, the light faded completely. He withdrew a penlight from his shirt pocket, but instead of flicking it on to read, he leaned back against the rocks. His escape from Plagio's Palm Springs home had unexpectedly drained him. He had planned to escape, then make his way to the main highway and thumb a ride to Los Angeles. Somehow—probably from crashing through the window, an act he found considerably more unnerving and more difficult than in the movies (it had taken two tries and the help of the rifle butt to get through the plate glass) —his sense of direction had become addled. Instead of striking out toward the highway, he had struck out across the desert. He had expected Plagio to follow immediately. Evidently, Plagio's henchman, Marvin The Extractor, a name referring to Marvin's occupation performing illicit engramectomies, had remained unconscious longer than expected. The glancing blow with the Ming vase, which had shattered the vase, had felt too light to put Marvin out long, but after an hour of walking, Eberly had looked back and seen no sign of pursuit. Only when he neared the rocks three hours later and

started his climb to reconnoiter and get his bearings did he
see the jeep, bouncing toward him across the desert.

"*Eberly.*"

Eberly noticed how the voice carried in the night air, making Plagio seem to be right on top of him. "*What?*"

"*Can we make a deal?*"

"*What kind of deal?*"

"*You submit and—*"

"*Never!*"

"*You submit and I'll give you three weeks paid vacation in Acapulco before you start on your next subject.*"

"*What good will Acapulco be if I don't know Spanish?*"

"*You don't have to talk to anyone.*"

"*I* like *talking to people.*"

"*Okay, make it Miami—anywhere.*"

Eberly thought about it. Plagio must be desperate. He had
never offered Eberly a vacation before. He always expected
Eberly to be back at the books the day after an extraction. The
client must be someone big, or the son of someone big, possibly one of Plagio's superiors. In spite of the dominating figure
Plagio had become in Eberly's life, Eberly knew Plagio was
small fry to the Organization, that vague and only obliquely
mentioned group who financed Plagio. When Congress outlawed engram transplants in the early 1990's, claiming it allowed the rich to become not only richer but smarter, organized crime moved in. The price to college students, harried
executives without time to take night classes, or any of the
myriad other slow learners in society had actually dropped
when people like Plagio took over. The American Medical
Association had maintained the cost of the operation at such
artificially high levels—they fought the criminalization of engram extraction tooth and nail, but popular sentiment and the
proximity of a congressional election carried the day—that
even the illegality of the procedure failed to sustain the high
price. Nowadays, a college student with five thousand dollars

and a disinclination to study—by the looks of Plagio's balance sheet, something close to eighty percent of the students in the country engaged in "cramming," as it was colloquially called —could buy French, German, Spanish or any Western language at a level sufficient to sustain them through graduate study. Slavic, Oriental and African languages, along with ancient languages, came slightly higher. Other subjects varied according to the job market. One year sciences would be expensive; the next, law or medicine. Liberal Arts seldom became economically interesting enough to transplant, except foreign languages, Eberly's specialty. Group rates were also available, allowing students to pass around skills as needed. Plagio preferred to sell to groups, fraternities and sororities. Though the fee per person was smaller, the total was larger and the overhead—supporting people like Eberly, who had a gift for language learning (he had once learned Kurdish in seven weeks), remained constant.

Still, if Plagio was so anxious to deliver, the customer must be important. Did that fact give Eberly some bargaining power? Maybe.

"Plagio."

"What?"

"Who's the customer?"

"What's it to you?"

"I've got a deal of my own to offer."

"Let's have it."

"You let me finish this book and I'll submit. Tell the customer to call in sick."

"He tried that already. His teacher doesn't give make-up exams. If he doesn't take the exam, he flunks. If he flunks, he's out of school— he's a borderline case already. If he's out of school, you know what that means."

"One fewer future customer for you."

"Right."

"Is that all you think about, Plagio—money?"

"It makes the world go round, Eberly."

"There's more to life than money."

"What?"

At a loss, Eberly hedged. *"Why can't you be reasonable?"*

"I think I am being reasonable. You're the one who's fighting the system and being unreasonable. What can you gain? A Pyrrhic victory?"

"A what?"

"Are you forgetting your English?"

Eberly shook his head. Pyrrhic? It was Greek to him. He shrugged and sat down, flicking on the penlight. Plagio would never understand. Things other than money drove some men, things with intrinsic merit, things without market value. He began to read. The dot of light danced across the page, illuminating accent marks and tildes. He read on. Don Quixote, once more mounted and questing, galloped, or rather, considering the nature of the sway-backed Rosinante, plodded through Eberly's brain. If only, mused Eberly, he had some modern equivalent to Rosinante, some charger, sound of limb and ready for flight, some jennet or jade or—

"Jeep," said Eberly.

He stood up and peered around the rocks. No sign of Plagio. Vaguely outlined below him, visible in the starlight only as a rectangular lump on the sand, stood the jeep.

"But how?" wondered Eberly aloud.

If he retraced his steps, crossing the rock ledge, Plagio would see him. Plagio's heat scanner worked even better at night. Searching the rocks for an alternate exit, he found the only possibility, a sheer descent to the desert floor. Looking at the drop, he felt himself sway. It would be difficult during the day. At night, it would be impossible. He decided to wait for dawn, and then descend and try for the jeep.

Dawn, tentative, gradual, then more assertive, arrived just as the battery in Eberly's penlight gave out, sending its faint emanations over the desert horizon. Though he had only ten pages to go to finish *Don Quixote,* he decided to postpone the pleasure. Dawn would rouse Plagio, too. If Plagio arrived before the end of the book—Eberly broke off, unwilling to let the thought appear in his mind.

He stuffed his belongings into his jacket, checked the rifle and prepared for the descent. If he was lucky, he would make it to the jeep and freedom before Plagio noticed.

"Eberly."

Should he answer? If he failed to answer, Plagio would boldly climb the rocks to inspect, thinking Eberly had escaped in the night. He wanted Plagio pinned in the rocks as long as possible.

"What is it now, mind raper?"

"Eberly, do you have to use insulting language like that? I have always treated you fairly."

"Like a prize stud, ready for milking."

"You're a confused man, Eberly."

"Call it what you will, brain picker! You understand what I mean."

"No, I don't, Eberly. I don't understand you at all. I thought I did, once. I thought you were like the rest of us. I thought you knew what was important in life."

"Money."

"That's right. What you can't sell in the marketplace isn't worth having."

"It's a form of intellectual prostitution, Plagio."

"Prostitution's a marketable skill, Eberly. If you think Gloria's game, I'm sure I can find a spot for—"

"INTELLECTUAL prostitution, I said."

"Oh. Sorry. It's hard to hear in these rocks."

"You drain people's minds for profit, Plagio."

"As I said, I harvest a crop. The crop is in demand. It's the way of the world, Eberly. Submit to it."

"Submit," muttered Eberly, jacking a shell into the chamber of the 30–30, about to pop up over the top of a rock and get off a shot. He controlled himself. Plagio probably wanted him to show himself. Though Plagio would have instructed his men to shoot for the torso, thus saving the brain and its engrams, Eberly felt little comfort in the idea. Plagio could extract the engrams for up to two or three hours after death. No, he would remain hidden.

"Eberly."

"What?"

"When did you suddenly get morality?"

"What do you mean?"

"You've worked with me for the last ten years. You've never complained before."

"I never complained because I was hooked."

"Narcotics? They will interfere with your learning capacity, Eberly."

"Not narcotics—money!"

A sarcastic edge came into Plagio's amplified voice. *"But now you're not hooked."*

Eberly thought about Gloria, about the kids, Ephraim and Ezekiel, both born when he was studying Biblical Greek. The money, arriving every Friday like clockwork, never late, never short, had kept him going. Each time he wanted to do something for himself—branch out into business, or go back to school and learn something unsalable (History or Literature) —money and the soft seduction of luxury, along with Gloria's spendthrift nature, kept his nose in a grammar book, conjugating Estonian verbs. Ten years without once doing something for himself. Ten years without taking his eyes from the demands of the marketplace. Ten years without doing something for its intrinsic worth. It was ten years too long. Plagio might know a stud from a milker—both could be sold on the market—but he would never understand the meaning of intrinsic worth, a thing done for itself, a windmill tilted. No, Eberly was no longer hooked, at least for the moment, on money. He was hooked on something more compelling, something he had to do, if only once, for himself. Casting his eyes up to the last fading star in the west, Eberly, hand in his jacket pocket, held tightly to *Don Quixote.*

"It's time to try for the jeep."

The descent was steeper than Eberly anticipated. He tore his pants leg on the rocks, almost dropped the rifle once, and hung by his fingertips innumerable times, sweating and scrambling for a foothold. Eventually, hands torn and bleeding from the sharp rocks, he dropped the last three meters to the desert, narrowly missing a kangaroo rat, which looked at him—frozen except for its twitching nose—then fled.

"You're lucky," said Eberly to the vanished rat. "No Plagios in your life."

During his descent, the sun had climbed up the sky. It baked the desert and broiled Eberly. June was a less than accommodating month in the Mohave. Eberly wished he had a hat. He wiped his forehead on his sleeve, planning his next move. Approach the jeep by stealth or rush it? Should he try for the jeep at all? Plagio or one of his men might be close to it. They could put a bullet through him before he could drop the jeep into low. Perhaps he should exploit his small advantage and head into the desert. And the keys—what if they were in Plagio's pocket? Eberly glanced at the sun. He could almost hear it crackling. No, the desert was out. It had to be the jeep, the jeep or surrend—

"Never."

The keys. If the keys were missing, he could sabotage the jeep and try to escape on foot. Either way, it was his only chance.

Keeping low, he worked his way around the base of the rock pile. With luck, Plagio would be above him, looking up and shouting into his bullhorn.

"Eberly."

Hypothesis proved. Plagio was still talking to him. Getting no answer, Plagio would be drawn farther up the rocks and farther away from the jeep.

"Eberly, answer me."

Eberly chuckled, amused at fooling Plagio, then tensed, freezing behind a man-sized boulder. The scraping footsteps of a man descending in gravel had frozen him. Cautiously, he peered around the boulder, keeping low. The jeep stood on a sand dune about twenty meters from the rocks. Marvin The Extractor, his elongated head like a loaf of bread with hair, approached it. Horrorstruck, Eberly watched as Marvin leaned across the driver's seat and plucked the keys from the ignition. Plagio was one step ahead of him.

Throwing caution, and, inadvertently, his penlight, to the wind, Eberly—leaving his crouch behind the rocks like a Marine leaving a landing craft, rifle gripped at the small of the stock and the barrel, holding it almost horizontal before him, a fearsome, bared-tooth leer on his face—charged. Charging on sand proved a slow business. Still, he managed to surprise Marvin, noting, before Marvin turned, the white bandage on the back of Marvin's head where the vase had landed.

Marvin turned, saw Eberly struggling up the dune, started to laugh—pointing his finger—as Eberly took a comic pratfall in the loose sand, changed his mind and went for his sidearm, a .45 in a flap holster. Marvin's attempted laugh fueled Eberly's rage. Eberly reached the top of the dune. Marvin had the holster flap up and the gun half-withdrawn. Eberly swung with the rifle butt, connecting with the side of Marvin's loaf-shaped head. Marvin, staring blankly, dazed, stood a moment after the blow, shook his head once, then wilted. His unconscious body began rolling down the dune like a log.

Rolling, Marvin's .45 went off.

"Damn it," muttered Eberly, frowning, "why don't you tell the whole world, Marvin?"

The shot would bring Plagio. Eberly scrambled after the rolling man. Abruptly, Marvin stopped rolling, almost tripping Eberly. Eberly knelt and gave the prone figure a slight nudge. It flopped on its back, snorting sand and beginning to breathe again. Quickly, Eberly rifled the pockets, coming up with two sets of keys, one presumably for the jeep and the other for Marvin's car.

He shook Marvin.

"Wake up, you creep."

Marvin's eyes started to open, narrow slits in the sand-matted face. Eberly dangled both sets of keys before Marvin's eyes.

"Which of these fits the jeep?"

The eyes closed. The head lolled.

"Marvin, damn it, wake up." He slapped Marvin once. The blow succeeded only in pushing Marvin farther down the dune.

Sand kicked up near Marvin's head, followed almost immediately by the sound of rifle fire. Eberly looked up. Plagio and two men, half-centimeter figures resting their rifles on rocks, fired at him.

Taking both sets of keys, he left Marvin and started up the dune. Sand hopped and jumped around his feet. He heard one stray round plink off the jeep. Only when he reached the relative safety of the opposite side of the jeep did he look back. Plagio, kneeling, and the two men, standing behind him and firing, had reached the base of the rock pile.

Eberly steadied the rifle across the hood of the jeep and fired four quick rounds. Though he could see none of them hit, Plagio, scurrying for the rocks, must have gotten the message.

Eberly reloaded and got into the jeep. Frantically, he tried the keys, innumerable keys on both chains. Why did Marvin carry so many keys? Vaguely, Eberly remembered a comment of Plagio's. Marvin, before setting up as an engram extractor, had stolen cars. It explained much of Marvin's character, the joy he took in his work. Stealing cars, stealing engrams—they both gave Marvin the same illicit thrill. A key fit.

Eberly stomped the clutch to the floor and twisted the key. The jeep ground, coughed and caught, coming alive. He jammed the gearshift into first and popped the clutch. The jeep lurched, almost seemed to hop, and then stopped, stalled.

Eberly restarted it, this time gently releasing the clutch. The engine uttered a decrescendo of slowing, labored, lugging noises, stalling.

Eberly checked the emergency brake—off—then leaned out to look at the front tire—flat. At the instant Eberly had popped the clutch, Plagio's aim had evidently proven true. It accounted for the hopping sensation.

"What now?" asked Eberly, staring at the flat tire.

A bullet shattered the windshield, leaving a hole surrounded by a spiderweb of cracked glass.

"Take cover," answered Eberly.

He got out of the jeep and crawled under it, positioning himself so Plagio would have to charge straight up the dune and into his rifle fire.

Furtively, Plagio attempted to dart from the rocks. Eberly fired. Sand spurted at Plagio's feet. The figure retreated, shaking its fist at Eberly. After several seconds, the bullhorn came on.

"Eberly."

Eberly cupped his hands around his mouth, answering. *"What?"*

"You can't escape now. You may have us pinned down, but we've got you pinned down, too. And that jeep isn't going anywhere. It's a standoff, Eberly. Give up."

Suddenly, inexplicably, doubt surfaced in Eberly's mind. Plagio was right, a standoff. What could he hope to gain by resisting Plagio? Actually, the man wanted nothing more than his due, completion of the illegal contract. What was wrong with that? In return, Eberly would get not only his life, something he had always found useful, but life in luxury.

Conscious of his own mortality, conscious of the shortness of life; conscious also that he was outgunned, Eberly considered submitting. He had responsibilities, Gloria and the children. Selfishness, a quality he abhorred on principle though practiced from time to time, was no reason to deny his family the good life, was it? He imagined Gloria in the welfare line, dress in rags, hair frazzled, people crowding in front of her. He imagined Ephraim and Ezekiel, selling pencils, begging from strangers, their eyes tear-filled and pitiful. And why?

Eberly crawled out from under the jeep, disgusted with himself, preparing to surrender. He stood up and took the copy of *Don Quixote* from his pocket, glaring at it.

"Because of *you*," he snarled. *"That's* why!"

He hurled the book to the sand and began hopping on it with both feet.

"You! You! You! Traitor! Seducer! What the hell good are you anyway?"

He stopped hopping, stepping back from the book. It had fallen on its spine, open to the page with Eberly's bookmark. He looked at the half-buried book, breathing deeply and trying to control his fury, pondering.

A bullet whizzed past his ear, jerking him from his ponderings. He dropped to the sand, nose a centimeter from the book. Plagio, unaware of Eberly's intent to surrender, was still firing.

"Plagio," shouted Eberly.

The firing ceased. *"What?"*

"I want—" The words seemed to stick in his throat.

"You want what?"

"I want to—" Eberly broke off, his attention attracted by the page in front of his nose. He began to read.

"You want to what?" coaxed Plagio.

"Just a minute."

"Eberly?"

"Just a minute!"

Eberly became lost in the knight's final return home. Sancho Panza's wife, Joan Panza, after asking about the health of Sancho's donkey (better, answered the squire, than that of the master), inquired what profit the squire had gained from his adventures, what dresses for Mrs. Panza, what shoes for the children?

I bring none of these things, good wife, quoth Sancho, *although I bring other things of more moment and estimation.*

"More moment and estimation," mumbled Eberly, sniffing, a tear beginning its journey down his cheek. Doubt again surfaced in his mind, this time challenging his desire to surrender. His voice changed, hardening, determination encrusting every syllable.

"More moment and estimation."

He looked over the top of the book. Plagio was nowhere in sight.

"Plagio!"

No answer. He looked down the sloping dune. Something odd, or rather, the lack of something odd—Marvin—attracted his attention. Had Marvin revived? Or—

Grasping the book in one hand and the rifle in the other, Eberly crawled under the jeep, elbows and knees dragging him forward. He reached the crest of the dune. Timorously, he looked over. The dune dipped in the area of Marvin's body, creating natural cover, obscuring Eberly's line of fire. He could see the tops of three heads behind the dip. While Eberly read, Plagio and his men had reached Marvin. They advanced out of the divot on their stomachs. Seeing him, they fired, rifles blazing in rapid succession. Sand hopped and skipped on all sides.

Repositioning the book slightly, Eberly rested the rifle barrel along the book's inner crease and aimed. He fired twice, halting Plagio's advance. He glanced down at the page next to the barrel, reading on.

Proceeding in this manner, firing and reading, pausing occasionally to turn a page or reload, Eberly impeded Plagio's advance and followed Don Quixote's. He read through the sonnets and epitaphs of the last few pages, eventually arriving at both the last paragraph and his last bullet.

A scholar, read Eberly, had been given the moldy, time-worn papers treating of the life and doings of *Don Quijote de la Mancha* and had, according to the author (someone named Cervantes), deciphered them. They promised to tell of further exploits, a third sally for the great knight.

"A third sally," said Eberly, closing the book and firing the last round. Another tear formed in his eye as he wistfully imagined the third sally.

"Eberly."

The voice of reality. *"What?"*

"By my count, you're out of ammunition. We're coming up."

Eberly rolled on his back, throwing his arms out to either side and letting the sun warm his face. He spoke quietly. "Come and get me, vulture. I'm ready."

He could hear Plagio marching up the dune. What had Plagio scheduled him for next time? Ah, yes, Russian. For the fifth time, Russian. In that word, Eberly saw his future. Russian would be harder than Spanish. First of all, that funny alphabet, like barbed-wire he would have to penetrate to get at the language. Secondly, it would take more time and effort to plan carefully, plus more endurance to carry out the plan. Momentarily, he shuddered at the rigors that lay ahead. At the same time, he welcomed them. What else could a man do who was driven from within? What else could a man do who was only on page fifteen of *War and Peace?*

Settling the World

by **M. JOHN HARRISON**

M. John Harrison, who makes his first appearance here in the pages of the annual *Best SF* volume, is a stalwart of the *New Wave* writing as exemplified in *New Worlds*. Your editor, who selfishly thinks one Harrison in science fiction is enough, bows to the inevitable when another Harrison comes along with fiction as good as this.

With the discovery of God on the far side of the Moon by a second-wave (Apollo B series) exploration team, and the subsequent gigantic and hazardous towing operation that brought Him back to start His reign anew, there began on Earth, as one might assume, a period of far-reaching change. I need not detail, for instance, the numerous climatic and political refinements, the New Medicine or the global basic minimum wage; or those modifications of geography itself which have been of so much benefit. However, despite the immediate, the "gross" progress, certain human institutions continued for a while to function as they always had; I think particularly of those edifices of a bureaucratic nature, whose very structure militates against devolution.

The Department to which I have given my services for so long was one of these: and so it was in a perfectly normal way that I received the call to visit my chief one Monday morning in the first April since the inception of the New Reign. The memo was issued, passed lethargically through the secretarial system and the typing pool, and reached me by way of my own secretary, Mrs. Padgett, who has since retired, I believe to help her mother in a market garden in Surrey. After dealing in a leisurely way with the rest of my post—we were all delightfully relaxed in those first days, settling our shoulders, as it were, into a larger size of coat—I took the lift up to the top of the building where by tradition the chief has his office, to find him in ruminative mood.

"Look at that, Oxlade," he invited, gesturing at the panoramic sweep of the city beneath. "How much fresher you must all find it down there, now the hurry has gone. Eh? The air refined, the man refreshed!"

Indeed, as I stared down at the clean and quiet streets, where a brisk wind and bright sunshine filled one with a corresponding inner vitality, I had been thinking precisely the same thing. In the parks, hundreds of daffodils were out, the benches were full of elderly citizens taking calm advantage of the new weather, and somewhere a great clock was striking ten in thoughtful, resonant tones. So different from the grey springs of previous years, with their heavy, slanting rains stripping the advertisements from the hoardings to flap dismally in the wind over the downcast heads of the hurrying crowd. There was so little joy in living then.

"Even you, sir, must find things changed," I ventured. "In the beginning—"

"Ah, Oxlade," he interrupted, "there is still so much to be done, and I have little opportunity to leave this wretched office. Events, however slowly, progress; and my time is not my own." My chief is given to these moments of reserve; perhaps it is his nature—who can tell?—or a nature forced on him by the exigencies of his position. But he allowed it to pass genially enough and turned the talk first to my wife, Mary, and the children—he is always perfectly solicitous—and then to the cultivation of orchids, a hobby of mine. The new climate

127

of Esher is perfect for this purpose, and I was able to inform him, with all due modesty, of some truly astonishing results in the outdoor hybridisation of English types like *Cephalanthera rubra* with their more exotic epiphytic cousins.

After a few minutes, we came to the business of the Department. "Oxlade," said the chief, "I would like you to look at some pictures that were brought to me by"—here he mentioned the name of one of our most trustworthy agents—"early this morning."

He darkened the room, and on one of the walls there appeared a rectangle of white light, shortly to be filled with a strange series of photographic slides. "You will observe, Oxlade, that these are still-shots of God's Motorway." It was in fact difficult to make out what they did show; I saw only certain apparently random blocks and slices of light and shadow, and, central to each frame, some blurred object which I could make no sense of; they were of a uniform graininess. "The quality isn't good, of course. But I have no reason to believe they represent anything other than a sudden intense surge of activity along the whole length of the Motorway." He paused reflectively and allowed the last picture to remain on the screen for a while (I thought for a moment that I could discern in it some mammoth organic shape) before replacing it with that passive, enduring oblong of white light.

"A perfect whiteness," he murmured, and we stared at it for some minutes of comfortable silence. Then he said: "I feel that may be as important as the affair of the eight-angstrom band, Oxlade."

A complicated business, with a solution perhaps more metaphysical than actual, which I well remembered, since it had led to my executive preferment.

"I want you to go down there. Look around. Test the air, so to speak. The Motorway must always be of interest to us."

God's Motorway: a lasting enigma. Certainly, none of us in the Department knew why God had caused His road to be constructed, why He should have need of a link between the lower reaches of the Thames estuary and a place somewhere in what used to be called the "industrial" Midlands; none of the executives, that is—and if my chief knew, he was for some reason of policy or private amusement keeping the knowledge from us. Our curiosity was at that time intense, but necessarily veiled; so I was elated to have an opportunity to catch a glimpse of that great artery. It ran, I knew, a hundred and twenty-five miles inland north-northwest from the front at Southend; it was by repute twenty lanes and a mile wide; all ordinary traffic was barred from it (indeed, there were no access points), and it was central to His purpose.

"Go down there tomorrow, Oxlade. Find out who else is there. Come back and tell me." The shutters slid back, and the chief was gazing once more out of the window. After the projector's harsh white rectangle of light, the sunshine seemed warm and mellow, for a moment more suited to autumn than to spring. "Still so much to be done, Oxlade," he mused, "but an inspiring sight, nonetheless. Good luck."

My chief's orders have been at times difficult of interpretation; but on this occasion I felt that he had made himself unusually plain.

I reached Southend, by way of Liverpool Street and one of the amazing new railway trains, at about seven-thirty the following morning—to find it full of white gulls, sun, and a curiously invigorating tranquillity. I decided to have a quiet breakfast on the seafront. I have always loved that row of archway cafés on the Shoeburyness Road, each with its strip of carefully tended forecourt crammed with gaudy umbrellas and gaily painted tables, from which you can hear the sailing boats bobbing against the sea-wall on a light, inviting swell. To choose one to eat in—if mere satisfaction of appetite is your object—is the matter of a moment; to select the *right* one, the one that best suits your mood of the hour, must be a serious business: for you may sit there all morning, captured by the sight of the sea before you.

It was in one of these that I met Estrades, lounging back

in his slatted chair with a bottle of mineral water and a long thin cigar.

Under the old order, Estrades had been perhaps my craftiest opponent. All that was dispensed with now, of course: but once, in a pitilessly cold room high above the old Margarethenstrasse of Berlin, I had had occasion to try to shoot off one of his kneecaps. Only a lucky accident of radio reception had saved him. We greeted each other now with a cautious pleasure: professionally speaking, we knew each other well but had little in common. He was a tall, elegant, but somewhat faded man, older than myself, and given to the most flamboyant of white linen suits and to buttonhole flowers of extravagant size (although I noticed that today his carnation in no way matched my own home-grown *Palaeonophis*). He hid his age well, but a faint pitting of the skin about the eyes was hindering his efforts, and in another year or so would betray him completely. Some said he was a Ukrainian, others a Kirghizian from the western slopes of the Tien Shan; but he had the lazy undeviating eye of the cultured Frenchman, and the morose, ironic sense of humour of a dispossessed Polish count. Estrades was certainly not his real name, but it is the only one we have to remember him by.

During my examination of the menu we exchanged courtesies and anecdotes of mutual friends and enemies. Estrades claimed that he was bored; he had come over, he said, on the strength of a rumour (he would place no greater weight than that on any information from Alexandria), and had been in Southend for some days. "You must," he said, "be interested in the Motorway, Oxlade, my friend—no, no, I can see it plainly in the set of your shoulders." He laughed in a peculiar restrained manner, his thin, scarred face remaining immobile but for a slight drawing back of the lips. "We are too old to play games. So take my advice, if you aren't too proud. I have been here for a week, and have seen nothing in daylight but that which is already known. Go at night, go at night."

"That which is already known"—how could I admit that I

knew so little? I determined immediately to do both, and turned the conversation to another subject.

Later, Estrades leaned back in his chair and yawned. "Tell me honestly, my friend, what you think of all this." And he made a gesture which took in the sea, the Shoeburyness Road, the gulls like white confetti at some marriage of water and air. I was puzzled: I thought that it was a remarkably fine sort of day; I thought that I had never eaten such large prawns. He stared at me for a moment, then threw back his head to laugh in earnest, revealing teeth of a miraculous regularity. "As evasive as ever," he said, wiping his eyes. "Oxlade, you are either the most stupid or the most careful of men. Look. Nobody is listening except the waitress, and she to her transistor radio. By 'this,' I mean this whole thing, this"—he paused thoughtfully—"this paradise for bad poets and old-age pensioners in which we now find ourselves (you and I, who have left toothmarks on the bone in half the gutters of Western Europe!); this warmed-over Eden in which we exercise ourselves by reading C. S. Lewis in a sunny garden in Kent—or, God forgive us all, grow flowers! 'Our reality is so much from His reality as He, moment by moment, projects into us. . . .' Is that all He's left to us?"

"And yet, Estrades," I said, a little pointedly, for I suspected that penultimate lapse of taste to be deliberate, and I saw that he was enjoying himself not a little at my expense, "you find yourself perfectly in place. I grow orchids, and that is sufficient—in the old days, I asked for nothing more; and you—why, you sit at a café table in Southend, or some *estaminet* of Antwerp, with perhaps more freedom than before to exercise your wit, your (if I may say so) rather impractical and gauzy cynicism. No one asks you to write bad poetry—or, indeed, to judge the poetry of others. All of us are satisfied in our individual ways."

He nodded slowly. "It is an argument. It is *the* argument. But it does not impress me. Can one find satisfaction in simply being dissatisfied? Is it that I am now *allowed* to be dissatisfied? I have considered it. I chafe." He gazed sadly out to sea, moved his hands. His face slackened, aged; for a brief moment, a hunger I can't describe illuminated his eyes, and I saw the whole superb pose—insouciance, iconoclasm and all —collapse into vacancy. Eventually he turned back to me, drew on his cigar, examined his graceful, nicotine-stained fingers. They shook a little as he strove to bring back that younger Estrades, the spoiled sophist and street-corner dandy. "Oxlade, I suspect we have been robbed, but I cannot discover how. As you say, each man is content. How then have I been passed over and left to wonder why?"

I paid my bill and got up to go. But then he was quite at ease again, smiling over my embarrassment, looking for the world as if he'd intended all along to give me this glimpse behind the shell. This, he seemed to be saying, is a secret between us; Estrades is not so brittle as he seems, old friend.

"I'm on my last throw here, Oxlade," he said, suddenly, squashing out the stub of his cigar. "There is only one thing left to be discovered." And when I failed to respond to this invitation, "Wait a minute." He came swiftly and gracefully to his feet and stared up and down the seafront. "Eisenburg!" he called. "You must remember Eisenburg," he said to me. "From the Piazzale Loreto riots—?"

I didn't. But I had met a hundred like him in the formless chaotic years immediately preceding the New Reign, when it seemed that every capital of the world was in ferment, throwing up its filth in unconscious anticipation of a cleansing sun that was yet to rise. He came ambling and soft-footed through the light morning traffic of the Shoeburyness Road, a huge muscular Sephardic Jew paying no attention to the drivers except to grin unnervingly in at them when they braked to avoid running him down. His forehead was furrowed, his eyebrows obliterated, by a long rumpled scar he had as a legacy from some Near Eastern oil coup or religious war.

As he stood on the pavement, grinning and posturing

wordlessly, he brought to the bright, mild coastal weather
something of the freezing winter heights of Mount Hermon.

Estrades watched both of us closely to see what effect he
had created. He seemed satisfied. "You can do nothing until
dark," he told me. "I thought the three of us might walk into
town together and remember things as they were before this
comic opera visitation—?"

Eisenburg began to laugh. "Bloody striped umbrellas,
eh?" he appealed suddenly. "That's good!"

"I think I'll take a look anyway," I said, and walked off. I
could feel Estrades staring after me, perhaps with contempt,
perhaps with amusement. If his motive had been simple dis-
comfiture, he had failed. Like a clever illusionist he had confused me for perhaps half a minute with his *Angst* and his
cheap linguistic philosophy and his lightning changes of
mood. But by importing the Jew into that otherwise perfect
morning, he had resurrected all the fakery, all the hollow
melodrama of the "games" he had himself warned me
against, and destroyed his own stature with innuendo and
mystification. Nothing could mar the eagerness I felt as I
strolled along the north bank of the estuary. My very first
glimpse of God's Own Road awaited me; the scent of my
Palaeonophis mingled deliciously with the scent of the sea; and
I found it easy to put him out of my mind.

God's Motorway rises out of the water almost exactly opposite the old refineries of the Sheerness promontory. No
houses are near it, and here the road to Shoeburyness ends.
It emerges along a vast but indistinct causeway, about which
the very air seems to hum with agitation: standing there in
awe on that pleasant day, I could not tell whether it was made
of stone, or some less palpable substance. I could see very
little of that crucial interface between Road and sea—there,
the water boiled and effervesced, and spray hung like some
diaphanous shifting curtain, full of the strangest hues. There
is no sight more impressive than those twenty lanes of me-

talled road emerging (as if from some other, longer journey) from the fume to race away inland, joyfully precise and resolute.

In a way (though in what a mean way) Estrades was proved right: nothing came up from the water; there was little concrete information to be gained there, and I had to turn elsewhere for something to take back to my chief. Yet I spent all morning watching the ever-changing, spectral colours of that spray and wondering what ecstatic energies had given them birth. Meanwhile, the herring gulls dived and gyred through it, apparently for the mere joy of the sensation, and after passage seemed whiter than before. Had I wings, I should certainly have followed them: how they spun and whirled!

That night I set out to discover more of the Motorway. It was my intention to strike inland behind the town and meet the road some three miles down its length. The thick sea-fog that hung over the suburbs as I left broke rapidly up into drifting and unpredictable banks. I carried a compact but powerful torch, a flask of hot tea. I had provided myself also with a warm coat and field-glasses of a remarkable resolution purchased in Dortmund some years before. In the chilly fields and abandoned housing estates between the northeastern peripheries of the town and God's Road, I became aware that I was not alone: yet I was sure, too, that none of the stealthy movements in the dark were aimed at myself. "The Motorway must always be of interest to us," my chief had said; it must have been of interest to many that night, for a continual procession of agents rustled through the fog toward it.

I lost my way (I have never been fond of the night, a serious weakness perhaps in a man of my profession, and one that I have often pondered), and consequently my line of travel intersected the Motorway a little sooner than I might have liked: but it did not matter in the end. A tall embankment towered up before me against the strange new constellation which, appearing in the skies about two years before, had heralded the Rediscovery of God; and as I struggled up that enormous earthwork, I could already hear the sound of heavy engines toiling north. The Road had woken up: I took my station close to the chain-link fence and wiped the condensation from the lenses of my night-glasses.

These now revealed that every one of the lanes was in use; at forty or more points along my field of vision, massive vehicles crawled and groaned northward up the slight gradient. None of them was less than two hundred feet long. The commonest type was composed of a single tractor unit coupled to the front of a great low-loading trailer, although many were built up like railway trains out of five or six of each component. They were of a uniform matte black colour, studded with large rivets; and while each tractor had what might be described as a cabin, nothing could be seen behind its windows. What sort of motor drives them, I have no idea—they seemed to toil; none moved at more than five or six miles an hour—and yet a sense of enormous power hung like a heat-haze over each carriageway, and the ground trembled beneath my feet.

Shifting fogs made my observations intermittent and superficial, and some actual distortion of the air rendered the carriageways of the far side difficult to see at all. At first, I experienced a sensation similar to that which I have already described in connection with the photographs shown me by my chief: while I could now make a little more sense of the general aspects of the picture before me, still the central object of each quick glimpse somehow defied interpretation. The road, I understood; the vehicles, I was able to perceive as such; it was their cargo that remained puzzling. What a strange commerce—what dim and ambiguous shapes in the night.

Suddenly, however, eye and brain seemed to perform the necessary trick of adjustment; I understood the problem to be one of scale; and I was able to see that the objects before me were in fact gigantic anthropoid limbs.

Quite close to me in the second or third lane, set upright

135

on its truncated wrist, a human fist moved slowly past, shrouded in tarpaulin. It was clenched, with palm toward me, a left hand perhaps thirty feet high—extended, it would have been twice that from the heel of the palm to the tips of the fingers. The tarpaulin flapped and fluttered round its deep contours; steel cables moored it to the bed of the vehicle. All was for a moment perfectly clear; then a fog bank occluded it forever. For a time my own excitement betrayed me. I neglected to refocus the glasses and, desperately scanning the more distant lanes, saw only slow mysterious movements, like those of some extinct reptile passing along an overgrown ride in a forest of cycadeoids.

Then a truly enormous forearm slipped by five lanes out, more than a hundred feet long and heavily muscled; and from then on I was witness to an astonishing parade of members —gargantuan calves and thighs, hands and feet, and some shapes difficult of definition that I took to be more private, possibly internal, organs; a parade accompanied by the groan and throb of God's Engines, by the shuddering of the earth and, above all, that sense of vast energies almost accidentally dissipated into the air.

Toward dawn the traffic became sporadic. One last limb crept past, supported by trestles and requiring two trailers to accommodate its length; the fog reasserted its grip; all movement ceased.

Stiffly, I rose from the crouch into which I had fallen, my knees aching and reluctant, my hands numb and cold. Minute beads of moisture clung to everything: my coat, the binoculars, the chain-link fence. My ears felt uncomfortable in the silence, as if some pressure on the inner passages had suddenly been relieved. For a minute or two I flapped my arms against my sides in an attempt to restore some warmth and vitality; but it was in a stupor of weariness that I stumbled away.

I stood for a moment at the foot of the embankment. Silence was no longer absolute—all about me were mysteri-

ous shiftings as other observers shrugged, yawned, put up
their instruments and prepared to leave the Motorway. Dawn
now illuminated the fog, filling it with a diffuse internal radi-
ance which in no way aided the eye. Two or three men passed
me within touching distance, conversing in low tones—they
were quite invisible. Then, faint and thin, a cry of despair
reached me through that drifting, luminous mist; running
footsteps thudded along the top of the embankment, moving
south. "Stop him!" someone shouted, then added something
made unintelligible by excitement.

I turned to look back. Estrades was suddenly standing
beside me, the mist seeming to give him up without sound.
A fur-lined leather jacket, the patched and oil-stained relic of
some European aerial war of his youth, bulked out his slim
figure. He was breathing heavily. He stared at me for a second
or two as if he hardly recognised me, then called urgently into
the mist, "He's yours, Eisenburg—about a hundred feet
ahead of you, now!" A shot rang out. The running man blun-
dered on.

"For God's sake," said Estrades disgustedly. He took his
cigar out of his mouth and frowned at it. "Never trust a Jew."
Then, in a different tone, "Think about what you've seen,
Oxlade," he advised me quietly. "Esher is no longer yours.
How can you go on, knowing what's happening up there?
How will you ever feel safe again?" He considered this; nodded; pulled a small revolver from the pocket of his flying
jacket. "Must I do it all myself?" he demanded of the man
Eisenburg. "It's all up if he gets away!" And he vanished once
more into the mist. Later, two more shots startled the bright
air. I waited, but Estrades did not return. I made my way back
across the damp fields, wondering if the poor wretch on the
embankment knew who was pursuing him. It was a dreary
trudge.

Somewhat later in the morning, I considered my position
carefully. I had made progress of a kind which may be
summed up in the following problem. At a maximum ob-

served speed of six miles an hour, it would be quite impossible for God's Vehicles to complete their entire journey in one night; and yet by day the Motorway lay silent, abandoned to the wind and sunshine along its whole length; where, then, did the traffic go? A fascinating and significant anomaly—but had I any assurance that it was not already known to my chief? Estrades was aware of it; there may have been others. It would be injudicious, I realised, to commit myself too early to one point of view and return to London with what would certainly be regarded as an incomplete report. It was safe to assume that my chief had some other interest—one that had appeared up until now to be peripheral.

Again, I thought of Estrades.

That saturnine expatriate, survivor of a thousand and one labyrinthine excursions beneath the political crust, liked to present his motives in terms of simple curiosity (and indeed there lay concealed behind his objectionable languor not only the keen and feral energy I had seen released that morning in the Essex mist but also, as I had discovered to my cost on more than one previous occasion, a mind subtle, relentless and unassuaged)—but only some specific objective could have drawn him from his retirement among the bleached river terraces of North Africa to kill by pistol on a cold morning in England. What tenuous thread had he followed through the brothels of Marseilles, the grey boulevards of Brussels, to Southend-on-Sea?

All the rest of the morning I sought him out along the crowded sea-wall, submerging myself in that fierce and unrestricted tide of bare red forearms and light opera, with its odours of fried fish, lavender and bottled stout. I knew he would be waiting for me. At noon, a light, uncustomary drizzle began to fall from a sky filled alternately with gunmetal cloud and weak, silvery sunshine. The esplanade was all of a sudden bleak and empty. In the shadow of the pier I sat on a stone, gazing up at the salt-caked fretwork of struts and warped boards that support the thumping slot-machines and shooting galleries. Shouting children hung over the white railings high above. When I looked toward the mercuric thread of the surf, Estrades stood at the end of the avenue of corroded iron supports, motionless and shining in a single watery ray of sun.

The rain died off as we walked toward one another. I wish sometimes that I had walked away instead. Up above, the planking thumped and rattled. By the time we met, the front was thick with people again, issuing, with no more than a single shiver to dispel the chilly interruption of their day, from the cafés and shop doorways that had sheltered them.

"I've been watching the faces on the beach," said Estrades, "hoping to recognise the old familiar ones. You remember, Oxlade? They were grey, as if moulded out of a flesh like soft wax, grey with insecurity and lost sleep, wincing from short tense encounters on windy street corners. (Can you remember even the corners, Oxlade, from the comfy recesses of your new dream?) They were sick, but real: they were our faces." He shook his head. "There must be fifty men out on that embankment every night. Many of them I must have known before. I look for them on the beach every day, but if they are there, they are burnt red like *rentiers* on holiday; they wear open-necked shirts and rolled sleeves. Like you, Oxlade, they have *relaxed.*"

He sighed, indicated the promenade crowds. "And there," he said, "you look for spirit. You watch them, you hear the noise and expect to find some visible motive for this happy, happy seething." He shrugged. "Ha. Their eyes are pale, blind. They have been robbed. They perform by rote, like some kind of animal."

"If that is true, Estrades—and I suspect it isn't—then it may simply be what they prefer. And look at the children. They seem happy enough. You can't deny that they seem happy enough, and aware of it."

He looked instead at the shingle, and hacked with his elegant heel at a tangle of bright green weed. He bent down quickly and prised something loose from it with his long, strong fingers. "Children ask less. Are they to remain children all their lives?" He flicked his fingers distastefully to remove a bit of seaweed, then held up an old threepenny piece, still somehow bright and untarnished. God knows how long it had rolled about the foreshore. "Even here there is spirit," he said gnomically, and flipped it away—it sped out of the shadow of the pier, glittered briefly in the exhausted light and vanished.

"Up there on the promenade is a festival of mediocrity, a feast of tolerance, an emptiness filled with wheel chair entertainers—" For a moment he watched them pass. "You don't want to know," he asked distantly, "who was killed this morning by the Motorway?" I must have revealed my tension in some way, for he turned back with a triumphant grin. "Oh, the Department is so careful with its executives. I killed your back-up operator. He sent a radio-message, 'All goes smoothly,' then I killed him before he could transmit again. Will you tell them?"

"I have never," I said carefully, "been informed that back-up operators are in use. You may have killed an innocent man."

"Then you are remarkably ill-informed. And no man on that embankment was entirely innocent." When my face remained blank, he laughed uproariously. "Oxlade, Oxlade!" he gasped. "If you could *see* yourself!" He recovered his composure. "Oh, how sick I am of all this faith," he muttered bitterly. I had, perhaps, succeeded in making him feel uncomfortable.

"Why did you kill him?"

He smiled off at something in the distance. The sun had come out fully; on the pier a small orchestra had begun to play selections from Gilbert and Sullivan.

"I intend to put an end to this half-wit's Utopia," he said quietly. "I want you with me, if only as a representative of your organisation; but I can allow no more reports until the thing is accomplished—your shadow was an embarrassment."

He studied me intently. "What do you say, Oxlade, old friend? Set against one another, we were always wasted." And before I could make the obvious answer: "Why, if you come you may even be able to stop me from doing it! What a coup! And all else failing, you will enter the most astonishing report on the episode. It will mean another promotion. More orchids will bloom in the quiet backwaters of Esher."

"Come where?" I asked.

"The Midlands," he said, "by way of the Road of God."

"What you are intending to do is more hopeless than blasphemous." I started to walk away.

He allowed me to leave the shadow of the pier before calling, "I will have you killed before you can reach a telephone, Oxlade." I looked up and down the front. Eisenburg the Jew stood negligently at the foot of the sea-wall. He grinned and lit a cigarette, staring at me over his cupped hands. Fifteen yards separated us. "I can't take the risk," said Estrades. I believed him.

"You are an evil man, Estrades," I told him. "The rest of us have forgotten how."

He laughed. "That is what is wrong with you," he said. Up above him children flocked into the shooting galleries. Their cries drowned the noise of the orchestra.

That was how I entered into my unwilling association with Estrades the European agent and became a party to the plot against God. Why that madman really wanted me with him, I don't know. Murder would have been so much easier. I believe now that it merely gratified his vanity to have a captive observer. He was an enormously vain man. At any rate, I could do nothing about it; and all that afternoon and part of the evening I watched passively as he prepared his ground in a series of visits to what were presumably "safe" houses scattered across Southend.

It was at one of these that Eisenburg took charge of the mysterious three-foot packing case upon which they had placed their hopes. It must have weighed half a hundred-

141

weight, if not more, but he carried it—together with a pair of long-handled bolt-cutters with which they intended to breach the fence at the summit of the embankment—under one arm, as if it were empty. I grew to loathe that crate (although I had no idea at that time of what it contained—had I done so, I might have taken my chances with him in one of the more crowded streets behind the esplanade), and he knew it. Whenever Estrades's attention was occupied elsewhere, Eisenburg would catch my eye and go through a long, complicated dumb-show of insinuation, tapping the thing significantly, making motions as if to open it—grinning ferociously all the time, so that his scar made ghastly furrows in his forehead. He never let it out of his sight, and he never tired of taunting me.

Meanwhile, Estrades, his pristine suit and carnation exchanged once more for flying jacket and revolver, had become tense and excited, given to Romantic gesture which constantly reaffirmed the emotional instability of his character. "So!" he exclaimed, as we made our way over the sodden fields behind the town. "Here we go! Everything staked on one throw! Three men against God!" Even the sunset seemed alarmed at this vast, childish vanity: the sky was one great inverted bowl of cloud, tilted up a little on the horizon over Shoeburyness to show a thin strip of blood-coloured light. "Oxlade, you think it can't be done. Pah. It can! We'll liberate Esher; and if the orchids are a little smaller next year, a little less gaudy—well, they will be *your* orchids, at least!"

"You aren't uneducated, Estrades. You must know it's been tried before."

"Not by a *man*, Oxlade." He nudged his accomplice. "Not by a man, eh, Eisenburg?" And they winked excruciatingly at one another like boys about to raid an orchard.

Up on the embankment we waited for the last shreds of light to be dispersed. A thin cold wind sprang up and hissed across the fields; for a moment, hung there between night and day, all seemed a grey and empty waste, an end to independent struggle under aimless airs—had God, I wondered, already lifted the protection of the New Reign from us three? Estrades shivered and zipped up his jacket. As darkness fell and the sound of God's Engines came throbbing up from the south, Eisenburg got to work with his bolt-cutters. The chain link proved tougher than expected; the Jew grunted and swore, Estrades fumed impatiently about; reluctantly, each strand of wire curled back on itself like burnt hair. By the time the first vehicle had crawled into view, we had our breach— but it was small and mean.

Estrades then replaced Eisenburg at the wire and remained crouched in the gap for perhaps half an hour, frequently consulting his watch. His face had become drawn and uncommunicative, as if he realised for the first or possibly the last time what his own actions meant, and the scars on his cheeks were lambent, raw. Did he see in the slow, enigmatic shapes crawling up the incline his own final annihilation, the Hand irrevocably withdrawn? The ground shuddered; the air above the Road shimmered and reverberated with its implication of awful energies. Suddenly, he seemed to gather himself. He showed me a hunted, almost panic-stricken face and shouted, "Now or never, Oxlade! If you want to live, *run!*"

And he squirmed through the breach.

I remember so little. For a second or two, I know, I watched as he sprinted for his life, a tiny energetic weaving and dodging under the threat of those huge wheels; then I felt a tremendous blow between the shoulder blades, and turned to find Eisenburg sweating and grinning at me in the gloom. "You next," he said, and gave me another push. We fled like insects across the broad back of the road, the Jew shoving me on before him; the wind eddying round those massive machines whipped at our clothing; black dizzy expanses of riveted steel towered above us. When I stumbled, he dragged me upright, raging incoherently in some foreign language.

Out in the third lane, Estrades, by dint it seemed of sheer hysterical strength, had gained the bed of an immense trailer. Eight feet above me, white-faced and peering, he extended a hand to haul me up. Eisenburg tossed us the crate and the bolt-cutters, but at his first attempt to ensure his own safety, he missed his stride. His jump took him six inches below Estrades's straining hand, and for a full half minute he had to run along behind the vehicle, gathering his course for a second try, laughing and sobbing, his face a perfect mask of panic and fear.

Panic and fear—all that remains to me of the journey.

How long we clung freezing and immobile to the back of that machine, I can't tell. Blue and waxy light pervaded all that space which might be described as the Road, and Time moved unreasonably along the warped perspectives into which we travelled. Estrades's watch, damaged in his mad scramble up the side of the vehicle, was useless. A regular, disturbing modulation of that cyanic light suggested we might have been aboard the thing for days rather than hours. What could be seen of the Motorway's environs, we saw transfigured, blurred, and it gave us neither help nor comfort. (The Road has, I suspect, little "real" existence in this way, little connection with what we know as reality. I was to confirm, for instance, on my eventual return to the World, that three days had passed since our breaching of the fence—but I place no significance on such crude measurements, since they are at best a device for the description of the human *Umwelt*. We travelled in the *Umwelt* of God, which, to my admittedly limited knowledge, no theologian has yet undertaken to define.)

To begin with, Estrades was determined to make some sort of study of the vehicle which we had infested like morose and frightened lice—even, I think, to gain access to the tractor cab and "commandeer" it; but this came to nothing. We shared the trailer with something unimaginable and shrouded. We were from the start too awed, too precarious. We sat apart, drew our knees up to our chins and stared silently before us. Eisenburg did once take a turn around the trailer, out of bravado or to ease some cramp of the joints, but even he didn't dare examine the thing beneath the tarpaulin, and Estrades soon called him back. He seemed glad enough to obey.

It was a wonder, finally, that any of us retained energy enough to make decisions, even to move (although move we did, and soon enough). The tarpaulin cracked and flapped dismally, like a tent pitched in a dark valley. Belts of fog came and went, to leave beads of condensation on the black metal; sudden winds chilled us to the bone. Our vehicle never left its precise position in the order of the convoy. We were stiff and tired and hungry; our ears were battered and stupefied by the constant beat of God's Engines. In that dreary blue suspension, we felt like the ghosts of the newly dead—who, filled with horror, stare numbly at one another in continual discovery of their irreversible state. Later, Estrades took to brooding for long periods over the crate, hoping perhaps to find his salvation there.

At last, Time, in an understandable human sense, was returned to us; the light ceased its steady fluctuation; ahead, the perspectives of the Road shifted and straightened, enabling us once more to estimate speed and distance; and for the first time the adjoining landscape became clearly visible to us. We found ourselves moving slowly across a great arid peneplain touched here and there by sourceless orange highlights and shadows of the profoundest purple. The earth was cracked and bare, like mudsoil on some abandoned African plateau. Nothing moved beyond the fence.

You will say, and quite reasonably, that there is no such view to be found in the British Isles. I can only agree. This was nothing to us. On the horizon had appeared the tall and awful shape of God.

Eisenburg the Jew bent his head and whimpered suddenly. Estrades stared astounded. "Christ, Oxlade!" he shouted, and lapsed immediately into some Magyar dialect I couldn't follow. He produced his revolver and for some reason began to wave it excitedly in my direction. Eisenburg, meanwhile, wept, choked and tried to kneel; Estrades saw this action from

145

the corner of his eye, and went at him like a snake. "None of that!" he hissed. "Get the bloody box open, Eisenburg! We've got him!" But his eyes were captured by that unbearable Enigma or apparition, and when the Jew failed to obey, he didn't seem to notice.

How can I describe Him?

He crouches there in my memory as He will crouch forever. He is in part profile, silhouetted against the sky. Ten square miles of earth lie between His six splayed legs. Rainbows of iridescence play across His vast black carapace. If He should ever spread the wings beneath those shimmering elytra! One compound eye a hundred yards across gazes fixedly into realms that we may never see. A mile in the air, gales thunder impotently about His stiff antennae and motionless, extended jaws. In the shadow of His long abdomen, the giant factories seem like toys, and it is as if He had brought with Him from the hidden obverse of the Moon an airlessness that makes the sky a harder, brighter place. We see that where His legs touch the earth, deep saucer-shaped depressions have formed. From each of these, huge fissures radiate. Can the World bear His weight without a groan?

What has He taken away from us, what has He come to give us in return? Estrades claimed to know—but Estrades had long been destroyed by his own despair. Staring up at that gargantuan entomic form, *Lucanus Cervus Omnipotens,* I knew there must be more. If I am no longer sure of that, it is because I am no longer sure of anything.

Eisenburg gaped, vomited. He wiped his mouth with the back of his hand and began to laugh. "It's a bloody beetle!" he shrieked. "It's only a bloody beetle!" Estrades winced, stared at his feet for a moment; then he started to laugh, too. They embraced, sobbing, rocking to and fro in a sort of clumsy dance. "Quick!" cried the Jew, disengaging himself. "Quick!" He grabbed the bolt-cutters and used them to lever off the lid of the crate. Grey-faced and shaking, the two of them knelt over its contents and began to make feverish ad-

justments to a nest of coloured wire and electrical components. In their haste, they fought briefly over the only tool
they had, a small screwdriver. Eisenburg won.

Estrades glanced over his shoulder and shuddered. "It's
about five miles," he said. "Set it for that."

He felt my gaze on him. "Freedom, Oxlade," he murmured. "Freedom." A fit of shivering got hold of him. Up
ahead, that enormous shape was coming closer and closer.

"An hour and twenty minutes," he told Eisenburg, "to be
on the safe side. We can't be certain what happens once it gets
there."

"You don't mean to carry on with this!" I found myself
shouting. I can't express the panic that had come over all
of us. It was almost physiological, some old fear etched into
the cells of the nervous system. "Estrades! Not so close to
Him—!" I clutched his shoulders. His trembling com-
municated itself to me, and for a second we clung to one
another, unable to speak. Estrades made noises. I tore myself
away. "What's *in* that crate, man? What are you going to do?"
Slowly, the trembling died away. Estrades drew a long, shuddering breath; his face writhed; he lifted the pistol. Then he
laughed bitterly and turned his back.

"Ask what all this is for," he suggested quietly, "instead."
And he gestured at the Motorway, at the impossible landscape
and the factories in the Shadow.

"Ask what this thing intends to do with *us*, why it has
turned us into tourists and parsons and performers of simper-
ing amateur dramatics in a world we no longer control.
Ask—" But he began to tremble again and couldn't go on. He
clenched his fists against the onset of the fit. Eisenburg, dropping the screwdriver, looked up in horror, his jaw muscles
quivering uncontrollably. Wracked and quaking, I thought, It
will get worse as we go closer; He cannot allow us any closer.
I was terrified in case I should see those gigantic mandibles
move. Estrades clutched at his gun with both hands, as if it
offered anchorage. "I have ten pounds of plutonium in that

box"—each word forced out between clenched teeth. "Eisenburg built the trigger. Twenty men died stealing the stuff, a hundred more are committed in Europe alone. I shall go . . . on . . . whatever happens. . . ."

He groaned and gave himself up to shivering.

I don't know quite what I intended to do. When I saw them both overcome, I threw myself at the bomb—I thought that if I could heave it over the side it would be broken, or at least irrecoverable. But they were on me in an instant, clubbing madly at my head and groin. Estrades's revolver went off with an enormous bang. Something smashed into my lower legs. The Jew roared, dropped his body squarely across mine and probed with stiffened fingers for the arteries in my neck. We flopped about like fish in the bottom of a rowing boat, panting and groaning. Then I discovered the discarded bolt-cutters under my hand and beat him repeatedly under the ear with them until he rolled away from me and stopped moving.

Scrambling to my feet, I discovered Estrades kneeling about two feet away. "For Christ's sake, Oxlade," he pleaded, "it's the *World!*" The pistol was pointed directly at my belly, but he was shivering so hard he couldn't pull the trigger. I opened his head up with the bolt-cutters. He knelt there, covered in blood, and said, "You shouldn't have done this." Then he went down like a dead man.

I took a step toward the bomb; my left leg folded up under me; and, clutching helplessly at the empty air, I fell into the Road—where I lay on my back for a moment unable to move, watching the vehicle draw inexorably away from me. Hot and stinking of rubber, huge wheels ground past, not a yard away from me through a fog of pain and nausea. About a minute later, the figure of Estrades reappeared on the trailer, looking small and desperately unsteady. His shoulders were a mantle of blood. He staggered about for a time, waving the revolver. A couple of rounds splattered into the metalling beside me; then he turned away and emptied the weapon defiantly into the air toward God. That was the last I saw of him.

The rest is nothing. I turned my back on it all and ran, despite the hole Estrades had put in the muscle of my calf (I still limp a little, although not now as proudly as I did in the weeks of my convalescence). "God," I remember praying, "let me get away before it goes off!" So close, it might even be that He heard me. I don't recall what I offered Him in exchange. Several times, I made some feeble attempt to cut my way through the fence; but I never managed to break more than a strand or two of wire before panic overtook me and I began to run again, timing my prayers to the sound of my own ragged breath. I was painfully conscious of the Mystery looming immobile and abiding behind me; but I never looked back.

Eventually, I fell down exhausted. There, where the Motorway ran through a cutting with broad, gently sloping sides of soft red earth, I scraped a shallow hole. Into this I thrust my face; I clasped my hands behind my neck, and in that submissive position I waited for Estrades's madness to find me out. A long time later, I passed out. Perhaps they had built the thing badly, or failed to complete the fusing sequence— perhaps after all I had killed them both. At any rate, the bomb never went off.

I suspect it never would have. I realise now that it was a failure of Faith to believe even for a second that they could have succeeded; and I suspect now that a dozen bombs would have made no difference to Him—I imagine Him spreading His great transparent wings to the blast, like a housefly in the sun.

The driver of a quite ordinary lorry, I am told, found me stumbling along the muddy verge of the A5 somewhere near Brownhills. How I got there, I am at a loss to explain. Presumably I succeeded at last in breaching the fence. God rises majestically above the suburbs of Birmingham and Wolverhampton, where His factories are: but He seems smaller than He does in that other place, that Simultaneous or Alternative Midlands which can only be seen from the other side of the chain link; and people live at ease within the sight of Him.

149

What a pure pleasure the convalescent experiences when he is at last released from his prison of a bed! The sheets, chains and fetters of his sapling vitality become mere sheets once more; his dull fellow-patients, now that he must leave them, seem the most interesting of human beings; and the view from his window—that sad fishbowl stage for his obsessive fantasies of recovery, peopled by actors whose motives he can only invent—becomes the World again, and he its newest participant. And what a world! What rediscoveries, what heartfelt reconsiderations! It was with just this profound sense of being made anew that, a little over a month after my adventures in the Realm of God, I made my way home from the offices of the Department.

I had been released from hospital that morning; my preliminary report was made—though there remained a necessary sharpening of its edges, the sketch, so to speak, was completed; and before me stretched the most poignant of May afternoons. I dawdled down Baker Street and paused for a while to admire the flowerbeds by the Clarence Gate. Regent's Park was full of cool laconic breezes, but beneath them there moved a heaviness, a languor, a promise of the summer to be. In my absence, cherry blossoms had sprung in every corner; the waterfowl had put on a fresh, dapper plumage and were waddling importantly about in the white sunlight that scoured the newly painted boards of the boat house.

Calm and happy, I let the faint cries of some large animal draw me across the jetty footbridge toward the distant Zoological Gardens. The wind brought me declamatory voices and the laughter of children—at the Open Air Theatre, they were presenting *A Midsummer Night's Dream;* and as I crossed the wide spaces north of the lake, the glowing phrases of my lunchtime interview with the chief mingled inextricably with strains of a Flanders and Swann medley issuing from the new bandstand: "A most genuine contribution . . . a hundred others rounded up in Europe alone; in Africa we move with speed and caution. We were of course well aware of Estrades and his cynical conspiracy. Nothing less than a victory, a triumph for decency and common sense . . . certain promotion." Old men were flying their kites from the benches by the pagoda; white and ecstatic as the gulls above God's Causeway, the kites danced and bobbed in tribute to the dashing air!

Since childhood, the elegant cages, the precise spaces, the immense colour and vitality of the Zoo have been a passion with me. Where else can be seen such relentless grace, such refined energy as we see in the leopard? Or such mysterious moonlit depths as those of the Small Mammal House? What a cacophony of wisdom the lories and macaws generate, what a deep spring of humour wells beneath the elephant's hide! That afternoon, I was remade. Mary and the children, I thought, would hardly begrudge me an hour; so I took it with the gibbons and the mountain sheep, and with the tiger who so reminded me of Estrades—pacing, hungry, so economical and dangerous that I caught myself trying to attract his eye. . . .

That was surely enough; the polar bear like a fixated ballet dancer run to fat, the sharp ammoniacal smell of the rhino, the flocking children, that sense of peaceful yet animal activity —these were surely enough: I shouldn't have gone to the Insect House.

I don't believe it was a beetle of any kind, much less *Lucanus Cervus,* that captured my attention—rather it was something grey and leafish, looking absurdly like a woman in muslin rags. It was resting on a twig, almost invisible and quite immobile, and perhaps this very quality of stillness—this perfectly alien perception of the passage of time—was sufficient. As I stared into the hot yellow recesses of the vivarium, I remembered the Mystery that lies at the end of God's Motorway, and I thought, What possible emotion could this thing have in common with us? I recalled the twisted perspectives and quaking blue light of the *Umwelt* of God, the factories in the Shadow, Estrades's final bitter suggestion—"Ask what this thing intends to do with *us,* in a world we no longer control."

In what continuum or sphere of reality would we find that nightmarish Simultaneous Midlands, with its pocked dreary landscape and vast presiding deity, if we once thought to look? Why is God building an enormous human body while we build bandstands? What does He want with us?

As I reread what I have written here I can see the progression of my loss mirrored in the very words I have used; Estrades began it, perhaps, as he had intended to, on the seafront at Southend—but that was only a moment's uncertainty, whereas this . . . Since the revelation in the Insect House, where the only sound is a shuffle of feet as visitors file past the specimens like communicants, I have been unable to recapture my sense of wonder. My attention wanders from my second-generation *Epipactis tetralix;* I grow bored and restless at rehearsals of the Esher Light Operatic Society; I chafe.

And I confess that it frightens me now to visit that penthouse office where my chief crouches high above the neat, the eternally bright and windy streets of the city, whispering "Still so much to do, Oxlade," as he grooms with quick strokes of his forelegs his feathery antennae, or flexes the horny wing-cases which, closed, look so much like an iridescent tail-coat—or in the gloom fixes his enigmatic compound eyes on that white, perfect rectangle of light cast by the slide projector, engaging in some renewal of the senses, some exploration of a consciousness I will never appreciate. I am his deputy now, and have risen as far as a man can rise. I look out over the pensioners in the trim parks below, and I should be proud.

What did Estrades know? He was an old man. He retired; he took himself off to North Africa and a study of Byzantine military history long before the Rediscovery. He had never stood above the streets of some familiar city, faced with one of the small energetic Replicas of Him that fill every responsible office in the World. He had no chance.

Why has God come to us in this way? We were so eager to accept Him.

The Chaste Planet

by **JOHN UPDIKE**

Here, from a modern master of English prose, is a brief look at some life forms we surely cannot expect to find on the largest planet in our solar system.

In 1999, space explorers discovered that within the warm, turbulent, semi-liquid immensity of Jupiter a perfectly pleasant little planet twirled, with argon skies and sparkling seas of molten beryllium. The earthlings who first arrived on the shores of this new world were shocked by the unabashed nakedness of the inhabitants. Not only were the inhabitants naked—their bodies cylindrical, slightly curved, and longitudinally ridged, like white pickles, with six toothpick-thin limbs stuck in for purposes of locomotion, and a kind of tasseled seventh concentrating the neural functions—but there appeared to be no sexual differentiation among them. Indeed, there was none. Reproduction took place by an absentee process known as "budding," and the inhabitants of Minerva (so the planet was dubbed, by a classics-minded official of the Sino-American Space Agency) thought nothing of it. Evidently, wherever a mathematical sufficiency of overlap-

*Reprinted by permission; © 1975 The New Yorker Magazine, Inc.

ping footsteps (or jabs, for their locomotion left marks rather like those of ski poles in crusty snow) impressed the porous soil of intermingled nickel and asbestos, a new pickleoid form slowly sprouted, or "budded." Devoid both of parentage and of progenitive desires, this new creature, when the three Minervan years (five of our weeks) of its maturation period brought it to full size (approximately eighteen of our inches), eagerly shook the nickel from its roots and assumed its place in the fruitful routines of agriculture, industry, trade, and government that on Minerva, as on Earth, superficially dominated life.

The erotic interests of the explorers and, as argon-breathing apparatus became perfected, of the ambassadors and investigators and mercantile colonists from our own planet occasioned amazement and misunderstanding among the Minervans. The early attempts at rape were scarcely more of a success than the later attempts, by some of the new world's economically marginal natives, to prostitute themselves. The lack of satisfactory contact, however, did not prevent the expatriate earthlings from falling in love with the Minervans, producing the usual debris of sonnets, sleepless nights, exhaustive letters, jealous fits, and supercharged dreams. The little pickle-shaped people, though no Pocahontas or Fayaway emerged among them to assuage the aliens' wonderful heat, were fascinated: How could the brief, mechanical event described (not so unlike, the scientists among them observed, the accidental preparation of their own ground for "budding") generate such giant expenditures of neural energy? "We live for love," they were assured. "Our spaceships, our skyscrapers, our stock markets are but deflections of this basic drive. Our clothes, our meals, our arts, our modes of transportation, even our wars, are made to serve the cause of love. An earthling infant takes in love with his first suck, and his dying gasp is clouded by this passion. All else is sham, disguise, and make-work."

The human colonies came to include females. This

subspecies was softer and more bulbous, its aggressions more intricate and its aura more complacent; the Minervans never overcame their distaste for women, who seemed boneless and odorous and parasitic after the splendid first impression made by the early space explorers carapaced in flashing sheets of aluminum foil. These females even more strongly paid homage to the power of love: "For one true moment of it, a life is well lost. Give us love, or give us death. Our dying is but a fleck within the continuous, overarching supremacy of *eros*. Love moves the stars, which you cannot see. It moves the birds, which you do not have, to song." The Minervans were dumbfounded; they could imagine no force, no presence beneath their swirling, argon-bright skies, more absolute than death—for which the word in their language was the same as for "silence."

Then the human females, disagreeably and characteristically, would turn the tables of curiosity. "And you?" they would ask their little naked auditors. "What is it that makes *you* tick? Tell us. There must be something hidden, or else Freud was a local oracle. Tell us, what do you dream of, when your six eyes shut?" And a blue-green blush would steal over the warty, ridged, colorless epiderms of the Minervans, and they would titter and rustle like a patch of artichokes, and on their slender stiff limbs scamper away, and not emerge from their elaborate burrows until the concealment of night— night, to earthling senses, as rapid and recurrent as the blinking of an eyelid.

The first clue arose from the sonnets the lovelorn spacemen used to recite. Though the words, however translated, came out as nonsense, the recitation itself held the Minervans' interest, and seemed to excite them with its rhythms. Students of the pioneer journals also noted that, by more than one account, before prostitution was abandoned as unfeasible the would-be courtesans offered from out of the depths of themselves a shy, strangulated crooning, a sort of pitch-speech analogous to Chinese. Then robot televiewers were sufficiently miniaturized to maneuver through the Minervans' elaborate burrows. Among the dim, shaky images beamed back from underground (the static from the nickel was terrific) were some of rods arranged roughly in sequence of size, and of other rods, possibly hollow, flared at one end or laterally punctured. The televiewer had stumbled, it turned out, upon an unguarded brothel; the objects were, of course, crude Minervan equivalents of xylophones, trumpets, and flutes. The ultimate reaches of many private burrows contained similar objects, discreetly tucked where the newly budded would not find them, as well as proto-harps, quasi-violins, and certain constructions percussive in purpose. When the crawling televiewers were fitted with audio components, the domestic tunnels, and even some chambers of the commercial complexes, were revealed as teeming with a constant, furtive music—a concept for which the only Minervan word seemed to be the same as their word for "life."

Concurrent with these discoveries, a team of SASA alienists had persuaded a number of Minervans to submit to psychoanalysis. The pattern of dreamwork, with its loaded symbolization of ladders, valves, sine curves, and hollow, polished forms, as well as the subjects' tendency under drugs to deform their speech with melodious slippage, and the critical case of one Minervan (nicknamed by the psychiatric staff Dora) who suffered from the obsessive malady known as "humming," pointed to the same conclusion as the televiewers' visual evidence: the Minervans on their sexless, muffled planet lived for music, of which they had only the most primitive inkling.

In the exploitative rush that followed this insight, tons of nickel were traded for a song. Spies were enlisted in the Earth's service for the bribe of a plastic harmonica; entire cabinets and corporation boards were corrupted by the promise of a glimpse of a clarinet-fingering diagram, or by the playing of an old 78-r.p.m. "Muskrat Ramble." At the first public broadcast of a symphony, Brahms' Fourth in E Minor, the audience of Minervans went into convulsions of ecstasy as the strings yielded the theme to the oboe, and would doubtless have perished *en masse* had not the sound engineer mercifully lifted the needle and switched to the Fred Waring arrangement of "American Patrol." Even so, many Minervans, in that epoch of violated innocence, died of musical overdose, and many more wrote confessional articles, formed liberational political parties, and engaged, with sometimes disappointing results, in group listening.

What music meant to the Minervans, it was beyond the ken of earthlings to understand. That repetitive mix of thuds, squeaks, and tintinnabulation, an art so mechanical that Mozart could scribble off some of the best between billiard shots, seemed perhaps to them a vibration implying all vibrations, a resolution of the most inward, existential antagonisms, a synthesizing interface—it has been suggested—between the nonconductivity of their asbestos earth and the high conductivity of their argon sky. There remained about the Minervans' musicality, even after it had been thoroughly exploited and rapaciously enlarged, something fastidious, balanced, and wary. A confused ancient myth gave music the resonance of the forbidden. In their Heaven, a place described as mercifully dark, music occurred without instruments, as it were inaudibly. An elderly Minervan, wishing to memorialize his life, would remember it almost exclusively in terms of music he had heard, or had made.

When the first Minervans were rocketed to Earth (an odyssey deserving its own epic: the outward flight through the thousands of miles of soupy hydrogen that comprised Jupiter's thick skull; the breakthrough into space and first sight of the stars, the black universe; the backward glance at the gaseous stripes and raging red spot dwindling behind them; the parabolic fall through the solar system, wherein the Minervans, dazzled by its brightness, mistook Venus for their destination, their invaders' home, instead of the watery brown sphere that expanded beneath them), the visitors were shocked by the ubiquitous public presence of music. Leaking from restaurant walls, beamed into airplanes as they landed and automobiles as they crashed, chiming from steeples, thundering from parade grounds, tingling through apartment walls, carried through the streets in small black boxes, violating even the peace of the desert and the forest, where drive-ins featured blue musical comedies, music at first overwhelmed, then delighted, then disgusted, and finally bored them. They removed the ear stopples that had initially guarded them from too keen a dose of pleasure; surfeit muffled them; they ceased to hear. The Minervans had discovered impotence.

End Game

by **JOE HALDEMAN**

Piece by piece, due to individual excellence of story, not design on the editors' part, we have been watching Haldeman chronicle his future war in these pages. These stories, each complete in its own right, make up a larger work. Each has been anthologized on its own merit, and this is the final one, for they are all part of his novel *The Forever War.*

Sometime in the twenty-third century they started calling it "the Forever War." Before that, it had just been the war, the only war.

And we had never met the enemy. The Taurans started the war at the end of the twentieth century, attacking our first starships with no provocation. We had never exchanged a word with the enemy; had never captured one alive.

I was drafted in 1997, and in 2458 still had three years to serve. I'd gone all the way from private to major in less than half a millennium. Without actually living all those years, of course; time dilation between collapsar jumps accounted for all but five of them.

Most of those five years I had been reasonably content, since the usual disadvantages of military service were offset by the fact that I was allowed to endure them in the company of the woman I loved. The three battles we had been in, we'd been in together; we'd shared a furlough on Earth, and had even had the luck to be wounded at the same time, winning a year-long vacation on the hospital planet Heaven. After that, everything fell apart.

We had known for some time that neither of us would live through the war. Not only because the fighting was fierce— you had about one chance in three of surviving a battle—but also, the government couldn't afford to release us from the Army; our back pay, compounded quarterly over the centuries, would cost them as much as a starship! But we did have each other, and there was always the possibility that the war might end.

But at Heaven, they separated us. On the basis of tests (and our embarrassing seniority) Marygay was made a lieutenant and I became a major. She was assigned to a Strike Force leaving from Heaven, though, and I was to go back to Stargate for combat officer training, eventually to command my own Strike Force.

I literally tried to move Heaven and Earth to get Marygay assigned to me; it didn't seem unreasonable for a commander to have a hand in the selection of his executive officer. But I found out later that the Army had good reason not to allow us together in the same company: heterosexuality was obsolete, a rare dysfunction, and we were too old to be "cured." The Army needed our experience, but the rule was one pervert per company; no exceptions.

We weren't simply lovers. Marygay and I were each other's only link to the real world, the 1990's. Everyone else came from a nightmare world that seemed to get worse as time went on. And neither was it simply separation: even if we were both to survive the battles in our future—not likely—time dilation would put us centuries out of phase with each other. There was no solution. One of us would die and the other would be alone.

My officer's training consisted of being immersed in a tank of oxygenated fluorocarbon with 239 electrodes attached to my brain and body. It was called ALSC, Accelerated Life Situation Computer, and it made my life accelerated and miserable for three weeks.

Want to know who Scipio Aemilianus was? Bright light of the Third Punic War. How to counter a knife-thrust to the abdomen? Crossed-wrists block, twist right, left side-kick to the exposed kidney.

What good all this was going to be, fighting perambulating mushrooms, was a mystery to me. But I was that machine's slave for three weeks, learning the best way to use every weapon from the sharp stick to the nova bomb, and absorbing two millennia's worth of military observation, theory and prejudice. It was supposed to make me a major. Kind of like making a duck by teaching a chicken how to swim.

My separation from Marygay seemed, if possible, even more final when I read my combat orders: Sade-138, in the Greater Magellanic Cloud, four collapsar jumps and 150,000 light-years away. But I had already learned to live with the fact that I'd never see her again.

I had access to all of my new company's personnel records, including my own. The Army's psychologist had said that I "thought" I was tolerant toward homosexuality—which was wounding, because I'd learned at my mother's knee that what a person does with his plumbing is his own business and nobody else's. Which is all very fine when you're in the majority, I found out. When you're the one being tolerated, it can be difficult. Behind my back, most of them called me "the Old Queer," even though no one in the company was more than nine years younger than me. I accepted the inaccuracy along with the irony; a commander always gets names. I should have seen, though, that this was more than the obligatory token disrespect that soldiers accord their officers. The name symbolized an attitude of contempt and estrangement more profound than any I had experienced during my years as a private and noncommissioned officer.

Language, for one thing, was no small problem. English had evolved considerably in 450 years; soldiers had to learn twenty-first century English as a sort of *lingua franca* with which to communicate with their officers, some of whom might be "old" enough to be their nine-times-great-grand-parents. Of course, they only used this language when talking to their officers, or mocking them, so they got out of practice with it.

At Stargate, maybe they should have spared some ALSC time to teach me the language of my troops. I had an "open door" policy, where twice weekly any soldier could come talk to me without going up through the chain of command, everything off the record. It never worked out well, and after a couple of months they stopped coming altogether.

There were only three of us who were born before the twenty-fifth century—the only three who had been *born* at all, since they didn't make people the sloppy old-fashioned way anymore. Each embryo was engineered for a specific purpose . . . and the ones that wound up being soldiers, although intelligent and physically perfect, seemed deficient in some qualities that I considered to be virtues. Attila would have loved them, though; Napoleon would have hired them on the spot.

The other two people "of woman born" were my executive officer, Captain Charlie Moore, and the senior medic, Lieutenant Diana Alsever. They were both homosexual, having been born in the twenty-second century, but we still had much in common, and they were the only people in the company whom I considered friends. In retrospect I can see that we insulated one another from the rest of the company, which might have been comfortable for them—but it was disastrous for me.

The rest of the officers, especially Lieutenant Hilleboe, my Field First, seemed only to tell me what they thought I wanted to hear. They didn't tell me that most of the troops thought I was inexperienced and cowardly and had only been made their commander by virtue of seniority. All of which was more or less true—after all, I hadn't volunteered for the position—but maybe I could have done something about it if my officers had been frank with me.

Our assignment was to build a base on Sade-138's largest planet, and defend it against Tauran attack. Tauran expansion was very predictable, and we knew that they would show up there sooner or later. My company, Strike Force Gamma, would defend the place for two years, after which a garrison force would relieve us. And I would theoretically resign my commission and become a civilian again—unless there happened to be a new regulation forbidding it. Or an old one that they had neglected to tell me about.

The garrison force would automatically leave Stargate two years after we had, with no idea what would be waiting for them at Sade-138. There was no way we could get word back to them, since the trip took 340 years of "objective" time, though ship-time was only seven months, thanks to time dilation.

Seven months was long enough, trapped in the narrow corridors and tiny rooms of *Masaryk II*. It was a relief to leave the ship in orbit, even though planetside meant four weeks of unrelenting hard labor under hazardous, uncomfortable conditions. Two shifts of 38.5 hours each, alternating shipboard rest and planetside work.

The planet was an almost featureless rock, an offwhite billiard ball with a thin atmosphere of hydrogen and helium. The temperature at the equator varied from 25° Kelvin to 17° on a 38.5-hour cycle, daytime heat being provided by the bright blue spark of S Doradus. When it was coldest, just before dawn, hydrogen would condense out of the air in a fine mist, making everything so slippery that you had to just sit down and wait it out. At dawn a faint pastel rainbow provided the only relief from the black-and-white monotony of the landscape.

The ground was treacherous, covered with little granular

chunks of frozen gas that shifted slowly, incessantly in the anemic breeze. You had to walk in a slow waddle to stay on your feet; of the four people who died during the construction of the base, three were the victims of simple falls.

From the sky down, we had three echelons of defense. First was the *Masaryk II,* with its six tachyon-drive fighters and fifty robot drones equipped with nova bombs. Commodore Antopol would take off after the Tauran ship when it flashed out of Sade-138's collapsar field. If she nailed it, we'd be home free.

If the enemy got through Antopol's swarm of fighters and drones, they would still have some difficulty attacking us. Atop our underground base was a circle of twenty-five self-aiming bevawatt lasers, with reaction times on the order of a fraction of a microsecond. And just beyond the laser's effective horizon was a broad ring with thousands of nuclear land mines that would detonate with any small distortion of the local gravitational field: a Tauran walking over one or a ship passing overhead.

If we actually had to go up and fight, which might happen if they reduced all our automatic defenses and wanted to take the base intact, each soldier was armed with a megawatt laser finger, and every squad had a tachyon rocket launcher and two repeating grenade launchers. And as a last resort, there was the stasis field.

I couldn't begin to understand the principles behind the stasis field; the gap between present-day physics and my Master's degree in the same subject was as long as the time that separated Galileo and Einstein. But I knew the effects.

Nothing could move at a speed greater than 16.3 meters per second inside the field, which was a hemispherical (in space, spherical) volume about fifty meters in radius. Inside, there was no such thing as electromagnetic radiation; no electricity, no magnetism, no light. From inside your suit, you could see your surroundings in ghostly monochrome—which phenomenon was glibly explained to me as being due to "phase transference of quasi-energy leaking through from an adjacent tachyon reality," which was so much phlogiston to me.

But inside the field, all modern weapons of warfare were useless. Even a nova bomb was just an inert lump. And any creature, Terran or Tauran, caught inside without proper insulation would die in a fraction of a second.

Inside the field we had an assortment of old-fashioned weapons and one fighter, for last-ditch aerial support. I made people practice with the swords and bows and arrows and such, but they weren't enthusiastic. The consensus was that we would be doomed if the fighting degenerated to where we were forced into the stasis field. I couldn't say that I disagreed.

For five months we waited around in an atmosphere of comfortably boring routine.

The base quickly settled into a routine of training and waiting. I was almost impatient for the Taurans to show up, just to get it over with one way or the other.

The troops had adjusted to the situation much better than I had, for obvious reasons. They had specific duties to perform and ample free time for the usual soldierly anodynes to boredom. My duties were more varied but offered little satisfaction, since the problems that percolated up to me were of the "buck stops here" type; the ones with pleasing, unambiguous solutions were taken care of in the lower echelons.

I'd never cared much for sports or games, but found myself turning to them more and more as a kind of safety valve. For the first time in my life, in these tense, claustrophobic surroundings, I couldn't escape into reading or study. So I fenced, quarterstaff and saber, with the other officers; worked myself to exhaustion on the exercise machines, and even kept a jump-rope in my office. Most of the other officers played chess, but they could usually beat me—whenever I won it gave me the feeling I was being humored. And word games were difficult because my language was an archaic dialect that they had trouble manipulating. And I lacked the time and talent to master "modern" English.

For a while I let Diana feed me mood-altering drugs, but the cumulative effect of them was frightening—I was getting addicted in a way that was at first too subtle to bother me— so I stopped short. Then I tried some systematic psychoanalysis with Lieutenant Wilber. It was impossible. Although he knew all about my problems in an academic kind of way, we didn't speak the same cultural language; his counseling me about love and sex was like my telling a fourteenth-century serf how best to get along with his priest and landlord.

And that, after all, was the root of my problem. I was sure I could have handled the pressures and frustrations of command, of being cooped up in a cave with these people who at times seemed scarcely less alien than the enemy; even the near-certainty that it could only lead to painful death in a worthless cause—if only I could have had Marygay with me. And the feeling got more intense as the months crept by.

Lieutenant Wilber got very stern with me at this point and accused me of romanticizing my position. He knew what love was, he said; he had been in love himself. And the sexual polarity of the couple made no difference—all right, I could accept that; that idea had been a cliché in my parents' generation (though it had run into some predictable resistance in my own). But love, he said, love was a fragile blossom; love was a delicate crystal; love was an unstable reaction with a half-life of about eight months. Crap, I said, and accused him of wearing cultural blinders; thirty centuries of prewar society taught that love was one thing that could last to the grave and even beyond, *and if he had been born instead of hatched he would know that without being told!* Whereupon he would assume a wry, tolerant expression and reiterate that I was merely a victim of self-imposed sexual frustration and romantic delusion.

In retrospect, I guess we had a good time arguing with each other. Cure me, he didn't.

2.

It was exactly 400 days since the day we had begun construction. I was sitting at my desk not checking out Hilleboe's new duty roster. Charlie was stretched out in a chair reading something on the viewer. The phone buzzed, and it was a voice from on high, the Commodore.

"They're here."

"What?"

"I said they're here. A Tauran ship just exited the collapsar field. Velocity .8 c. Deceleration thirty G's. Give or take."

Charlie was leaning over my desk. "What?"

"How long before you can pursue?" I asked.

"Soon as you get off the phone." I switched off and went over to the logistic computer, which was a twin to the one on *Masaryk II* and had a direct data link to it. While I tried to get numbers out of the thing, Charlie fiddled with the visual display.

The display was a hologram about a meter square by half a meter thick and was programmed to show the positions of Sade-138, our planet, and a few other chunks of rock in the system. There were green and red dots to show the positions of our vessels and the Taurans'.

The computer said that the minimum time it could take the Taurans to decelerate and get back to this planet would be a little over eleven days. Of course, that would be straight maximum acceleration and deceleration all the way; Commodore Antopol could pick them off like flies on a wall. So, like us, they'd mix up their direction of flight and degree of acceleration in a random way. Based on several hundred past records of enemy behavior, the computer was able to give us a probability table:

DAYS TO CONTACT	PROBABILITY
11	.000001
15	.001514

20	.032164
25	.103287
30	.676324
35	.820584
40	.982685
45	.993576
50	.999369

MEDIAN

28.9554	.500000

Unless, of course, Antopol and her gang of merry pirates managed to make a kill. The chances for that, I had learned in the can, were slightly less than fifty-fifty.

But whether it took 28.9554 days or two weeks, those of us on the ground had to just sit on our hands and watch. If Antopol was successful, then we wouldn't have to fight until the regular garrison troops replaced us here, and we moved on to the next collapsar.

"Haven't left yet." Charlie had the display cranked down to minimum scale; the planet was a white ball the size of a large melon, and *Masaryk II* was a green dot off to the right some eight melons away; you couldn't get both on the screen at the same time.

While we were watching, a small green dot popped out of the ship's dot and drifted away from it. A ghostly number "2" drifted beside it, and a key projected on the display's lower left-hand corner identified it as 2—PURSUIT DRONE. Other numbers in the key identified the *Masaryk II,* a planetary defense fighter, and fourteen planetary defense drones. Those sixteen ships were not yet far enough away from one another to have separate dots.

"Tell Hilleboe to call a general assembly. Might as well break it to everyone at once."

The men and women didn't take it very well, and I couldn't really blame them. We had all expected the Taurans to attack much sooner—and when they persisted in not coming, the feeling grew that Strike Force Command had made a mistake, and they'd never show up at all.

I wanted them to start weapons training in earnest; they hadn't used any high-powered weapons in almost two years. So I activated their laser-fingers and passed out the grenade and rocket launchers. We couldn't practice inside the base, for fear of damaging the external sensors and defensive laser ring. So we turned off half the circle of bevawatt lasers and went out about a klick beyond the perimeter; one platoon at a time, accompanied by either me or Charlie. Rusk kept a close watch on the early-warning screens. If anything approached, she would send up a flare, and the platoon would have to get back inside the ring before the unknown came over the horizon, at which time the defensive lasers would come on automatically. Besides knocking out the unknown, they would fry the platoon in less than .02 second.

We couldn't spare anything from the base to use as a target, but that turned out to be no problem. The first tachyon rocket we fired scooped out a hole twenty meters long by ten wide by five deep; the rubble gave us a multitude of targets from twice-man-sized on down.

They were good, a lot better than they had been with the primitive weapons in the stasis field. The best laser practice turned out to be rather like skeet-shooting: pair up the people and have one stand behind the other, throwing rocks at random intervals. The one who was shooting had to gauge the rock's trajectory and zap it before it hit the ground. Their eye-hand coordination was impressive (maybe the Eugenics Council had done something right). Shooting at rocks down to pebble-size, most of them could do better than nine out of ten. Old non-bioengineered me could hit maybe seven out of ten, and I'd had a good deal more practice than they'd had.

They were equally facile at estimating trajectories with the grenade launcher, which was a more versatile weapon than it had been in the past. Instead of just shooting one-microton bombs with a standard propulsive charge, it had four different charges and a choice of one-, two-, three- or four-microton bombs. For really close infighting, where it was dangerous to use the lasers, the barrel of the launcher would unsnap, and you could load it with a magazine of "shotgun" rounds. Each shot would send out an expanding cloud of a thousand tiny flechettes that were instant death out to five meters and turned to harmless vapor at six.

The tachyon rocket launcher required no skill whatsoever. All you had to do was be careful no one was standing behind you when you fired it; the backwash from the rocket was dangerous for several meters behind the launching tube. Otherwise, you just lined up your target in the crosshairs and pushed the button. You didn't have to worry about trajectory; for all practical purposes, the rocket just traveled in a straight line. It reached escape velocity in less than a second.

It improved the troops' morale to get out and chew up the landscape with their new toys. But the landscape wasn't fighting back. No matter how physically impressive the weapons were, their effectiveness would depend on what the Taurans could throw back. A Greek phalanx must have looked pretty impressive, but it wouldn't do too well against a single man with a flamethrower.

And as with any engagement, because of time dilation, there was no way to tell what sort of weaponry they would have. It depended on what the Tauran level of technology had been when their mission had begun; they could be a couple of centuries ahead of us or behind us. They might never have heard of the stasis field. Or they might be able to say a magic word and make us disappear.

I was out with the fourth platoon, burning rocks, when Charlie called and asked me to come back in, urgent. I left Heimoff in charge.

"Another one?" The scale of the holograph display was such that our planet was pea-sized, about five centimeters from the X that marked the position of Sade-138. There were forty-one red and green dots scattered around the field; the key identified number forty-one as TAURAN CRUISER (2).

"That's right." Charlie was grim. "Appeared a few minutes ago. When I called. It has the same characteristics as the other one: 30 G's, .8 *c.*"

"You called Antopol?"

"Yeah." He anticipated the next question. "It'll take almost a day for the signal to get there and back."

"It's never happened before." But of course Charlie knew that.

"Maybe this collapsar is especially important to them."

"Likely." So it was almost certain we'd be fighting on the ground. Even if Antopol managed to get the first cruiser, she wouldn't have a fifty-fifty chance on the second one. Low on drones and fighters. "I wouldn't like to be Antopol now."

"She'll just get it earlier."

"I don't know. We're in pretty good shape."

"Save it for the troops, William." He turned down the display's scale to where it showed only two objects: Sade-138 and the new red dot, slowly moving.

We spent the next two weeks watching dots blink out. And if you knew when and where to look, you could go outside and see the real thing happening, a hard bright speck of white light that faded in about a second.

In that second, a nova bomb had put out over a million times the power of a bevawatt laser. It made a miniature star half a klick in diameter and as hot as the interior of the Sun. Anything it touched it would consume. The radiation from a near miss could botch up a ship's electronics beyond repair —two fighters, one of ours and one of theirs, had evidently suffered that fate; silently drifting out of the system at a constant velocity, without power.

We had used more powerful nova bombs earlier in the war, but the degenerate matter used to fuel them was unstable in large quantities. The bombs had a tendency to explode while they were still inside the ship. Evidently the Taurans had the same problem—or they had copied the process from us in the first place—because they had also scaled down to nova bombs that used less than a hundred kilograms of degenerate matter. And they deployed them much the same way we did, the warhead separating into dozens of pieces as it approached the target, only one of which was the nova bomb.

They would probably have a few bombs left over after they finished off *Masaryk II* and her retinue of fighters and drones. So it was likely that we were just wasting time and energy in weapons practice.

The thought did slip by my conscience that I could gather up eleven people and board the fighter we had hidden safely behind the stasis field. It was preprogrammed to take us back to Stargate.

I even went to the extreme of making a mental list of the eleven, trying to think of that many people who meant more to me than the rest. Turned out I'd be picking six at random.

I put the thought away, though. We did have a chance, maybe a damned good one, even against a fully armed cruiser. It wouldn't be easy to get a nova bomb close enough to include us inside its kill-radius.

Besides, they'd just space me for desertion. So why bother?

Spirits rose when one of Antopol's drones knocked out the first Tauran cruiser. Not counting the ships left behind for planetary defense, she still had eighteen drones and two fighters. They wheeled around to intercept the second cruiser, by then a few light-hours away, still being harassed by fifteen enemy drones.

One of the drones got her. Her ancillary craft continued the attack, but it was a rout. One fighter and three drones fled the battle at maximum acceleration, looping up over the plane of the ecliptic, and were not pursued. We watched them with morbid interest while the enemy cruiser inched back to do battle with us. The fighter was headed back for Sade-138, to escape. Nobody blamed them. In fact, we sent them a farewell/good-luck message; they didn't respond, naturally, being zipped up in the acceleration tanks. But it would be recorded.

It took the enemy five days to get back to the planet and be comfortably ensconced in a stationary orbit on the other side. We settled in for the inevitable first phase of the attack, which would be aerial and totally automated: their drones against our lasers. I put a force of fifty men and women inside the stasis field, in case one of the drones got through. An empty gesture, really; the enemy could just stand by and wait for them to turn off the field; fry them the second it flickered out.

Charlie had a weird idea that I almost went for.

"We could boobytrap the place."

"What do you mean?" I said. "This place is boobytrapped, out to twenty-five klicks."

"No, not the mines and such. I mean the base itself, here, underground."

"Go on."

"There are two nova bombs in that fighter." He pointed at the stasis field through a couple of hundred meters of rock. "We can roll them down here, boobytrap them, then hide everybody in the stasis field and wait."

In a way it was tempting. It would relieve me from any responsibility for decision-making; leave everything up to chance. "I don't think it would work, Charlie."

He seemed hurt. "Sure it would."

"No, look. For it to work, you have to get every single Tauran inside the kill-radius before it goes off—but they wouldn't all come charging in here once they breached our defenses. Least of all if the place seemed deserted. They'd suspect something, send in an advance party. And after the advance party set off the bombs—"

"We'd be back where we started, yeah. Minus the base. Sorry."

I shrugged. "It was an idea. Keep thinking, Charlie." I turned my attention back to the display, where the lopsided space war was in progress. Logically enough, the enemy wanted to knock out that one fighter overhead before he started to work on us. About all we could do was watch the red dots crawl around the planet and try to score. So far the pilot had managed to knock out all of the drones; the enemy hadn't sent any fighters after him yet.

I'd given the pilot control over five of the lasers in our defensive ring. They couldn't do much good, though. A beva-watt laser pumps out a billion kilowatts per second at a range of a hundred meters. A thousand klicks up, though, the beam was attenuated to ten kilowatts. Might do some damage if it hit an optical sensor. At least confuse things.

"We could use another fighter. Or six."

"Use up the drones," I said. We did have a fighter, of course, and a swabbie attached to us who could pilot it. But it might turn out to be our only hope, if they got us cornered in the stasis field.

"How far away is the other guy?" Charlie asked, meaning the fighter pilot who had turned tail. I cranked down the scale, and the green dot appeared at the right of the display. "About six light-hours." He had two drones left, too near to him to show as separate dots, having expended one in covering his getaway. "He's not accelerating anymore, but he's doing .9 c."

"Couldn't do us any good if he wanted to." Need almost a month to slow down.

At that low point, the light that stood for our own defensive fighter faded out. "Crap."

"Now the fun starts. Should I tell the troops to get ready, stand by to go topside?"

"No . . . have them suit up, in case we lose air. But I expect it'll be a little while before we have a ground attack." I turned the scale up again. Four red spots were already creeping around the globe toward us.

I got suited up and came back to Administration to watch the fireworks on the monitors.

The lasers worked perfectly. All four drones converged on us simultaneously; were targeted and destroyed. All but one of the nova bombs went off below our horizon (the visual horizon was about ten kilometers away, but the lasers were mounted high and could target something at twice that distance). The bomb that detonated on our horizon had melted out a semicircular chunk that glowed brilliantly white for several minutes. An hour later, it was still glowing dull orange, and the ground temperature outside had risen to 50° Absolute, melting most of our snow, exposing an irregular dark gray surface.

The next attack was also over in a fraction of a second, but this time there had been eight drones, and four of them got within ten klicks. Radiation from the glowing craters raised the temperature to nearly 300°. That was above the melting point of water, and I was starting to get worried. The fighting suits were good to over 1000°, but the automatic lasers depended on low-temperature superconductors for their speed.

I asked the computer what the lasers' temperature limit was, and it printed out TR 398–734–009–265, "Some Aspects Concerning the Adaptability of Cryogenic Ordnance to Use in Relatively High-Temperature Environments," which had lots of handy advice about how we could insulate the weapons if we had access to a fully equipped armorer's shop. It did note that the response time of automatic-aiming devices increased as the temperature increased, and that above some "critical temperature," the weapons would not aim at all. But there was no way to predict any individual weapon's behavior, other than to note that the highest critical temperature recorded was 790° and the lowest was 420°.

Charlie was watching the display. His voice was flat over the suit's radio: "Sixteen this time."

"Surprised?" One of the few things we knew about Tauran

psychology was a certain compulsiveness about numbers, especially primes and powers of two.

"Let's just hope they don't have thirty-two left." I queried
the computer on this; all it could say was that the cruiser had
thus far launched a total of forty-four drones, and some cruisers had been known to carry as many as 128.

We had more than a half hour before the drones would
strike. I could evacuate everybody to the stasis field, and they
would be temporarily safe if one of the nova bombs got
through. Safe, but trapped. How long would it take the crater
to cool down, if three or four—let alone sixteen—of the
bombs made it through? You couldn't live forever in a
fighting suit, even though it recycled everything with re-
morseless efficiency. One week was enough to make you
thoroughly miserable. Two weeks, suicidal. Nobody had ever
gone three weeks, under field conditions.

Besides, as a defensive position, the stasis field could be
a death trap. The enemy has all the options, since the dome
is opaque; the only way you can find out what they're up to
is to stick your head out. They didn't have to wade in with
primitive weapons unless they were impatient. They could
just keep the dome saturated with laser fire and wait for you
to turn off the generator. Meanwhile harassing you by throwing spears, rocks, arrows into the dome—you could return
fire, but it was pretty futile.

Of course, if one man stayed inside the base, the others
could wait out the next half hour in the stasis field. If he didn't
come get them, they'd know the outside was hot. I chinned
the combination that would give me a frequency available to
everybody Echelon 5 and above.

"This is Major Mandella." That still sounded like a bad
joke.

I outlined the situation to them and asked them to tell
their troops that everyone in the company was free to move
into the stasis field. I would stay behind and come retrieve

them if things went well—not out of nobility, of course; I preferred taking the chance of being vaporized in a nanosecond, rather than almost certain slow death under the gray dome.

I chinned Charlie's frequency. "You can go, too. I'll take care of things here."

"No, thanks," he said slowly. "I'd just as soon . . . hey, look at this."

The cruiser had launched another red dot, a couple of minutes behind the others. The display's key identified it as being another drone. "That's curious."

"Superstitious bastards," he said without feeling.

It turned out that only eleven people chose to join the fifty who had been ordered into the dome. That shouldn't have surprised me, but it did.

As the drones approached, Charlie and I stared at the monitors, carefully not looking at the holograph display, tacitly agreeing that it would be better not to know when they were one minute away, thirty seconds . . . and then, like the other times, it was over before we knew it had started. The screens glared white and there was a yowl of static, and we were still alive.

But this time there were fifteen new holes on the horizon —or closer!—and the temperature was rising so fast that the last digit in the readout was an amorphous blur. The number peaked in the high 800's and began to slide down.

We had never seen any of the drones, not during that tiny fraction of a second it took the lasers to aim and fire. But then the seventeenth one flashed over the horizon, zigzagging crazily, and stopped directly overhead. For an instant it seemed to hover, and then it began to fall. Half the lasers had detected it, and they were firing steadily, but none of them could aim; they were all stuck in their last firing position.

It glittered as it dropped, the mirror polish of its sleek hull reflecting the white glow from the craters and the eerie flickering of the constant, impotent laser fire. I heard Charlie take one deep breath and the drone fell so close you could see spidery Tauran numerals etched on the hull, and a transparent porthole near the tip—then its engine flared and it was suddenly gone.

"What the hell?" Charlie said quietly.

The porthole. "Maybe reconnaissance."

"I guess. So we can't touch them, and they know it."

"Unless the lasers recover." Didn't seem likely. "We better get everybody under the dome. Us, too."

He said a word whose vowel had changed over the centuries, but whose meaning was clear. "No hurry. Let's see what they do."

We waited for several hours. The temperature outside stabilized at 690°—just under the melting point of zinc, I remembered to no purpose—and I tried the manual controls for the lasers, but they were still frozen.

"Here they come," Charlie said. "Eight again."

I started for the display. "Guess we'll—"

"Wait! They aren't drones." The key identified all eight with the legend TROOP CARRIER.

"Guess they want to take the base," he said. "Intact."

That, and maybe try out new weapons and techniques. "It's not much of a risk for them. They can always retreat and drop a nova bomb in our laps."

I called Brill and had her go get everybody who was in the stasis field; set them up with the remainder of her platoon as a defensive line circling around the northeast and northwest quadrants.

"I wonder," Charlie said. "Maybe we shouldn't put everyone topside at once. Until we know how many Taurans there are."

That was a point. Keep a reserve, let the enemy underestimate our strength. "It's an idea . . . there might be just sixty-four of them in eight carriers." Or 128 or 256. I wished our spy satellites had a finer sense of discrimination. But you can only cram so much into a machine the size of a grape.

179

I decided to let Brill's seventy people be our first line of defense, and ordered them into a ring in the ditches we had made outside the base's perimeter. Everybody else would stay downstairs until needed.

If it turned out that the Taurans, either through numbers or new technology, could field an unstoppable force, I'd order everyone into the stasis field. There was a tunnel from the living quarters to the dome, so the people underground could go straight there in safety. The ones in the ditches would have to fall back under fire. If any of them were still alive when I gave the order.

I called in Hilleboe and had her and Charlie keep watch over the lasers. If they came unstuck, I'd call Brill and her people back. Turn on the automatic aiming system again, then just sit back and watch the show. But even stuck, the lasers could be useful. Charlie marked the monitors to show where the rays would go; he and Hilleboe could fire them manually whenever something moved into a weapon's line-of-sight.

We had about twenty minutes. Brill was walking around the perimeter with her men and women, ordering them into the ditches a squad at a time, setting up overlapping fields of fire. I broke in and asked her to set up the heavy weapons so that they could be used to channel the enemy's advance into the path of the lasers.

There wasn't much else to do but wait. I asked Charlie to measure the enemy's progress and try to give us an accurate countdown, then sat at my desk and pulled out a pad, to diagram Brill's arrangement and see whether I could improve on it.

The first line that I drew ripped through four sheets of paper. It had been some time since I'd done any delicate work in a suit. I remembered how, in training, they'd made us practice controlling the strength-amplification circuits by passing eggs from person to person, messy business. I wondered if they still had eggs on Earth.

The diagram completed, I couldn't see any way to add to it. All those reams of theory crammed in my brain; there was plenty of tactical advice about envelopment and encirclement, but from the wrong point of view. If you were the one who was being encircled, you didn't have many options. Just sit tight and fight. Respond quickly to enemy concentrations of force, but stay flexible so the enemy can't employ a diversionary force to divert strength from some predictable section of your perimeter. *Make full use of air and space support:* always good advice. Keep your head down and your chin up and pray for the cavalry. Hold your position and don't contemplate Dienbienphu, the Alamo, the Battle of Hastings.

"Eight more carriers out," Charlie said. "Five minutes. Until the first eight get here."

So they were going to attack in two waves. At least two. What would I do, in the Tauran commander's position? That wasn't too far-fetched; the Taurans lacked imagination in tactics and tended to copy human patterns.

The first wave could be a throwaway, a kamikaze attack to soften us up and evaluate our defenses. Then the second would come in more methodically and finish the job. Or vice versa; the first group would have twenty minutes to get entrenched, then the second could skip over their heads and hit us hard at one spot—breach the perimeter and overrun the base.

Or maybe they sent out two forces simply because two was a magic number. Or they could only launch eight troop carriers at a time (that would be bad, implying that the carriers were large; in different situations they had used carriers holding as few as four troops or as many as 128).

"Three minutes." I stared at the cluster of monitors that showed various sectors of the mine field. If we were lucky, they'd land out there, out of caution. Or maybe pass over it low enough to detonate mines.

I was feeling vaguely guilty. I was safe in my hole, doodling, ready to start calling out orders. How did those seventy sacrificial lambs feel about their absentee commander?

Then I remembered how I had felt about Captain Stott, that first mission, when he'd elected to stay safely in orbit while we fought on the ground. The rush of remembered hate was so strong I had to bite back nausea.

"Hilleboe, can you handle the lasers by yourself?"

"I don't see why not, sir."

I tossed down the pen and stood up. "Charlie, you take over the unit coordination; you can do it as well as I could. I'm going topside."

"I wouldn't advise that, sir."

"Hell no, William. Don't be an idiot."

"I'm not taking orders, I'm giv—"

"You wouldn't last ten seconds up there," Charlie said.

"I'll take the same chance as everybody else."

"Don't you hear what I'm saying? *They'll* kill you!"

"The troops? Nonsense. I know they don't like me especially, but—"

"You haven't listened in on the squad frequencies?" No, they didn't speak my brand of English when they talked among themselves. "They think you put them out on the line for punishment, for cowardice. After you'd told them anyone was free to go into the dome."

"Didn't you, sir?" Hilleboe said.

"To punish them? No, of course not." Not consciously. "They were just up there when I needed . . . hasn't Lieutenant Brill said anything to them?"

"Not that I've heard," Charlie said. "Maybe she's been too busy to tune in."

Or she agreed with them. "I'd better get—"

"There!" Hilleboe shouted. The first enemy ship was visible in one of the mine field monitors; the others appeared in the next second. They came in from random directions and weren't evenly distributed around the base. Five in the northeast quadrant and only one in the southwest. I relayed the information to Brill.

But we had predicted their logic pretty well; all of them were coming down in the ring of mines. One came close enough to one of the tachyon devices to set it off. The blast caught the rear end of the oddly streamlined craft, causing it to make a complete flip and crash nose-first. Side ports opened up and Taurans came crawling out. Twelve of them; probably four left inside. If all the others had sixteen as well, there were only slightly more of them than of us.

In the first wave.

The other seven had landed without incident, and yes, there were sixteen each. Brill shuffled a couple of squads to conform to the enemy's troop concentration, and we waited.

They moved fast across the mine field, striding in unison like bowlegged, top-heavy robots, not even breaking stride when one of them was blown to bits by a mine, which happened eleven times.

When they came over the horizon, the reason for their apparently random distribution was obvious: they had analyzed beforehand which approaches would give them the most natural cover, from the rubble that the drones had kicked up. They would be able to get within a couple of kilometers of the base before we got any clear line-of-sight on them. And their suits had augmentation circuits similar to ours, so they could cover a kilometer in less than a minute.

Brill had her troops open fire immediately, probably more for morale than out of any hope of actually hitting the enemy. They probably were getting a few, though it was hard to tell. At least the tachyon rockets did an impressive job of turning boulders into gravel.

The Taurans returned fire with some weapon similar to the tachyon rocket, maybe exactly the same. They rarely found a mark, though; our people were at and below ground level, and if the rocket didn't hit something, it would keep on going forever, amen. They did score a hit on one of the bevawatt lasers, though, and the concussion that filtered down to us was strong enough to make me wish we had burrowed a little deeper than twenty meters.

The bevawatts weren't doing us any good. The Taurans must have figured out the lines of sight ahead of time, and gave them wide berth. That turned out to be fortunate, because it caused Charlie to let his attention wander from the laser monitors for a moment.

"What the hell?"

"What's that, Charlie?" I didn't take my eyes off the monitors. Waiting for something to happen.

"The ship, the cruiser—it's gone." I looked at the holograph display. He was right; the only red lights were those that stood for the troop carriers.

"Where did it go?" I asked inanely.

"Let's play it back." He programmed the display to go back a couple of minutes and cranked out the scale to where both planet and collapsar showed on the cube. The cruiser showed up, and with it, three green dots. Our "coward," attacking the cruiser with only two drones.

But he'd had a little help from the laws of physics.

Instead of going into collapsar insertion, he had skimmed *around* the collapsar field in a slingshot orbit. He had come out going .9 c; the drones were going .99 c, headed straight for the enemy cruiser. Our planet was about a thousand light-seconds from the collapsar, so the Tauran ship had only ten seconds to detect and stop both drones. And at that speed, it didn't matter whether you'd been hit by a nova bomb or a spitball.

The first drone disintegrated the cruiser, and the other one, .01 second behind, glided on down to impact on the planet. The fighter missed the planet by a couple of hundred kilometers and hurtled on into space, decelerating with the maximum twenty-five G's. He'd be back in a couple of months.

But the Taurans weren't going to wait. They were getting

close enough to our lines for both sides to start using lasers, but they were also within easy grenade range. A good-sized rock could shield them from laser fire, but the grenades and rockets were slaughtering them.

At first, Brill's troops had the overwhelming advantage; fighting from ditches, they could only be harmed by an occasional lucky shot or an extremely well aimed grenade (which the Taurans threw by hand, with a range of several hundred meters). Brill had lost four, but it looked as if the Tauran force were down to less than half its original size.

Eventually, the landscape had been torn up enough so that the bulk of the Tauran force was also able to fight from holes in the ground. The fighting slowed down to individual laser duels, punctuated occasionally by heavier weapons. But it wasn't smart to use up a tachyon rocket against a single Tauran, not with another force of unknown size only a few minutes away.

Something had been bothering me about that holographic replay. Now, with the battle's lull, I knew what it was.

When that second drone crashed at near-light speed, how much damage had it done to the planet? I stepped over to the computer and punched it up; found out how much energy had been released in the collision, and then compared it with geological information in the computer's memory.

Twenty times as much energy as the most powerful earthquake ever recorded. On a planet three-quarters the size of Earth.

On the general frequency: "Everybody—topside! Right now!" I palmed the button that would cycle and open the airlock and tunnel that led from Administration to the surface.

"What the hell, Will—"

"Earthquake!" How long? "Move!"

Hilleboe and Charlie were right behind me.

"Safer in the ditches?" Charlie said.

"I don't know," I said. "Never been in an earthquake."

Maybe the walls of the ditch would close up and crush us.

I was surprised at how dark it was on the surface. S Dora-dus had almost set; the monitors had compensated for the low light level.

An enemy laser raked across the clearing to our left, making a quick shower of sparks when it flicked by a bevawatt mounting. We hadn't been seen yet. We all decided yes, it would be safer in the ditches, and made it to the nearest one in three strides.

There were four men and women in the ditch, one of them badly wounded or dead. We scrambled down the ledge, and I turned up my image amplifier to log two, to inspect our ditchmates. We were lucky; one was a grenadier, and they also had a rocket launcher. I could just make out the names on their helmets. We were in Brill's ditch, but she hadn't noticed us yet. She was at the opposite end, cautiously peering over the edge, directing two squads in a flanking movement. When they were safely in position, she ducked back down. "Is that you, Major?"

"That's right," I said cautiously. I wondered whether any of the people in the ditch were among the ones after my scalp.

"What's this about an earthquake?"

She had been told about the cruiser's being destroyed, but not about the other drone. I explained in as few words as possible.

"Nobody's come out of the airlock," she said. "Not yet. I guess they all went into the stasis field."

"Yeah, they were just as close to one as the other." Maybe some of them were still down below, hadn't taken my warning seriously. I chinned the general frequency to check, and then all hell broke loose.

The group dropped away and then flexed back up; slammed us so hard that we were airborne, tumbling out of the ditch. We flew several meters, going high enough to see the pattern of bright orange and yellow ovals, the craters where nova bombs had been stopped. I landed on my feet, but the ground was shifting and slithering so much that it was impossible to stay upright.

With a basso grinding I could feel through my suit, the cleared area above our base crumbled and fell in. Part of the stasis field's underside was exposed when the ground subsided; it settled to its new level with aloof grace.

I hoped everybody had had time and sense enough to get under the dome.

A figure came staggering out of the ditch nearest to me, and I realized with a start that it wasn't human. At this range, my laser burned a hole straight through his helmet; he took two steps and fell over backward. Another helmet peered over the edge of the ditch. I sheared the top of it off before he could raise his weapon.

I couldn't get my bearings. The only thing that hadn't changed was the stasis dome, and it looked the same from any angle. The bevawatt lasers were all buried, but one of them had switched on, a brilliant flickering searchlight that illuminated a swirling cloud of vaporized rock.

Obviously, though, I was in enemy territory. I started across the trembling ground toward the dome.

I couldn't raise any platoon leaders. All of them but Brill were probably inside the dome. I did get Hilleboe and Charlie; told Hilleboe to go inside the dome and roust everybody out. If the next wave also had 128, we were going to need everybody.

The tremors died down, and I found my way into a "friendly" ditch—the cooks' ditch, in fact, since the only people there were Orban and Rudkoski.

I got a beep from Hilleboe and chinned her on. "Sir . . . there were only ten people there. The rest didn't make it."

"They stayed behind?" Seemed like they'd had plenty of time.

"I don't know, sir."

"Never mind. Get me a count, how many people we have,

all totaled." I tried the platoon leaders' frequency again and it was still silent.

The three of us watched for enemy laser fire, for a couple of minutes, but there was none. Probably waiting for reinforcements.

Hilleboe called back. "I only get fifty-three, sir. Some others may be unconscious."

"All right. Have them sit tight until—" Then the second wave showed up, the troop carriers roaring over the horizon with their jets pointed our way, decelerating. *"Get some rockets on those bastards!"* Hilleboe yelled to everyone in particular. But nobody had managed to stay attached to a rocket launcher while he was being tossed around. No grenade launchers, either, and the range was too far for the hand lasers to do any damage.

These carriers were four or five times the size of the ones in the first wave. One of them grounded about a kilometer in front of us, barely stopping long enough to disgorge its troops. Of which there were over fifty, probably sixty-four—times eight made 512. No way we could hold them back.

"Everybody listen, this is Major Mandella." I tried to keep my voice even and quiet. "We're going to retreat into the dome, quickly but in an orderly way. I know we're scattered all over hell. If you belong to the second or fourth platoon, stay put for a minute and give covering fire while the first and third platoons, and support, fall back.

"First and third and support, fall back to about half your present distance from the dome, then take cover and defend the second and fourth as they come back. They'll go to the edge of the dome and cover you while you come back the rest of the way." I shouldn't have said "retreat"; that word wasn't in the book. Retrograde action.

There was a lot more retrograde than action. Eight or nine people were firing, and all the rest were in full flight. Rudkoski and Orban had vanished. I took a few carefully aimed shots, to no great effect, then ran down to the other end of the ditch, climbed out and headed for the dome.

The Taurans started firing rockets, but most of them seemed to be going too high. I saw two of us get blown away before I got to my halfway point; found a nice big rock and hid behind it. I peeked out and decided that only two or three of the Taurans were close enough to be even remotely possible laser targets, and the better part of valor would be in not drawing unnecessary attention to myself. I ran the rest of the way to the edge of the field and stopped to return fire. After a couple of shots, I realized that I was just making myself a target; as far as I could see there was only one other person who was still running toward the dome.

A rocket zipped by, so close I could have touched it. I flexed my knees and kicked, and entered the dome in a rather undignified posture.

3.

Inside, I could see the rocket that had missed me drifting lazily through the gloom, rising slightly as it passed through to the other side of the dome. It would vaporize the instant it came out the other side, since all of the kinetic energy it had lost in abruptly slowing down to 16.3 meters per second would come back in the form of heat.

Nine people were lying dead, face-down just inside of the field's edge. It wasn't unexpected, though it wasn't the sort of thing you were supposed to tell the troops.

Their fighting suits were intact—otherwise they wouldn't have made it this far—but sometime during the past few minutes' rough-and-tumble, they had damaged the coating of special insulation that protected them from the stasis field. So as soon as they entered the field, all electrical activity in their bodies ceased, which killed them instantly. Also, since no molecule in their bodies could move faster than 16.3 m/sec, they instantly froze solid, their body temperatures stabilized at a cool 0.426° Absolute.

I decided not to turn any of them over to find out their names, not yet. We had to get some sort of defensive position worked out, before the Taurans came through the dome. If they decided to slug it out rather than wait.

With elaborate gestures, I managed to get everybody collected in the center of the field, under the fighter's tail, where the weapons were racked.

There were plenty of weapons, since we had been prepared to outfit three times this number of people. After giving each person a shield and short-sword, I traced a question in the snow: GOOD ARCHERS? RAISE HANDS. I got five volunteers, then picked out three more so that all the bows would be in use. Twenty arrows per bow. They were the most effective long-range weapon we had; the arrows were almost invisible in their slow flight, heavily weighted and tipped with a deadly sliver of diamond-hard crystal.

I arranged the archers in a circle around the fighter (its landing fins would give them partial protection from missiles coming in from behind) and between each pair of archers put four other people: two spear-throwers, one quarterstaff, and a person armed with battleax and a dozen chakram throwing knives. This arrangement would theoretically take care of the enemy at any range from the edge of the field to hand-to-hand combat.

Actually, at some 600-to-42 odds, they could probably walk in with a rock in each hand, no shields or special weapons, and still beat the crap out of us.

Assuming they knew what the stasis field was. Their technology seemed up to date in all other respects.

For several hours nothing happened. We got about as bored as anyone could, waiting to die. No one to talk to, nothing to see but the unchanging gray dome, gray snow, gray spaceship and a few identically gray soldiers. Nothing to hear, taste or smell but yourself.

Those of us who still had any interest in the battle were keeping watch on the bottom edge of the dome, waiting for the first Taurans to come through. So it took us a second to realize what was going on when the attack did start. It came from above, a cloud of catapulted darts swarming in through the dome some thirty meters above the ground, headed straight for the center of the hemisphere.

The shields were big enough that you could hide most of your body behind them by crouching slightly; the people who saw the darts coming could protect themselves easily. The ones who had their backs to the action, or were just asleep at the switch, had to rely on dumb luck for survival; there was no way to shout a warning, and it took only three seconds for a missile to get from the edge of the dome to its center.

We were lucky, losing only five. One of them was an archer, Shubik. I took over her bow and we waited, expecting a ground attack immediately.

It didn't come. After a half hour, I went around the circle and explained with gestures that the first thing you were supposed to do, if anything happened, was to touch the person on your right. He'd do the same, and so on down the line.

That might have saved my life. The second dart attack, a couple of hours later, came from behind me. I felt the nudge, slapped the person on my right, turned around and saw the cloud descending. I got the shield over my head and they hit a split-second later.

I set down my bow to pluck three darts from the shield, and the ground attack started.

It was a weird, impressive sight. Some three hundred of them stepped into the field simultaneously, almost shoulder-to-shoulder around the perimeter of the dome. They advanced in step, each one holding a round shield barely large enough to hide his massive chest. They were throwing darts

191

similar to the ones we had been barraged with.

I set the shield up in front of me—it had little extensions on the bottom to keep it upright—and with the first arrow I shot, I knew we had a chance. It struck one of them in the center of his shield, went straight through and penetrated his suit.

It was a one-sided massacre. The darts weren't very effective without the element of surprise—but when one came sailing over my head from behind, it did give me a crawly feeling between the shoulderblades.

With twenty arrows I got twenty Taurans. They closed ranks every time one dropped; you didn't even have to aim. After running out of arrows, I tried throwing their darts back at them. But their light shields were quite adequate against the small missiles.

We'd killed more than half of them with arrows and spears, long before they got into range of the hand-to-hand weapons. I drew my sword and waited. They still outnumbered us by better than three to one.

When they got within ten meters, the people with the chakram throwing knives had their own field day. Although the spinning disc was easy enough to see, and it took more than a half second to get from thrower to target, most of the Taurans reacted the same ineffective way, raising up the shield to ward it off. The razor-sharp, tempered heavy blade cut through the light shield like a buzz-saw through cardboard.

The first hand-to-hand contact was with the quarterstaffs, which were metal rods two meters long, that tapered at the ends to a double-edged, serrated knife blade. The Taurans had a cold-blooded—or valiant, if your mind works that way—method for dealing with them. They would simply grab the blade and die. While the human was trying to extricate his weapon from the frozen death-grip, a Tauran swordsman, with a scimitar over a meter long, would step in and kill him.

Besides the swords, they had a bolo-like thing that was a

length of elastic cord that ended with about ten centimeters of something like barbed wire, and a small weight to propel it. It was a dangerous weapon for all concerned; if they missed their target it would come snapping back unpredictably. But they hit their target pretty often, going under the shields and wrapping the thorny wire around ankles.

I stood back-to-back with Private Erikson, and with our swords we managed to stay alive for the next few minutes. When the Taurans were down to a couple of dozen survivors, they just turned around and started marching out. We threw some darts after them, getting three, but we didn't want to chase after them. They might turn around and start hacking again.

There were only twenty-eight of us left standing. Nearly ten times that number of dead Taurans littered the ground, but there was no satisfaction in it.

They could do the whole thing over, with a fresh 300. And this time it would work.

We moved from body to body, pulling out arrows and spears, then took up places around the fighter again. Nobody bothered to retrieve the quarterstaffs. I counted noses: Charlie and Diana were still alive (Hilleboe had been one of the quarterstaff victims) as well as two supporting officers, Wilber and Szydlowska. Rudkoski was still alive, but Orban had taken a dart.

After a day of waiting, it looked as if the enemy had decided on a war of attrition, rather than repeating the ground attack. Darts came in constantly, not in swarms anymore, but in twos and threes and tens. And from all different angles. You couldn't stay alert forever; they'd get somebody every three or four hours.

We took turns sleeping, two at a time, on top of the stasis field generator. Sitting directly under the bulk of the fighter, it was the safest place in the dome.

Every now and then, a Tauran would appear at the edge of the field, evidently to see whether any of us were left.

Sometimes we'd shoot an arrow at him, for practice.

The darts stopped falling after a couple of days. I supposed it was possible that they'd simply run out of them. Or maybe they'd decided to stop when we were down to twenty survivors.

There was a more likely possibility. I took one of the quarterstaffs down to the edge of the field and poked it through, a centimeter or so. When I drew it back, the point was melted off. When I showed it to Charlie, he just rocked back and forth (the only way you can nod in a suit); this sort of thing had happened before, one of the first times the stasis field hadn't worked. They simply saturated it with laser fire and waited for us to go stir-crazy and turn off the generator. They were probably sitting in their ships playing the Tauran equivalent of pinochle.

I tried to think. It was hard to keep your mind on something for any length of time in that hostile environment, sense-deprived, looking over your shoulder every few seconds. Something Charlie had said. Only yesterday. I couldn't track it down. It wouldn't have worked then; that was all I could remember. Then finally it came to me.

I called everyone over and wrote in the snow:
GET NOVA BOMBS FROM SHIP.
CARRY TO EDGE OF FIELD.
MOVE FIELD.

Szydlowska knew where the proper tools would be, aboard ship. Luckily, we had left all of the entrances open before turning on the stasis field; they were electronic and would have been frozen shut. We got an assortment of wrenches from the engine room and climbed up to the cockpit. He knew how to remove the access plate that exposed a crawl space into the bomb bay. I followed him in through the meter-wide tube.

Normally, I supposed, it would have been pitch black. But the stasis field illuminated the bomb bay with the same dim, shadowless light that prevailed outside. The bomb bay was too small for both of us, so I stayed at the end of the crawl space and watched.

The bomb-bay doors had a "manual override," so they were easy; Szydlowska just turned a hand-crank and we were in business. Freeing the two nova bombs from their cradles was another thing. Finally, he went back down to the engine room and brought back a crowbar. He pried one loose and I got the other, and we rolled them out the bomb bay.

Sergeant Anghelov was already working on them by the time we climbed back down. All you had to do to arm the bomb was to unscrew the fuse on the nose of it and poke something around in the fuse socket to wreck the delay mechanism and safety restraints.

We carried them quickly to the edge, six people per bomb, and set them down next to each other. Then we waved to the four people who were standing by at the field generator's handles. They picked it up and walked ten paces in the opposite direction. The bombs disappeared as the edge of the field slid over them.

There was no doubt that the bombs had gone off. For a couple of seconds it was as hot as the interior of a star outside, and even the stasis field took notice of the fact: about a third of the dome glowed a dull pink for a moment, then was gray again. There was a slight acceleration, like you would feel in a slow elevator. That meant we were drifting down to the bottom of the crater. Would there be a solid bottom? Or would we sink down through molten rock to be trapped like a fly in amber—didn't pay to even think about that. Perhaps if it happened, we could blast our way out with the fighter's bevawatt laser.

Twelve of us, anyhow.

HOW LONG? Charlie scraped in the snow at my feet.

That was a damned good question. About all I knew was the amount of energy two nova bombs released. I didn't know how big a fireball they would make, which would determine the temperature at detonation and the size of the crater. I didn't know the heat capacity of the surrounding rock, or its boiling point. I wrote ONE WEEK, SHRUG? HAVE TO THINK.

The ship's computer could have told me in a thousandth of a second, but it wasn't talking. I started writing equations in the snow, trying to get a maximum and minimum figure for the length of time it would take for the outside to cool down to 500°. Anghelov, whose physics was much more up to date, did his own calculations on the other side of the ship.

My answer said anywhere from six hours to six days (although for six hours, the surrounding rock would have to conduct heat like pure copper), and Anghelov got five hours to four and a half days. I voted for six and nobody else got a vote.

We slept a lot. Charlie and Diana played chess by scraping symbols in the snow. I was never able to hold the shifting positions of the pieces in my mind. I checked my figures several times and kept coming up with six days. I checked Anghelov's computations, too, and they seemed all right, but I stuck to my guns. It wouldn't hurt us to stay in the suits an extra day and a half. We argued goodnaturedly in terse shorthand.

There had been nineteen of us left the day we tossed the bombs outside. There were still nineteen six days later, when I paused with my hand over the generator's cutoff switch. What was waiting for us out there? Surely we had killed all the Taurans within several klicks of the explosion. But there might have been a reserve force farther away, now waiting patiently on the crater's lip. At least you could push a quarterstaff through the field and have it come back whole.

I dispersed the people evenly around the area, so they might not get us with a single shot. Then, ready to turn it back on immediately if anything went wrong, I pushed.

4.

My radio was still tuned to the general frequency; after more than a week of silence my ears were suddenly assaulted with loud, happy babbling.

We stood in the center of a crater almost a kilometer wide and deep. Its sides were a shiny black crust shot through with red cracks, hot but no longer dangerous. The hemisphere of earth that we rested on had sunk a good forty meters into the floor of the crater, while it had still been molten, so now we stood on a kind of pedestal.

Not a Tauran in sight.

We rushed to the ship, sealed it and filled it with cool air and popped our suits. I didn't press seniority for the one shower; just sat back in an acceleration couch and took deep breaths of air that didn't smell like recycled Mandella.

The ship was designed for a maximum crew of twelve, so we stayed outside in shifts of seven to keep from straining the life support systems. I sent a repeating message to the other fighter, which was still over six weeks away, that we were in good shape and waiting to be picked up. I was reasonably certain he would have seven free berths, since the normal crew for a combat mission was only three.

It was good to walk around and talk again. I officially suspended all things military for the duration of our stay on the planet. Some of the people were survivors of Brill's mutinous bunch, but they didn't show any hostility toward me.

We played a kind of nostalgia game, comparing the various eras we'd experienced on Earth, wondering what it would be like in the 700-years-future we were going back to. Nobody mentioned the fact that we would at best go back to a few months' furlough, and then be assigned to another Strike Force, another turn of the wheel.

Wheels. One day Charlie asked me from what country my name originated; it sounded weird to him. I told him it originated from the lack of a dictionary and that if it were spelled right, it would look even weirder.

I got to kill a good half hour explaining all the peripheral details to that. Basically, though, my parents were "hippies" (a kind of subculture in late twentieth century America that rejected materialism and embraced a broad spectrum of odd ideas) who lived with a group of other hippies in a small agricultural community. When my mother got pregnant, they wouldn't be so conventional as to get married: this entailed the woman taking the man's name, and implied that she was his property. But they got all intoxicated and sentimental and decided they would both change their names to be the same. They rode into the nearest town, arguing all the way as to what name would be the best symbol for the love bond between them—I narrowly missed having a much shorter name —and they settled on Mandala.

A mandala is a wheel-like design the hippies had borrowed from a foreign religion, that symbolized the cosmos, the cosmic mind, God, or whatever needed a symbol. Neither my mother nor my father really knew how to spell the word, and the magistrate in town just wrote it down the way it sounded to him. And they named me William in honor of a wealthy uncle, who unfortunately died penniless.

The six weeks passed rather pleasantly; talking, reading, resting. The other ship landed next to ours and did have nine free berths. We shuffled crews so that each ship had someone who could get it out of trouble if the preprogrammed jump sequence malfunctioned. I assigned myself to the other ship, hoping it would have some new books. It didn't.

We zipped up in the tanks and took off simultaneously.

We wound up spending a lot of time in the tanks, just to keep from looking at the same faces all day long in the crowded ship. The added periods of acceleration got us back to Stargate in ten months, subjective. Of course it was still 340 years (minus seven months) to the hypothetical objective observer.

There were hundreds of cruisers in orbit around Stargate. Bad news: with that kind of backlog we probably wouldn't get any furlough at all.

I supposed I was more likely to get a court-martial than a furlough, anyhow. Losing eighty-eight percent of my company, many of them because they didn't have enough confidence in me to obey that direct earthquake order. And we were back where we'd started on Sade-138; no Taurans there, but no base, either.

We got landing instructions and went straight down, no shuttle. There was another surprise waiting at the spaceport. More dozens of cruisers were standing around on the ground —they'd never done that before for fear that Stargate would be hit—and two captured Tauran cruisers as well. We'd never managed to get one intact.

Seven centuries could have brought us a decisive advantage, of course. Maybe we were winning.

We went through an airlock under a "returnees" sign. After the air cycled and we'd popped our suits, a beautiful young woman came in with a cartload of tunics and told us, in perfectly accented English, to get dressed and go to the lecture hall at the end of the corridor to our left.

The tunic felt odd, light yet warm. It was the first thing I'd worn besides a fighting suit or bare skin in almost a year.

The lecture hall was about a hundred times too big for the twenty-two of us. The same girl was there, and asked us to move down to the front. That was unsettling; I could have sworn she had gone down the corridor the other way—I *knew* she had; I'd been captivated by the sight of her clothed behind.

Hell, maybe they had matter transmitters. Or teleportation. Wanted to save herself a few steps.

We sat for a minute, and a man clothed in the same kind

of unadorned tunic we and the girl were wearing walked across the stage with a stack of thick notebooks under each arm.

The same girl followed him on, also carrying notebooks.

I looked behind me, and she was still standing in the aisle. To make things even more odd, the man was virtually a twin to both of the women.

The man riffled through one of the notebooks and cleared his throat. "These books are for your convenience," he said, also with perfect accent, "and you don't have to read them if you don't want to. You don't have to do anything you don't want to do, because . . . you're free men and women. The war is over."

Disbelieving silence.

"As you will read in this book, the war ended 221 years ago. Accordingly, this is the year 220. Old style, of course, it is A.D. 3138.

"You are the last group of soldiers to return. When you leave here, I will leave as well. And destroy Stargate. It exists only as a rendezvous point for returnees, and as a monument to human stupidity. And shame. As you will read. Destroying it will be a cleansing."

He stopped speaking, and the woman started without a pause. "I am sorry for what you've been through and wish I could say that it was for a good cause, but as you will read, it was not.

"Even the wealth you have accumulated, back salary and compound interest, is worthless, as I no longer use money or credit. Nor is there such a thing as an economy, in which to use these . . . things."

"As you must have guessed by now," the man took over, "I am, we are, clones of a single individual. Some 250 years ago, my name was Kahn. Now it is Man.

"I had a direct ancestor in your company, a Corporal Larry Kahn. It saddens me that he didn't come back."

"I am over ten billion individuals but only one consciousness," she said. "After you read, I will try to clarify this. I know that it will be difficult to understand.

"No other humans are quickened, since I am the perfect pattern. Individuals who die are replaced. There are planets, however, on which humans are born in the normal, mammalian way. If my society is too alien for you, you may go to one of these planets. If you wish to take part in procreation, we will not discourage it. Many veterans ask us to change their polarity to heterosexual so that they can more easily fit into these other societies. This I can do very easily."

Don't worry about that, Man, just make out my ticket.

"You will be my guest here at Stargate for ten days, after which you will be taken wherever you want to go," he said. "Please read this book in the meantime. Feel free to ask any questions, or request any service." They both stood and walked off the stage.

Charlie was sitting next to me. "Incredible," he said. "They let . . . they encourage . . . men and women to do *that* again? Together?"

The female aisle Man was sitting behind us, and she answered before I could frame a reasonably sympathetic, hypocritical reply. "It isn't a judgment on your society," she said, probably not seeing that he took it a little more personally than that. "I only feel that it's necessary as a eugenic safety device. I have no evidence that there is anything wrong with cloning only one ideal individual, but if it turns out to have been a mistake, there will be a large genetic pool with which to start again."

She patted him on the shoulder. "Of course, you don't have to go to these breeder planets. You can stay on one of my planets. I make no distinction between heterosexual play and homosexual."

She went up on the stage to give a long spiel about where we were going to stay and eat and so forth while we were on Stargate. "Never been seduced by a computer before," Charlie muttered.

The 1143-year-long war had been begun on false pretenses and only continued because the two races were unable to communicate.

Once they could talk, the first question was "Why did you start this thing?" and the answer was "Me?"

The Taurans hadn't known war for millennia, and toward the beginning of the twenty-first century it looked as if mankind were ready to outgrow the institution as well. But the old soldiers were still around, and many of them were in positions of power. They virtually ran the United Nations Exploratory and Colonization Group, which was taking advantage of the newly discovered collapsar jump to explore interstellar space.

Many of the early ships met with accidents and disappeared. The ex-military men were suspicious. They armed the colonizing vessels, and the first time they met a Tauran ship, they blasted it.

They dusted off their medals, and the rest was going to be history.

You couldn't blame it all on the military, though. The evidence they presented for the Taurans' having been responsible for the earlier casualties was laughably thin. The few people who pointed this out were ignored.

The fact was, Earth's economy needed a war, and this one was ideal. It gave a nice hole to throw buckets of money into, but would unify humanity rather than divide it.

The Taurans relearned war, after a fashion. They never got really good at it, and would eventually have lost.

The Taurans, the book explained, couldn't communicate with humans because they had no concept of the individual; they had been natural clones for millions of years. Eventually, Earth's cruisers were manned by Man, Kahnclones, and they were for the first time able to get through to one another.

The book stated this as a bald fact. I asked a Man to explain what it meant, what was special about clone-to-clone communication, and he said that I *a priori* couldn't understand it.

There were no words for it, and my brain wouldn't be able to accommodate the concepts even if there were words.

All right. It sounded a little fishy, but I was willing to accept it. I'd accept that up was down if it meant the war was over.

I'd just finished dressing after my first good night's sleep in years, when someone tapped lightly on my door. I opened it and it was a female Man, standing there with an odd expression on her face. Almost a leer; was she trying to look seductive?

"Major Mandella," she said, "may I come in?" I motioned her to a chair, but she went straight to the bed and sat daintily on the rumpled covers.

"I have a proposition for you, Major." I wondered whether she knew the word's archaic second meaning. "Come sit beside me, please."

Lacking Charlie's reservations about being seduced by a computer, I sat. "What do you propose?" I touched her warm thigh and found it disappointingly easy to control myself. Can reflexes get out of practice?

"I need permission to clone you, and a few grams of flesh. In return, I offer you immortality."

Not the proposition I'd expected. "Why me? I thought you were already the perfect pattern."

"For my own purposes, and within my powers to judge, I am. But I need you for a function . . . contrary to my own nature. And contrary to my Tauran brother's nature."

"A nasty job." Spend all eternity cleaning out the sewers; immortality of a sort.

"You might not find it so." She shifted restlessly, and I removed my hand. "Thank you. You have read the first part of the book?"

"Scanned it."

"Then you know that both Man and Tauran are gentle

203

beings. We do not fight among ourselves or with each other, because physical aggressiveness has been bred out of our sensibilities. Engineered out."

"A laudable accomplishment." I saw where this was leading, and the answer was going to be no.

"But it was just this lack of aggressiveness that allowed Earth, in your time, to successfully wage war against a culture uncountable millennia older. I am afraid it could happen again."

"This time to Man."

"Man and Tauran; philosophically there is little difference."

"What you want, then, is for me to provide you with an army. A band of barbarians to guard your frontiers."

"That's an unpleasant way of—"

"It's not a pleasant idea." My idea of hell. "No. I can't do it."

"Your only chance to live forever."

"Absolutely not." I stared at the floor. "Your aggressiveness was bred out of you. Mine was knocked out of me."

She stood up and smoothed the tunic over her perfect hips. "I cannot use guile. I will not withhold this body from you, if you desire it."

I considered that but didn't say anything.

"Besides immortality, all I can offer you is the abstract satisfaction of service. Protecting humanity against unknown perils."

I'd put in my thousand-odd years of service, and hadn't got any great satisfaction. "No. Even if I thought of you as humanity, the answer would still be no."

She nodded and went to the door.

"Don't worry," I said. "You can get one of the others."

She opened the door and addressed the corridor outside. "No, the others have already declined. You were the least likely, and the last one I approached."

Man was pretty considerate, especially so in light of our refusal to cooperate. Just for us twenty-two throwbacks, he went to the trouble of rejuvenating a little restaurant/tavern and staffing it at all hours (I never saw a Man eat or drink—guess they'd discovered a way around it). I was sitting in there one evening, drinking beer and reading their book, when Charlie came in and sat down.

Without preamble, he said, "I'm going to give it a try."

"Give what a try?"

"Women. Hetero." He shuddered. "No offense . . . it's not really very appealing." He patted my hand, looking distracted. "But the alternative . . . have you tried it?"

"Well . . . no, I haven't." Female Man was a visual treat, but only in the same sense as a painting or a piece of sculpture. I just couldn't see them as human beings.

"Don't." He didn't elaborate. "Besides, they say—he says, she says, it says—that they can change me back just as easily. If I don't like it."

"You'll like it, Charlie."

"Sure, that's what *they* say." He ordered a stiff drink. "Just seems unnatural. Anyway, since, uh, I'm going to make the switch, do you mind if . . . why don't we plan on going to the same planet?"

"Sure, Charlie, that'd be great." I meant it. "You know where you're going?"

"Hell, I don't care. Just away from here."

"I wonder if Heaven's still as nice—"

"No." Charlie jerked a thumb at the bartender. *"He* lives there."

"I don't know. I guess there's a list."

A Man came into the tavern, pushing a car piled high with folders. "Major Mandella? Captain Moore?"

"That's us," Charlie said.

"These are your military records. I hope you find them of interest. They were transferred to paper when your Strike Force was the only one outstanding, because it would have

205

been impractical to keep the normal data retrieval networks running to preserve so few data."

They always anticipated your questions, even when you didn't have any.

My folder was easily five times as thick as Charlie's. Probably thicker than any other, since I seemed to be the only trooper who'd made it through the whole duration. Poor Marygay. "Wonder what kind of report old Stott filed about me." I flipped to the front of the folder.

Stapled to the front page was a small square of paper. All the other pages were pristine white, but this one was tan with age and crumbling around the edges.

The handwriting was familiar, too familiar even after so long. The date was over 250 years old.

I winced and was blinded by sudden tears. I'd had no reason to suspect that she might be alive. But I hadn't really known she was dead, not until I saw that date.

"William? What's—"

"Leave me be, Charlie. Just for a minute." I wiped my eyes and closed the folder. I shouldn't even read the damned note. Going to a new life, I should leave old ghosts behind.

But even a message from the grave was contact of a sort. I opened the folder again.

11 Oct 2878

William—

All this is in your personnel file. But knowing you, you might just chuck it. So I made sure you'd get this note.

Obviously, I lived. Maybe you will, too. Join me.

I know from the records that you're out at Sade-138 and won't be back for a couple of centuries. No problem.

I'm going to a planet they call Middle Finger, the fifth planet out from Mizar. It's two collapsar jumps, ten months subjective. Middle Finger is a kind of Coventry for heterosexuals. They call it a "eugenic control baseline."

No matter. It took all of my money, and all the money of five other old-timers, but we bought a cruiser from UNEF. And we're using it as a time machine.

So I'm on a relativistic shuttle, waiting for you. All it does is go out five light-years and come back to Middle Finger, very fast. Every ten years I age about a month. So if you're on schedule and still alive, I'll only be twenty-eight when you get here. Hurry!

I never found anybody else and I don't want anybody else. I don't care whether you're ninety years old or thirty. If I can't be your lover, I'll be your nurse.

—Marygay

"Say, bartender."

"Yes, Major?"

"Do you know of a place called Middle Finger? Is it still there?"

"Of course it is. Where would it be?" Reasonable question. "A very nice place. Garden planet. Some people don't think it's exciting enough."

"What's this all about?" Charlie said.

I handed the bartender my empty glass. "I just found out where we're going."

5. Epilog
From *The New Voice,*
Paxton, Middle Finger 24–6
14/2/3143
OLD-TIMER HAS FIRST BOY

Marygay Potter-Mandella (24 Post Road, Paxton) gave birth Friday last to a fine baby boy, 3.1 kilos.

Marygay lays claim to being the second-"oldest" resident of Middle Finger, having been born in 1977. She fought through most of the Forever War and then waited for her mate on the time shuttle, 261 years. Her mate, William Mandella-Potter, is two years older.

The baby, not yet named, was delivered at home with the help of a friend of the family, Dr. Diana Alsever-Moore.

The Lop-Eared Cat That Devoured Philadelphia

by **LOUIS PHILLIPS**

Even a cat may look at a king,
But this feline is ridiculous,
300 feet high.
A mutation we understand
& still growing.
Radioactive isotopes
Fell into its milk, so now its purr
Can be heard all the way to Cleveland;
Its meow shatters glass
& bullets do not stop
It. All of us

Feel a bit like mice,
Dreading the thought of it
Ever going into heat.
We'd like to have it altered,
But the vet
Can't get
Close enough. As for now,
When its droopy ears drag the street,
Cars topple,
Houses fall & trees.
As for fleas,

They've discovered heaven
& whine in black fur
Driving us berserk.

The Lop-Eared Cat that Devoured Philadelphia

None of us have slept for nights,
Its claws
Scratching windows
Like shavings from a moon.
There is a tense beauty to her
In the light,
But nothing that I'd care to own.
She has grown

Too large for us to handle.
We've petitioned the President
To drop the Bomb
Or send in troops,
But there are big wars on
& it is difficult to gain attention.
All the foolish cat does
Is glare into the sun
& scoop
Up segments of our population
For a snack. One solution
Is to create a super St. Bernard,
But frankly
We lack heart
& the council is a bit conservative.
Perhaps we've been too hard.
After all, she does
Keep herself clean,
& when she leaps
There is such grace
Our hearts keen to our throats
In anticipation.

Besides, if giant rats ever appear,
We'll be far ahead of other cities.

A Dead Singer

by **MICHAEL MOORCOCK**

SF and music are often seen as close allies; Kingsley Amis long ago pointed out parallels between jazz and science fiction. The two have rarely been embodied in one man as they are in the person of the versatile Michael Moorcock. He is a fantasist with a world audience, and a musician. His LP with The Deep Fix entitled *The New World's Fair* was released on the UA label this year.

Despite their kinship, SF stories about musicians are rare. In this superbly understated story, Moorcock brings the great rock guitarist, Jimi Hendrix, back from the dead. As well as sketching the Hendrix ambience with sympathetic understanding, he presents a chilly picture of what it means to live outside one's own time.

I

It's not the speed, Jimi," said Shakey Mo, "it's the H you got to look out for."

Jimi was amused. "Well, it never did me much good."

"It didn't do you no harm in the long run." Shakey Mo laughed. He could hardly hold on to the steering wheel.

The big Mercedes camper took another badly lit bend. It was raining hard against the windscreen. Mo switched on the lamps. With his left hand he fumbled a cartridge from the case on the floor beside him and slotted it into the stereo. The heavy, driving drumming and moody synthesisers of Hawkwind's latest album made Mo feel much better. "That's the stuff for energy," said Mo.

Jimi leaned back. Relaxed, he nodded. The music filled the camper.

Shakey Mo kept getting speed hallucinations on the road ahead. Armies marched across his path; Nazis set up road blocks; scampering children chased balls; big fires suddenly started and ghouls appeared and disappeared. He had a bad time controlling himself sufficiently to keep on driving through it all. The images were familiar and he wasn't freaked out by them. He was content to be driving for Jimi. Since his comeback (or resurrection, as Mo privately called it) Jimi hadn't touched a guitar or sung a note, preferring to listen to other people's music. He was taking a long while to recover from what had happened to him in Ladbroke Grove. Only recently his colour had started to return, and he was still wearing the white silk shirt and jeans in which he'd been dressed when Shakey Mo first saw him, standing casually on the cowling of the Imperial Airways flying boat as it taxied towards the landing stage on Derwent Water. What a summer that had been, thought Mo. Beautiful.

The tape began to go round for the second time. Mo touched the stud to switch tracks, then thought better of it. He turned the stereo off altogether.

"A nice one." Jimi was looking thoughtful again. He was almost asleep as he lay stretched out over the bench seat, his hooded eyes fixed on the black road.

"It's got to build up again soon," said Mo. "It can't last, can it? I mean, everything's so dead. What have we got apart from Hawkwind really? And Bowie, maybe. Where's the energy going to come from, Jimi?"

"It's where it keeps going to that bothers me, man. You know?"

"I guess you're right." Mo didn't understand. But Jimi had to be right.

Jimi had known what he was doing, even when he died. Eric Burden had gone on TV to say so. "Jimi knew it was time to go," he'd said. It was like that with the records and performances. Some of them hadn't seemed to be as tight as others; some of them were even a bit rambling. Hard to turn on to. But Jimi had known what he was doing. You had to have faith in him.

Mo felt the weight of his responsibilities. He was a good roadie, but there were better roadies than he. More together people who could be trusted with a big secret. Jimi hadn't spelt it out, but it was obvious he felt that the world wasn't yet ready for his return. But why hadn't Jimi chosen one of the really ace roadies? Everything had to be prepared for the big gig. Maybe at Shea Stadium or the Albert Hall or the Paris Olympia? Anyway, some classic venue. Or at a festival? A special festival celebrating the resurrection. Woodstock or Glastonbury. Probably something new altogether, some new holy place. India, maybe? Jimi would say when the time came. After Jimi had contacted him and told him where to be picked up, Mo had soon stopped asking questions. With all his old gentleness, Jimi had turned the questions aside. He had been kind, but it was clear he hadn't wanted to answer.

Mo respected that.

The only really painful request Jimi had made was that Mo stop playing his old records, including, "Hey, Joe!" the first single. Previously there hadn't been a day when Mo hadn't put something of Jimi's on. In his room in Lancaster Road, in the truck when he was roading for Light and later The Deep Fix, even when he'd gone to the House during his short-lived conversion to Scientology he'd been able to plug his earbead into his cassette recorder for an hour or so. While Jimi's physical presence made up for a lot and stopped the worst of the withdrawal symptoms, it was still difficult. No amount of mandrax, speed or booze could counter his need for the music, and consequently the shakes were getting just a little bit worse each day. Mo sometimes felt that he was paying some kind of price for Jimi's trust in him. That was good karma, so he didn't mind. He was used to the shakes anyway. You could get used to anything. He looked at his sinewy, tattooed arms stretched before him, the hands gripping the steering wheel. The world snake was wriggling again. Black, red and green, it coiled slowly down his skin, round his wrist and began to inch towards his elbow. He fixed his eyes back on the road.

2

Jimi had fallen into a deep sleep. He lay along the seat behind Mo, his head resting on the empty guitar case. He was breathing heavily, as if something were pressing down on his chest.

The sky ahead was wide and pink. In the distance was a line of blue hills. Mo was tired. He could feel the old paranoia creeping in. He took a fresh joint from the ledge and lit it, but he knew that dope wouldn't do a lot of good. He needed a couple of hours sleep himself.

Without waking Jimi, Mo pulled the truck into the side of the road, near a wide, shallow river full of flat white limestone rocks. He opened his door and climbed slowly to the grass. He wasn't sure where they were; maybe somewhere in Yorkshire. There were hills all around. It was a mild autumn morning but Mo felt cold. He clambered down to the bank and knelt there, cupping his hands in the clear water, sucking up the river. He stretched out and put his tattered straw hat over his face. It was a very heavy scene at the moment. Maybe that was why it was taking Jimi so long to get it together.

Mo felt much better when he woke up. It must have been noon. The sun was hot on his skin. He took a deep breath of the rich air and cautiously removed his hat from his face. The black Mercedes camper with its chrome trimming was still on the grass near the road. Mo's mouth felt dry. He had another drink of water and rose, shaking the silver drops from his brown fingers. He trudged slowly to the truck, pulled back the door and looked over the edge of the driver's seat. Jimi wasn't there, but sounds came from behind the partition. Mo climbed across the two seats and slid open the connecting door. Jimi sat on one of the beds. He had erected the table and was drawing in a big red notebook. His smile was remote as Mo entered.

"Sleep good?" he asked.

Mo nodded. "I needed it."

"Sure," said Jimi. "Maybe I ought to do a little driving."

"It's okay. Unless you want to make better time."

"No."

"I'll get some breakfast," said Mo. "Are you hungry?"

Jimi shook his head. All through the summer, since he had left the flying boat and got into the truck beside Mo, Jimi appeared to have eaten nothing. Mo cooked himself some sausages and beans on the little Calor stove, opening the back door so that the smell wouldn't fill the camper. "I might go for a swim," he said as he brought his plate to the table and sat as far away from Jimi as possible, so as not to disturb him.

"Okay," said Jimi, absorbed in his drawing.

"What you doing? Looks like a comic strip. I'm really into comics."

Jimi shrugged. "Just doodling, man. You know."

Mo finished his food. "I'll get some comics next time we stop on the motorway. Some of the new ones are really far out, you know. Big machines. Mutants. The New Gods. Seen that?"

"No." Jimi's smile was sardonic.

"Really far out. Cosmic wars, time warps. All the usual stuff but different, you know. Better. Bigger. More spectacular. Sensational, man. Oh, you want to see them. I'll get some."

"Far out," said Jimi distantly, but it was obvious he hadn't been listening. He closed the notebook and sat against the vinyl cushions, folding his arms across his white silk chest. As if it occurred to him that he might have hurt Mo's feelings, he added: "Yeah, I used to be into comics a lot. You seen the Jap kind? Big fat books. Oh, man—they are *really* far out. Kids burning. Rape. All that stuff." He laughed, shaking his head. "Oh, man!"

"Yeah?" Mo laughed hesitantly.

"Right!" Jimi went to the door, placing a hand on either side of the frame and looking into the day. "Where are we, Mo? It's a little like Pennsylvania. The Delaware Valley. Ever been there?"

"Never been to the States."

"Is that right?"

"Somewhere in Yorkshire, I think. Probably north of Leeds. That could be the Lake District over there."

"Is that where I came through?"

"Derwent Water."

"Well, well." Jimi chuckled.

Jimi was livelier today. Maybe it was taking him time to store up all the energy he'd need when he finally decided to reveal himself to the world. Their driving had been completely at random. Jimi had let Mo decide where to go. They had been all over Wales, the Peaks, the West Country, most parts of the Home Counties, everywhere except London. Jimi had been reluctant to go to London. It was obvious why. Bad memories. Mo had been into town a few times, leaving the Mercedes and Jimi in a suburban layby and walking and hitching into London to get his mandies and his speed. When he could he scored some coke. He liked to get behind a snort or two of coke once in a while. In Finch's on the corner of Portobello Road he'd wanted to tell his old mates about Jimi, but Jimi had said to keep quiet about it, so when people had asked him what he was doing, where he was living these days, he'd had to give vague answers. There was no problem about money. Jimi didn't have any, but Mo had got a lot selling the white Dodge convertible. The Deep Fix had given it to him after they'd stopped going on the road. And there was a big bag of dope in the truck, too. Enough to last two people for months, though Jimi didn't seem to have any taste for that, either.

Jimi came back into the gloom of the truck. "What d'you say we get on the road again?"

Mo took his plate, knife and fork down to the river, washed them and stashed them back in the locker. He got into the driver's seat and turned the key. The Wankel engine started at once. The Mercedes pulled smoothly away, still heading north, bumping off the grass and back onto the asphalt. They were on a narrow road suitable only for the one-way traffic, but there was nobody behind them and nobody ahead of them until they left this road and turned onto the A65, making for Kendal.

"You don't mind the Lake District?" Mo asked.

"Suits me," said Jimi. "I'm the mad Gull Warrior, man." He smiled. "Maybe we should make for the ocean?"

"It's not far from here." Mo pointed west. 'Morecambe Bay?"

3

The cliff tops were covered in turf as smooth as a fairway. Below them the sea sighed. Jimi and Mo were in good spirits, looning around like kids.

In the distance, round the curve of the bay, were the towers and fun fairs and penny arcades of Morecambe, but here it was deserted and still, apart from the occasional cry of a gull.

Mo laughed, then cried out nervously as Jimi danced so near to the cliff edge it seemed he'd fall over.

"Take it easy, Jimi."

"Shit, man. They can't kill me."

He had a broad, euphoric smile on his face and he looked really healthy. "They can't kill Jimi, man!"

Mo remembered him on stage. In total command. Moving through the strobes, his big guitar stuck out in front of him, pointing at each individual member of the audience, making each kid feel that he was in personal touch with Jimi.

"Right!" Mo began to giggle.

Jimi hovered on the edge, still flapping his outstretched arms. "I'm the boy they boogie to. Oh, man! There ain't nothin' they can do to me!"

"Right!"

Jimi came zooming round and flung himself down on the turf next to Mo. He was panting. He was grinning. "It's coming back, Mo. All fresh and new."

Mo nodded, still giggling.

"I just know it's there, man."

Mo looked up. The gulls were everywhere. They were screaming. They took on the aspect of an audience. He hated them. They were so thick in the sky now.

"Don't let them fucking feathers stick in your throat," said Mo, suddenly sullen. He got up and returned to the truck.

"Mo. What's the matter with you, man?"

Jimi was as concerned as ever, but that only brought Mo down more. It was Jimi's kindness which had killed him the first time. He'd been polite to everyone. He couldn't help it. Really hung-up people had got on him. And they'd drained Jimi dry.

"They'll get you again, man," said Mo. "I know they will. Every time. There isn't a thing you can do about it. No matter how much energy you build up, you know, they'll still suck it all out of you and moan for more. They want your blood, man. They want your sperm and your bones and your flesh, man. They'll take you, man. They'll eat you up again."

"No. I'll—no, not this time."

"Sure." Mo sneered.

"Man, are you trying to bring me down?"

Mo began to twitch. "No. But . . ."

"Don't worry, man, okay?" Jimi's voice was soft and as-sured.

"I can't put it into words, Jimi. It's this, sort of, premoni-tion, you know."

"What good did words ever do for anybody?" Jimi laughed his old, deep laugh. "You are crazy, Mo. Come on, let's get back into the truck. Where do you want to head for?"

But Mo couldn't reply. He sat at the steering wheel and stared through the windscreen at the sea and the gulls.

Jimi was conciliatory. "Look, Mo, I'll be cool about it, right? I'll take it easy. Or maybe you think I won't need you?"

Mo didn't know why he was so down all of sudden.

"Mo, you stay with me, wherever I go," said Jimi.

4

Outside Carlisle they saw a hitchhiker, a young guy who looked really wasted. He was leaning on a signpost. He had enough energy to raise his hand. Mo thought they should stop for him. Jimi said: "If you want to," and went into the back of the truck, closing the door as Mo pulled in for the hitch-hiker.

Mo said: "Where you going?"

The hitchhiker said: "What about Fort William, man?"

Mo said: "Get in."

The hitchhiker said his name was Chris. "You with a band, man?" He glanced round the cabin at the old stickers and the stereo, at Mo's tattoos, his faded face paint, his Cawthorn T-shirt, his beaded jacket, his worn jeans with washed-out patches on them, the leather cowboy boots which Mo had bought at the Emperor of Wyoming in Notting Hill Gate last year.

"Used to road for The Deep Fix," said Mo.

The hitchhiker's eyes were sunken and the sockets were red. His thick black hair was long and hung down to his pale face. He wore a torn Wrangler denim shirt and a dirty white Levi jacket, and both legs of his jeans had holes in the knees. He had moccasins on his feet. He was nervous and eager.

"That's a really good band. Very heavy."

"Right," said Mo.

'What's in the back?" Chris turned to look at the door. "Gear?"

"You could say that."

"I've been hitching for three days, night and day," said Chris. He had an oil- and weather-stained khaki pack on his lap.

"D'you mind if I get some kip sometime?"

"No," said Mo. There was a service station ahead. He decided to pull in and fill the Merc up. By the time he got to the pumps Chris was asleep.

As he waited to get back into the traffic, Mo crammed his mouth full of pills. Some of them fell from his hand onto the floor. He didn't bother to pick them up. He was feeling bleak.

Chris woke when they were going through Glasgow.

"Is this Glasgow?"

Mo nodded. He couldn't keep the paranoia down. He glared at the cars ahead as they moved slowly through the streets. Every window of every shop had a big steel mesh grille on it. The pubs were like bunkers. He was really pissed off without knowing why.

"Where you going yourself?" Chris asked.

"Fort William," said Mo.

"Lucky for me. Know where I can score any grass in Fort William?"

Mo reached forward and pushed a tobacco tin along the edge towards the hitchhiker. "You can have that."

Chris took the tin and opened it. "Far out! You mean it? And the skins?"

"Sure," said Mo. He hated Chris. He hated everybody. He knew the mood would pass.

"Oh, wow! Thanks, man." Chris put the tin in his pack. "I'll roll one when we're out of the city, okay?"

"Okay."

"Who are you working for now?" said Chris. "A band?"

"No."

"You on holiday?"

The kid was talking so much, Mo wondered if he'd picked up a speed freak. Probably though it was just his lack of sleep. "Sort of," he said.

"Me, too. Well, it started like that. I'm at university. Exeter. Or was. I decided to drop out. I'm not going back to that shit heap. One term was enough for me. I thought of heading for the Hebrides. Someone I know's living in a commune out there, on one of the islands. They got their own sheep, goats, a cow. Nobody getting off on them. You know. Really free. It seems okay to me."

Mo nodded.

Chris pushed back his black, greasy hair. "I mean compare something like that with a place like this. How do people stand it, man? Fucking hell."

Mo didn't answer. He moved forward, changing gear as the lights changed.

"Amazing," said Chris. He saw the case of cartridges at his feet. "Can I play some music?"

"Go ahead," said Mo.

Chris picked out an old album, "Who's Next." He tried to slide it into the slot the wrong way round. Mo took it from his hand and put it in the right way. He felt better when the music started. He noticed, out of the corner of his eye, that Chris tried to talk for a while before he realised he couldn't be heard.

Mo let the tape play over and over again as they drove away from Glasgow. Chris rolled joints and Mo smoked a little, beginning to get on top of his paranoia. By about four in the afternoon he was feeling better, and he switched off the stereo. They were driving beside Loch Lomond. The bracken was turning brown and shone like brass where the sun touched it. Chris had fallen asleep again, but he woke up as the music stopped. "Far out." He dug the scenery. "Fucking far out." He wound his window down. "This is the first time I've been to Scotland."

"Yeah?" said Mo.

"How long before we reach Fort William, man?"

"A few hours. Why are you heading for Fort William?"

"I met this chick. She comes from there. Her old man's a chemist or something."

Mo said coldly, on impulse: "Guess who I've got in the back."

"What, a chick?"

"No."

"Who?"

"Jimi Hendrix."

Chris's jaw dropped. He looked at Mo and snorted, willing to join in the joke. "No? Really? Hendrix, eh? What is it, a refrigerated truck?" He was excited by the fantasy. "You think if we thaw him out he'll play something for us?" He shook his head, grinning.

"He is sitting in the back there. Alive. I'm roading for him."

"Really?"

"Yeah."

"Fantastic." Chris was half-convinced. At the same time Mo knew he was wondering if Mo were freaking out on him. Mo laughed. Chris looked at the door. After that, he was silent for a while.

Something like a half an hour later, he said: "Hendrix was

the best, you know. He was the king, man. Not just the music,
but the style, too. I couldn't believe it when I heard he died.
I still can't believe it, you know."

"Sure," said Mo. "Well, he's back."

"Yeah?" Again Chris laughed uncertainly. "In there? Can
I see him?"

"He's not ready yet."

"Sure," said Chris.

It was dark when they reached Fort William. Chris staggered down from the truck. "Thanks man. That's really nice,
you know. Where are you staying?"

"I'm moving on," said Mo. "See you."

"Yeah. See you." Chris still had that baffled look on his
face.

Mo smiled to himself as he started the camper, heading for
Oban. Once they were moving, the door opened and Jimi
clambered over the seats to sit beside him.

"You told that kid about me?"

"He didn't believe me," said Mo.

Jimi shrugged.

It began to rain again.

5

They lay together in the damp heather looking out over
the hills. There was nobody for miles; no roads, towns or
houses. The air was still and empty save for a hawk drifting
so high above them it was almost out of sight.

"This'll do, eh?" said Mo. "It's fantastic."

Jimi smiled gently. "It's nice," he said.

Mo took a Mars Bar from his pocket and offered it to Jimi,
who shook his head. Mo began to eat the Mars Bar.

"What d'you think I am, man?" said Jimi.

"How d'you mean?"

"Devil or angel? You know."

"You're Jimi," said Mo. "That's good enough for me, man."

"Or just a ghost," said Jimi. "Maybe I'm just a ghost."

Mo began to shake. "No," he said.

"Or a killer?" Jimi got up and struck a pose. "The Sonic Assassin. Or the Messiah, maybe." He laughed. "You wanna hear my words of wisdom?"

"That's not what it's about," said Mo, frowning. "Words. You just have to be there, Jimi. On the stage. With your guitar. You're above all that stuff—all the hype. Whatever you do—it's right, you know."

"If you say so, Mo." Jimi was on some kind of downer. He lowered himself to the heather and sat there cross-legged, smoothing his white jeans, picking mud off his black patent leather boots. "What is all this *Easy Rider* crap, anyway? What are we doing here?"

"You didn't like *Easy Rider*?" Mo was astonished.

"The best thing since *Lassie Come-Home.*" Jimi shrugged. "All it ever proved was that Hollywood could still turn 'em out, you know. They got a couple of fake freaks and made themselves a lot of money. A ripoff, man. And the kids fell for it. What does that make me?"

"You never ripped anybody off, Jimi."

"Yeah? How d'you know?"

"Well, you never did."

"All that low-energy shit creeping in everywhere. Things are bad." Jimi had changed the subject, making a jump Mo couldn't follow. "People all over the Grove playing nothing but Byrds crap. Simon and Garfunkel. Jesus Christ! Was it ever worth doing?"

"Things go in waves. You can't be up the whole time."

"Sure," Jimi sneered. "This one's for all the soldiers fighting in Chicago. And Milwaukee. And New York. And Vietnam. Down with War and Pollution. What was all that about?"

"Well . . ." Mo swallowed the remains of the Mars Bar.

223

"Well—it's important, man. I mean, all those kids getting killed."

"While we made fortunes. And came out with a lot of sentimental crap. That's where we were wrong. You're either in the social conscience business or show business. You're just foolish if you think you can combine them like that."

"No, man. I mean, you can say things which people will hear."

"You say what your audience wants. A Frank Sinatra audience gets their shit rapped back to them by Frank Sinatra. Jimi Hendrix gives a Jimi Hendrix audience what they want to hear. Is that what I want to get back into?"

But Mo had lost him. Mo was watching the tattoos crawl up his arms. He said vaguely: "You need different music for different moods. There's nothing wrong with the Byrds if you're trying to get off some paranoia trip. And you get up on Hendrix. That's what it's like. Like uppers and downers, you know."

"Okay," said Jimi. "You're right. But it's the other stuff that's stupid. Why do they always want you to keep saying things? If you're just a musician that's all you should have to be. When you're playing a gig, anyway, or making a record. Anything else should come out of that. If you wanna do benefits, free concerts, okay. But your opinions should be private. They want to turn us into politicians."

"I told you," said Mo, staring intensely at his arms. "Nobody asks that. You do what you want to do."

"Nobody asks it, but you always feel you got to give it to 'em." Jimi rolled over and lay on his back, scratching his head. "Then you blame them for it."

"Not everyone thinks they owe anything to anyone," said Mo mildly as his skin undulated over his flesh.

"Maybe that's it," said Jimi. "Maybe that's what kills you. Jesus Christ. Psychologically, man, you know, that means you must be in one hell of a mess. Jesus Christ. That's suicide, man. Creepy."

"They killed you," said Mo.

"No, man. It was suicide."

Mo watched the world snake crawl. Could this Hendrix be an impostor?

6

"So what you going to do, then?" said Mo. They were on the road to Skye and the Merc was running low on fuel.

"I was a cunt to come back," said Jimi. "I thought I had some kind of duty."

Mo shrugged. "Maybe you have, you know."

"And maybe I haven't."

"Sure." Mo saw a filling station ahead. The gauge now read Empty and a red light was flashing on the panel. It always happened like that. He'd hardly ever been stranded. He glanced in the mirror and saw his own mad eyes staring back at him. Momentarily he wondered if he should turn the mirror a little to see if Jimi's reflection was there too. He pushed the thought away. More paranoia. He had to stay on top of it.

While the attendant was filling the truck, Mo went to the toilet. Amongst the more common bits of graffiti on the wall was the slogan "Hawkwind is Ace." Maybe Jimi was right. Maybe his day was over and he should have stayed dead. Mo felt miserable. Hendrix had been his only hero. He did up his flies, and the effort drained off the last of his energy. He staggered against the door and began to slide down towards the messy floor. His mouth was dry; his heart was thumping very fast. He tried to remember how many pills he'd swallowed recently. Was he about to O.D.?

He put his hands up to the door handle and hauled himself to his feet. He bent over the lavatory bowl and shoved his finger down his throat. Everything was moving. The bowl was alive. A greedy mouth trying to swallow him. The walls heaved and moved in on him. He heard a whistling noise.

225

Nothing came up. He stopped trying to vomit, turned, steadied himself as best as he could, brushed aside the little white stick men who tried to grab at him, dragged the door open and plunged through. Outside, the attendant was putting the cap back on the tank. He wiped his big hands on a piece of rag and put the rag back into his overalls, saying something. Mo found some money in his back pocket and gave it to him. He heard a voice:

"You okay, laddie?"

The man had offered him a genuine look of concern.

Mo mumbled something and clambered into the cab.

The man ran up as Mo started the engine, waving money and green stamps.

"What?" said Mo. He managed to wind the window down. The man's face changed to a malevolent devil's mask. Mo knew enough not to worry about it. "What?"

He thought he heard the attendant say: "Your friend's already paid."

"That's right, man," said Jimi from beside him.

"Keep it," said Mo. He had to get on the road quickly. Once he was driving he would be more in control of himself. He fumbled a cartridge at random from the case. He jammed it into the slot. The tape started halfway through a Stones album. Jagger singing "Let It Bleed" had a calming influence on Mo. The snakes stopped winding up and down his arms and the road ahead became steady and clearer. He'd never liked the Stones much. A load of wankers, really, though you had to admit Jagger had a style of his own which no one could copy. But basically wankers like the rest of the current evil-trippers, like Morrison and Alice Cooper, like Bolan in a different way. It occurred to him he was wasting his time thinking about nothing but bands. But what else was there to think about? Anyway, how else could you see your life? The mystical thing didn't mean much to him. Scientology was a load of crap. At any rate, he couldn't see anything in it. The guys running all that stuff seemed to be more hung-up than the people they were supposed to be helping. That was true of a lot of things. Most people who told you they wanted to help you were getting off on you in some way. He'd met pretty much every kind of freak by now. Sufis, Hare Krishnas, Jesus freaks, Meditators, Processors, Divine Lighters. They could all talk better than him, but they all seemed to need more from him than they could give. You got into people when you were tripping. Acid had done a lot for him that way. He could suss out the hype-merchants so easily these days. And by that test Jimi couldn't be a fake. Jimi was straight. Fucked up now, possibly, but okay.

The road was long and white and then it became a big boulder. Mo couldn't tell if the boulder was real or not. He drove at it, then changed his mind, braking sharply. A red car behind him swerved and hooted as it went past him through the boulder, which disappeared. Mo shook all over. He took out the Stones tape and changed it for the Grateful Dead's "American Beauty," turned down low.

"You okay, man?" said Hendrix.

"Sure. Just a bit shaky." Mo started the Merc up.

"You want to stop and get some sleep?"

"I'll see how I feel later."

It was sunset when Jimi said: "We seem to be heading south."

"Yeah," said Mo. "I need to get back to London."

"You got to score?"

"Yeah."

"Maybe I'll come in with you this time."

"Yeah?"

"Maybe I won't."

7

By the time Mo had hitched to the nearest tube station and reached Ladbroke Grove he was totally wasted. The images were all inside his head now; pictures of Jimi from the first time he'd seen him on TV playing "Hey, Joe" (Mo had still been at school then), pictures of Jimi playing at Woodstock, at festivals and gigs all over the country. Jimi in big, feathered hats, bizarre multicoloured shirts, several rings on each finger, playing the white Fender, flinging the guitar over his head, plucking the strings with his teeth, shoving it under his straddled legs, making it wail and moan and throb, doing more with a guitar than anyone had done before. Only Jimi could make a guitar come alive in that way, turning the machine into an organic creature, simultaneously a prick, a woman, a white horse, a sliding snake. Mo glanced at his arms, but they were still. The sun was beginning to set as he turned into Lancaster Road, driven more by a mixture of habit and momentum than any energy or sense of purpose. He had another image in his head now, of Jimi as a soul thief, taking the energy away from the audience. Instead of the martyr, Jimi became the vampire. Mo knew that the paranoia was really setting in, and the sooner he got hold of some uppers the better. He couldn't blame Jimi for how he felt. He hadn't slept for two days. That was all it was. Jimi had given everything to the people in the audience, including his life.

He crawled up the steps of the house in Lancaster Road and rang the third bell down. There was no answer. He was shaking badly. He held on to the concrete steps and tried to calm himself, but it got worse and he thought he was going to pass out.

The door behind him opened.

"Mo?"

It was Dave's chick, Jenny, wearing a purple brocade dress. Her hair was bright with wet henna.

"Mo? You all right?"

Mo swallowed and said: "Hullo, Jenny. Where's Dave?"

"He went down to the Mountain Grill to get something to

eat. About half an hour ago. Are you all right, Mo?"

"Tired," said Mo. "Dave got any uppers?"

"He had a lot of mandies in yesterday."

Mo accepted the news. "Can you let me have a couple of quids' worth?"

"You'd better ask him yourself, Mo. I don't know who he's promised them to."

Mo nodded and got up carefully.

"You want to come in and wait, man?" said Jenny.

Mo shook his head. "I'll go down the Mountain. See you later, Jenny."

"See you later, Mo. Take care, now."

Mo shuffled slowly up Lancaster Road and turned the corner into Portobello Road. He thought he saw the black and chrome Merc cross the top of the street. The buildings were all crowding on him. They were grey and huge, and everyone he passed was out to get him. He saw them grinning at him, leering. He heard them talking about him. There were fuzz everywhere. A woman threw something at him. He kept going until he reached the Mountain Grill and had stumbled through the door. The café was crowded with freaks, but there was nobody there he knew. They all had evil, secretive expressions and they were whispering.

"You fuckers," he mumbled, but they pretended they weren't listening. He saw Dave.

"Dave? Dave, man!"

Dave looked up, grinning privately. "Hi, Mo. When did you get back to town?" He had a round, smooth, sneaky face. He was dressed in new, clean denims with fresh patches on them. One of the patches said "Star Rider."

"Just got in." Mo leaned across the table, careless of the intervening people, and whispered in Dave's ear. "I hear you got some mandies."

Dave's face became serious. "Sure. Now?"

Mo nodded.

Dave rose slowly and paid his bill to the dark, fat lady at the till. "Thanks, Maria."

Dave took Mo by the shoulder and led him out of the café. Mo wondered if Dave was about to finger him. He remembered that Dave had been suspected more than once.

Dave said softly as they went along: "How many d'you need, Mo?"

"How much are they?"

Dave said: "You can have them for two bob each."

"I'll have five quids' worth. Yeah?"

"Okay."

They got back to Lancaster Road and Dave let himself in with two keys, a Yale and a maltis. They went up a dark, dangerous stairway. Dave's room was gloomy, thick with incense, with painted blinds covering the windows. Jenny sat on a mattress in the corner listening to Stray Dog on the stereo. She was knitting.

"Hi, Mo," she said. "So you found him."

Mo sat down on the mattress in the opposite corner. "How's it going, Jenny?" he said. He didn't like Dave, but he liked Jenny. He made a big effort to be polite. Dave was standing by a chest of drawers, dragging a box from under a pile of tasselled curtains. Mo looked past him and saw Jimi standing there. He was dressed in a hand-painted silk shirt with roses all over it. There was a jade talisman on a silver chain round his throat. He had the white Strat in his hands. His eyes were closed as he played it. Almost immediately, Mo guessed he was looking at a poster.

Dave counted a hundred mandies into an aspirin bottle. Mo reached into his jeans and found some money. He gave Dave a five-pound note and Dave gave him the bottle. Mo opened the bottle and took out a lot of the pills, swallowing them fast. They didn't act right away, but he felt better for taking them. He got up.

"See you later, Dave."

"See you later, man," said Dave. "Maybe in Finch's to-night."

"Yeah."

8

Mo couldn't remember how the fight started. He'd been sitting quietly in a corner of the pub drinking his pint of bitter when that big fat fart who was always in there making trouble decided to pick on him. He remembered getting up and punching the fat fart. There had been a lot of confusion then, and he had somehow knocked the fat fart over the bar. Then a few people he knew pulled him away and took him back to a basement in Latimer Road where he listened to some music.

It was "Band of Gypsies" that woke him up. Listening to "Machine Gun," he realised suddenly that he didn't like it. He went to the pile of records and found other Hendrix albums. He played "Are You Experienced," the first album, and "Electric Ladyland" and he liked them much better. Then he played "Band of Gypsies" again.

He looked round the dark room. Everyone seemed to be totally spaced out.

"He died at the right time," he said. "It was over for him, you know. He shouldn't have come back."

He felt in his pocket for his bottle of mandies. There didn't seem to be that many left. Maybe someone had ripped them off in the pub. He took a few more and reached for the bottle of wine on the table, washing them down. He put "Are You Experienced" on the deck again and lay back. "That was really great," he said. He fell asleep. He shook a little bit. His breathing got deeper and deeper. When he started to vomit in his sleep nobody noticed. By that time everyone was right out of it. He choked quietly and then stopped.

9

About an hour later a black man came into the room. He was tall and elegant. He radiated energy. He wore a white silk shirt and white jeans. There were shiny patent leather boots on his feet. A chick started to get up as he came into the room. She looked bemused.

"Hi," said the newcomer. "I'm looking for Shakey Mo. We ought to be going."

He peered at the sleeping bodies and then looked closer at one which lay a little apart from the others. There was vomit all over his face and over his shirt. His skin was a ghastly, dirty green. The black man stepped across the others and knelt beside Mo, feeling his heart, taking his pulse.

The chick stared stupidly at him. "Is he all right?"

"He's O-D'ed," the newcomer said quietly. "He's gone. D'you want to get a doctor or something, honey?"

"Oh, Jesus," she said.

The black man got up and walked to the door.

"Hey," she said. "You look just like Jimi Hendrix, you know that?"

"Sure."

"You can't be—you're not, are you? I mean, Jimi's dead."

Jimi shook his head and smiled his old, rich smile. "Shit, lady. They can't kill Jimi." He laughed as he left.

The chick glanced down at the small, ruined body covered in its own vomit. She swayed a little, rubbing at her thighs. She frowned. Then she went as quickly as she could from the room, hampered by her long cotton dress, and into the street. It was nearly dawn and it was cold. The tall figure in the white shirt and jeans didn't seem to notice the cold. It strode up to a big Mercedes camper parked near the Bingo Hall.

The chick began to run after the black truck as it started up and rolled a little way before it had to stop on the red light at the Ladbroke Grove intersection.

"Wait," she shouted. "Jimi!"

But the camper was moving before she could reach it. She saw it heading north towards Kilburn.

She wiped the clammy sweat from her face. She must be freaking out. She hoped when she got back to the basement that there wouldn't really be a dead guy there. She didn't need it.

In memory of Smiling Mike and John the Bog

Afterword: Science Fiction on the Titanic

by **BRIAN W. ALDISS**

Readers who follow the Hugo and Nebula Awards, science fiction's reply to the Roman *panem et circenses,* are given an annual delight. True, the delight tells us more about human nature than about literature, but that is to be expected. Aldiss's second law of thermo-linguistics states that what is most popular is rarely best and that what is best is rarely most popular.

Anyhow, students of form in the Nebula stakes will recall that one of the contenders for the Dramatic Presentation in 1974 was a TV play shown on CBS Playhouse, *Catholics,* by Brian Moore. *Catholics* concerned some Irish monks who were in conflict with the future Roman Catholic Church.

Nineteen seventy-five has seen the publication of a novel by Brian Moore, *The Great Victorian Collection. The Great Victorian Collection* is not sf, but it is certainly fantasy, and that of a high order.

Mr. Moore is a Canadian novelist, and his central character, Tony Maloney, is a Canadian academic from McGill enjoying a brief holiday in California after attending a symposium there. Maloney checks into the Sea Winds Motel at Carmel-by-the-Sea for a night. During the night, he dreams that the world's largest and most precious collection of Victoriana is assembled on the empty lot outside his bedroom window. He awakes in the morning, and the collection is there in all its glory. He walks among the aisles and stalls. Everything is real, as genuine as the originals. Experts are called in from London and New York. They vouch for the authenticity of every item.

It's an alluring idea. Maloney finds that the collection will not survive if he leaves Carmel; driving eight miles out of town, he phones the motel, to be told to come back quickly, as the collection is being ruined by a heavy rainstorm. He returns just as the rain ceases.

The complications that follow are well worked out, as Maloney becomes increasingly involved in the show-business aspect of his creation, and the great Victorian collection becomes an increasingly tawdry sideshow. All this aspect of the novel is a logical unfolding. Much as I enjoyed the novel (and felt envious of an author who had hit on such a theme), the logic of the miraculous I found less persuasive. After we have been shown that the collection cannot survive Maloney's absence, we are later told that it can: a weakness which seriously mars this kind of story. We appreciate that only one small boy recognizes that the king's new clothes are nonexistent; the story would be lessened, not heightened, if we discovered that in fact a cobbler, the hangman, a local whore, and a three-legged donkey also fail to see the clothes.

However, *The Great Victorian Collection* remains very enjoyable. As a metaphor for a man tied by one leg to his dream, it is effective.

We are all clear that such a novel is not sf, or, if we aren't, Mr. Moore seeks to make it clear to us. When Maloney is puzzling over how the collection could have materialized, he reflects that this could hardly be a miracle; he does not believe in God. "Nor did he believe in evil spirits, extrasensory perception, or creatures from another planet."

Despite which, the novel toys with the idea that ESP is involved. The president of the International Society for Parakinesic Research phones Maloney and is helpful. The episode is not treated satirically. And Maloney himself is shown to have powers of divination.

This sort of novel, in which the miraculous happens, is clearly of interest to sf readers. It is their meat, even if no science is directly involved in the rationale of events, right down to the way in which the splendors of the Victorian collection represent a kind of time travel to the past. This having been said, such a novel would have seemed far from our interest only a few years ago. That matters have changed in this respect is not merely because our tastes have become more catholic (no reference to Mr. Moore's play) as the readership has widened. Other factors have entered, factors belonging to a wider stage than literary taste.

Speaking in the United States this year, Alexander Solzhenitsyn explained why he believes that the West has already lost World War III. He charges us with seeking to prolong prosperity at the price of illusory concessions; the United States and the countries of Europe have handed over or "abandoned to violence without bounds" whole countries such as the Baltic states, Moldavia, Mongolia, Albania, Bulgaria, Hungary, Czechoslovakia, and other nations in Europe and the Far East. Solzhenitsyn sees the Kremlin triumphing by this widespread failure of the will to resist, and notes how, at the time of the energy crunch, "when valiant Israel was defending itself to the death with faultless solidarity, Europe was capitulating, country after country, before the menace of a reduction in Sunday motoring."

One may look askance at this praise of solidarity in a polemic inveighing against the state where solidarity takes iron precedence over individuality, without necessarily disagreeing with the tenor of Solzhenitsyn's complaint.

Certainly the energy crisis to which Solzhenitsyn refers has had a remarkable effect on Western confidence. Oil equals our culture's life-blood. That's not my gasoline tank you're holding, it's my heart, as the old song nearly had it. All things are related. Coincidentally with the crisis came a wish to believe in alternate power sources, like Uri Geller. All the old hab-dab about father figures from Outer Space, parapsychology, telepathy, and spoon-bending came forth again, along with a plea from responsible figures in public life for more research investment in windmills, waterwheels, and, for all I know, breaking wind, that yet untapped source of natural gas.

All of which makes one feel that the centuries of science upon which our Western culture are based have traveled unmarked through the popular mind. A surprising number of people are willing to junk the entire accumulation of knowledge since ancient Greece after watching Uri Geller perform for five minutes on their 23-inch screen. Fantastic.

The fun we're having is being watched by an alien culture. Slowly and surely, our weaknesses are being studied and plans are being laid against us. Intellects vast and cool and unsympathetic—I refer to the Chinese, of course—are viewing us across the media.

Scientica Sinica, China's most prestigious science journal, has recently reported that the decline of the West (in which, from their advantageous perspective, they include the USSR) is exemplified by the widespread scientific interest in spoon-bending, telepathy, and other related claptraps. (I hereby pronounce that "claptrap" shall have a plural form, in order to cope with present-day conditions.) Just as General Turgidson in *Dr. Strangelove* feared a mineshaft gap between the two superpowers, so the Chinese see an ESP race between them . . . "The Pentagon and the CIA constantly keep themselves well informed on new developments in parapsychology."

Harsher words are in store. "Parapsychology," according to Hsin Ping, the writer of the article, "peddles the rotten products of superstitition and religion," forming a belt of pseudoscience which "serves the interests of the bourgeois and revisionist politics."

Well, we don't have to take any notice of what the Chinese say. Nevertheless, the general indictment reminds us of how readily sf espouses pseudoscience, even while it likes to talk of itself as if it were defending the frontiers of scientific truth, which is rather like patrolling the perimeters of Fort Knox after having detonated a firebomb in the central strongroom. Have a look at the sf shelves in any bookstore; they're generally placed next to the nut cult section, the cash-crop books on the Bermuda Triangle, the Great Pyramid, Stonehenge as prehistoric computer, UFO's, Did the Incas Come from Outer Space?, Was God an Astronaut?, Was Jesus a Junkie? How We Are Ruled by Our Stars, and similar feasts for the intellect. Booksellers know their clientele.

So in this respect, sf has proved itself prophetic. Campbell's *Astounding,* in the forties and fifties, went in heavily for psi, mad machines, weirdo explanations of man's origins, applied magic. The rest of the population is following where we led.

One of our leading catastrophe experts, Professor Paul Ehrlich, author of *The Population Bomb,* has devoted much time and ingenuity to warning the West of its blindness to ecological limits. When Professor Ehrlich was in London recently, a sneaky interviewer from the *Guardian* asked him why it was, when preaching the doctrine that we were set for disaster, he flew in in his private plane and stayed at the Hilton. To which Ehrlich gave the memorable answer, "If you are on the *Titanic,* why travel steerage?"

My growing belief is that sf enjoys its trip on the *Titanic,* but that, if anything, it speeds the rendezvous with the iceberg. By unwittingly undermining the very foundations of our culture—foundations which are surely scientific—we may contribute to the general malaise afflicting that culture. This is just a supposition: the sort of supposition we enjoy using in sf. Perhaps someone would care to embody it in a story. Self-scrutiny is occasionally a better exercise than beating the drum.

Maybe Moore's *Great Victorian Collection* is to be preferred as it is, with the miracle presented as such. We then accept the story as a metaphor for the not uncommon condition of a man shackled to his dream. Supposing Moore had decided to write his novel as an sf story. He could have had the collection planted in the parking lot by aliens from a superculture, busy re-creating our recent past. Or he could have justified it, Dick-wise, by explaining the whole business as a psychotic hallucination in which Maloney remains trapped. Maybe Maloney could be a genuine Victorian dreaming up the twentieth century.

All these artful dodges we sf writers get up to—these tricks with reality—reflect an uncertainty regarding what is true, what is of ultimate value, which is entirely contemporary. If a copy of Philip Dick's *Flow My Tears the Policeman Said* was dispatched through time to the year 1911, before the *Titanic* sailed, nobody then would understand it. Whereas *The Great Victorian Collection* would be immediately comprehensible: there has always been a belief in miracles in the popular mind. As L. Sprague de Camp once said, the public would rather be bunked than debunked.

Our uncertainties about the present have given sf readers one delightful bonus. This year is memorable for the proliferation of books looking back on the pictorial side of sf as it has unrolled over the decades. The past is always safer than the future. The plushiest of these volumes is James Gunn's *Alternate Worlds,* which includes not only artwork and a considerable text but photographs of authors and artists. There is also a translation of Jacques Sadoul's *Hier, l'An 2000,* under the more prosaic and misleading title of *2000 A.D.*; a large paperback of Anthony Frewin's, *One Hundred Years of Science Fiction Illustration;* Franz Rottensteiner's *The Science Fiction Book,* and my own *Science Fiction Art.* Other books are due, including one by Lester del Rey.

Although five books or more may seem something of a glut, I believe this is far from the truth. Each adopts an individual approach to a wide subject which has scarcely been touched on so far. Although, for my tastes, Rottensteiner's text is both silly and bombastic, his illustrations are varied and include a few from parts of the world which the other books ignore.

Science fiction art has had its influence. The sets and decor of films like *Metropolis* and *Things to Come* have left their mark on our times. In general, however, the art has been too little appreciated outside the field—and even inside the field, where its vigor and inventiveness have rarely received attention, except perhaps on a rather fannish level. All these books are immensely enjoyable in their own right, revealing a wealth of material. I could hardly take my eyes off Sadoul's volume when I received a copy of the French edition, and suffered the same happy disability when my own book rolled off the press. But all are mainly pictorial anthologies, and should be seen as forerunners of a proper critical appreciation of the dozens of artists who have excelled in this difficult medium. Such an appreciation is badly needed. The Bok Foundation does well by the art of Hannes Bok. There is a multitude of other artists who merit individual studies.

Sf criticism is now getting into its stride; it should not neglect the visual aspect of the genre. Many readers may have forgotten the first story they read, or have graduated to something more demanding, but the chances are that they still recall their first Paul painting, their first Finlay interior, their first Emsh cover, or their first brush with Flash Gordon, Buck Rogers, or Dan Dare. This was where they encountered a different way of looking at the world. Much of the early artwork in the field carries an immediate conviction still, whereas the stories they illustrated may no longer hold the interest.

It is also significant that this renewed attention in the art of the past comes at a time when so many vital new illustrators are at work. If anyone has any doubts about that, I recommend an inspection of recent LP sleeves as well as recent paperbacks. The *Titanic* may be encountering fog, but the decor in the stateroom is tremendously impressive.